DARK GODDESS

SARWAT CHADDA

PENGUIN BOOKS

PENGUIN BOOKS

Published by the Penguin Group
Penguin Books Ltd, 80 Strand, London WC2R 0RL, England
Penguin Group (USA) Inc., 375 Hudson Street, New York, New York 10014, USA
Penguin Group (Canada), 90 Eglinton Avenue East, Suite 700, Toronto, Ontario, Canada M4P 2Y3
(a division of Pearson Penguin Canada Inc.)
Penguin Ireland, 25 St Stephen's Green, Dublin 2, Ireland (a division of Penguin Books Ltd)
Penguin Group (Australia), 250 Camberwell Road, Camberwell, Victoria 3124, Australia
(a division of Pearson Australia Group Pty Ltd)
Penguin Books India Pvt Ltd, 11 Community Centre, Panchsheel Park, New Delhi – 110 017, India
Penguin Group (NZ), 67 Apollo Drive, Rosedale, North Shore 0632, New Zealand
(a division of Pearson New Zealand Ltd)
Penguin Books (South Africa) (Pty) Ltd, 24 Sturdee Avenue, Rosebank, Johannesburg 2196, South Africa

Penguin Books Ltd, Registered Offices: 80 Strand, London WC2R 0RL, England

penguin.com

First published 2010
1

Copyright © Sarwat Chadda, 2010
All rights reserved

The moral right of the author has been asserted

Set in Sabon MT 11/15pt by Palimpsest Book Production Limited, Falkirk, Stirlingshire
Made and printed in England by Clays Ltd, St Ives plc

British Library Cataloguing in Publication Data
A CIP catalogue record for this book is available from the British Library

ISBN: 978-0-141-32588-0

www.greenpenguin.co.uk

Mixed Sources
Product group from well-managed
forests and other controlled sources
www.fsc.org Cert no. SA-COC-1592
© 1996 Forest Stewardship Council

Penguin Books is committed to a sustainable future
for our business, our readers and our planet.
The book in your hands is made from paper
certified by the Forest Stewardship Council.

To my wife and daughters

I came upon a small child, the daughter of a local farmer. She was no more than four, with shining eyes and curling auburn hair.

I devoured her. Her flesh was most delicious.

Confession of Pierre de Gévaudan, 1767

CHAPTER 1

The Rottweiler's head lay in a bush, just off the snow-sprinkled path. One eye was gone, leaving a blood-encrusted socket. Its tongue hung out stupidly from a broken jaw. The body was a few metres further, its chest carved open so the ribs stuck out of the skin like a row of gruesome lollipops.

Billi covered her face with her sleeve. The cold night air was fresh with January frost, but the corpse stank of spilt intestines. The dog was, had been, brutishly big, but its size had not saved it from being torn apart.

'Well?' asked Pelleas as he searched further along the path, scanning the ground with his torch. They were on the edge of the woods, spiny trees to one side and a low hedge bordering a white-coated field to the other. The dense snow clouds of the day had lifted, leaving the velvet-black sky hazy with starlight and the crescent moon. The sky over London never looked like this – vast and fathomless.

Billi snapped off a twig and used it to bind her long, black hair in a loose bun. She leaned over the corpse, directing her torch at the wounds. She'd seen the pictures of the other slaughtered victims, but the artificial eye of the lens had made them seem remote, fake even. This was sickeningly real. She poked at the body with a stick and grimaced as semi-congealed blood oozed from the gaping tears. They hadn't been made with knives – that much was obvious.

They'd been made with claws.

Without touching, Billi spread her hand carefully over the line of the wounds. Five ragged talons had been dragged through the dog's guts. Judging by the width of the wounds, the beast was big. 'Definitely a Loony,' she said.

Pelleas peered over his shoulder. 'You mean "were-wolf", of course.'

'Of course.'

Pelleas was a stickler and didn't like the slang she and the other squires used. They had a whole directory for the Unholy. Loony. Fang-face. Goat-head. Casper. The list went on and on, each squire adding something new. Billi straightened and adjusted the sword tucked into her belt, resting her hand on the leather-bound hilt. She'd brought a *wakizashi*, a single-edged Japanese short-sword. It had been her godfather's and she hoped that something of his strength still lingered in it. She clicked the blade out a few centimetres, just enough to see the torch glisten on the deadly, mirror-like surface, then slammed it back in place.

'This the one?' Billi asked.

Pelleas inspected the corpse. He'd been hunting Loonies most of his adult life, and to him a claw wound was as individual as a fingerprint. He lowered his fingers into the gaping holes, checking the depth of the cuts. He smiled grimly.

'Yes, it's Old Grey,' he said, wiping his bloody fingers in the snow. 'At last.' Pelleas scratched his arm and peered around. He'd come close to it in Dartmoor, only for it to escape and leave him with a scar that ran from his elbow to his wrist. Billi knew Pelleas had very personal reasons for hunting this creature down. He wasn't the first to disguise revenge as duty.

They'd been hunting this werewolf for over four months, following its bloody trail from Cornwall, Devon, through the south-east, all the way to here – Thetford Forest in East Anglia. Thirteen dead across five counties. Werewolves were territorial and only went off reservation if they were hunting something, or someone, very special.

'I wonder if it's an Oracle they're looking for?' said Billi as she peered into the thicket of branches, seeing nothing but darkness.

'Another one like Kay?' Pelleas tapped his rapier against his leg. 'Doesn't seem likely, does it?'

No, it didn't. People like Kay only came along once in a lifetime, if you were lucky. Billi stared down at the dog and her hand locked rigid round the sword hilt. Kay had been more than an Oracle. He'd been her best friend since they were ten and he'd been the one person she'd

3

cared about. Then he'd turned into something more. She'd loved him more than anyone else. But now he was lying in a grave on the Kent coast. For a moment Billi felt lost; she wiped her face, but there was nothing there to wipe away. Kay was gone and she had a job to do, here and now. Dwelling on the past solved nothing.

'You sure it's not one of the Bodmin pack?' Billi asked, wanting to think about something else. But Pelleas shook his head.

'The Bodmin werewolves aren't the problem. They haven't hunted humans for the last six years. Arthur saw to that, remember?'

'I remember.' How could she not? Her father had fought the alpha male and chopped its arm off. God, she could picture that severed limb, dripping blood all over the kitchen table, like it was yesterday. That night she'd learned her father and his friends weren't just porters at the Inns of Court. Maybe her life would have been better if they were really servants, cleaners and handymen. Instead of being the Poor Fellow Soldiers of Jesus Christ and of the Temple of Solomon.

The Knights Templar.

Like her.

Ever since that duel the Bodmin werewolves had stuck to the Accord between Templar and wolf; the Templars left them alone and they left humans alone.

No, this was a rogue, a wolf driven mad by bloodlust. It needed to be put down.

Billi scanned the bloodied snow around the body. A

row of pawprints ran alongside the ripped-up torso. The imprints were deep, just the balls of the feet with wide-splayed toes. The snow hadn't settled into them, meaning they'd been made recently. Billi shivered as she peered into the black net of bristly trees.

'I'm calling the others,' she said. 'The werewolf could still be –'

A branch creaked.

Instantly the Templars clicked off their torches.

Bad bad bad.

Ever so slowly Billi and Pelleas sank down to their knees. Something snorted loudly and a growl rattled out of the darkness. Billi went down on to her belly, burying herself in the muddy snow, using it to cover her scent. Some of it trickled down her collar, but she didn't dare shiver. Her fingers tightened round her scabbard and she forced every muscle still, and held her breath.

A brittle twig snapped as the Loony came out on to the path, five or six metres from where they hid. All Billi could see was a huge, black silhouette, almost two metres tall, wrapped in sinewy muscle and dressed in a ragged pelt. It raised its face skywards and howled at the sickle-edged moon.

Old scars were carved into its mangy grey fur. Pelleas's monster, just as he'd described it. It stepped forward on reverse-kneed legs, coiled and ever ready to leap, its disproportionately long arms ending in uneven, yellow-ivory talons. Its tail must have been bitten or torn off in some fight a long time ago, leaving just a stub. Billi took in the demonic green eyes that gazed at the moon. The werewolf turned its snout this way and that, its black lips peeled back into a grotesque grin, fangs slimy with spittle.

Billi pushed further into the snow as the beast's gaze lingered over her. The werewolf's body tensed and its long hairs quivered as it gave a guttural hiss. Had it seen her? Billi dragged her hand over the sword hilt. Despite her training, despite the steel, she felt a dread slide over her, colder than the snow.

A bush shook as a second werewolf emerged. Billi let slip a sigh as the Old Grey's attention shifted to the new arrival. This beast was in its prime, heavily muscled, its fur thick and red, claws bright and razor-sharp. Its eyes were the same green as the older monster, and instantly Billi knew they were kin, not just by the eyes but in the way the Big Red mimicked the elder's stance and movements. The Old Grey grunted at the younger werewolf.

They launched forward, bursting through the hedge and loping over the field in a blur. Moonlight lay silver on their backs, but within seconds they were fading.

Pelleas sprang up. 'Quick, Billi! What's over there?' He pointed his rapier towards the far edge of the field where the wolves had run.

Out there? Billi racked her brain. She'd checked the Ordnance Survey only an hour ago . . .

'A farmhouse.' *Oh no*.

Pelleas swore and pushed himself through the hedge. 'Pelleas,' Billi hissed. 'The others.' Their eyes met. Two knights might take one werewolf, but the odds shifted badly one-to-one. They should wait for reinforcements. But she could see the fire in his gaze. Pelleas was rake-thin, but as tough and as fast as a whiplash. He wasn't going to let the werewolves go, not after having lost them the last time.

'It's our duty, Billi.' He jumped over the hedge and ran.

Duty. Always duty. It was their duty to fight, no matter what the odds, no matter who the foe. To fight and, if necessary, to die.

Wasn't that what Templars did best? They called it martyrdom, but it amounted to the same thing. Wasn't it one of the Rules of the Order?

You shall keep the company of martyrs.

They needed backup, and now. Billi's thumb hammered out F-A-R-M-H-O-U-S-E on her mobile as she flicked her sword free from its scabbard. *Wakizashi* aloft, she turned her body sideways and tried to use her long legs to clamber over the hedge. It scratched and pulled at her, but eventually she broke through. She ran after Pelleas.

CHAPTER 2

A howl, part bestial cry and part human scream, ripped through the night air. Billi pumped her long legs harder, closing the gap between her and Pelleas. But as she caught the glint of moonlight on her naked blade, the dread slowly gave way to something else – excitement. Fire rose up through her guts, along her arteries and into her heart. Her knuckles whitened as they gripped the sword hilt tighter.

Ahead she heard glass shatter, then more screams – and these very human.

'Come on, Billi!' shouted Pelleas. He was over a low wooden fence in an instant.

She hadn't gone far, but Billi's heart pounded in her chest like she'd run a marathon. She tumbled the last few metres and crashed into the fence. She knelt there, shaking her head clear. Howls, screams and Pelleas's battle cry echoed. She wiped the snow off her face and saw Pelleas charge into the house, rapier raised. Then she heard a man's cry, cut off suddenly and ending with a spluttering cough.

Any sane person would turn around and get the hell out of there.

But what part of Billi's life had ever been sane?

'*Deus vult!*' she screamed, scrambling over the fence and steaming towards the farmhouse. Broken glass from the French windows littered the yellow paving slabs. Billi jumped through the doorframe and into the kitchen.

A man was dead. He lay askew on the flagstone floor, his chest ripped open and his lifeblood pooling round him. His legs, still in a pair of striped pyjamas, twitched, but just for a moment.

The Old Grey, snout and teeth red from its kill, moved warily in front of Pelleas, searching for an opening past his deadly steel. Behind it the Big Red had finished its own murderous work. A woman wearing a blood-washed dressing gown leaned against the coarse brick wall. Her eyes bore only the dimmest life. The Big Red seemed to be holding her up, its right paw pressed against her chest. Then it slowly pulled out its talons, each one coming free of her body with a wet, sticky slurp. The woman slid gently down the wall.

Billi froze. Suddenly her sword seemed puny against those dripping talons. These were natural-born killers, bred to it through thousands of generations. Every kilogram of muscle, every centimetre of bone, was built to slaughter.

'Mummy!' The scream drew everyone's attention. Kneeling at the top of the wooden stairs was a blonde girl, maybe eight or nine, wearing a pair of pony-print pyjamas. She stared at her parents' corpses, her face deathly white. Then she turned and ran.

And so did Old Grey.

Pelleas slashed the air and the old werewolf backed away. Billi darted through the sudden gap. The werewolf spun and Billi ducked as its claws swiped the air. The five lethal blades clicked together, but caught only a few strands of her black hair. Billi took the stairs in three bounds, leaving the carnage in the kitchen behind her. She reached the top of the stairs just in time to see the furthest door down the landing slam shut. She ran to it and twisted the handle. Locked.

'Open up!' Billi cried. The white-painted door had the wooden letters VASILISA fixed to it. A few bounced off as Billi smashed her sword hilt into the thick wood. 'Let me in, Vasilisa!'

The stairs creaked.

'Pelleas?' Billi looked down the corridor. *Please, please let it be him.* 'Pelleas?'

The shape turned its long, lupine head and out of the darkness predatory green eyes glowed. Its snarl was deep and low, so elemental that the air quivered. Big Red stepped closer, dragging its long, still-bloody claws along the plaster, digging deep grooves along both walls. There was no way past it. Behind Billi was a window and a four-metre drop. She was trapped.

'Vasilisa . . .' But the door remained firmly locked. Billi backed away, *wakizashi* held firmly in her right hand, its tip pointed directly at the werewolf's heart.

They were a few metres apart. Red's black lips crept into a snarl, letting Billi see each of those murderous canines. It leapt.

The charge knocked Billi over and sent the sword flying. Red dug its claws into her shoulders. Billi shoved her feet into its belly and pushed as she rolled backwards. She almost didn't make it; the beast was heavier than she'd thought. Her legs trembled, but she squeezed every ounce of power she had into the throw and suddenly the werewolf tumbled over her and crashed through the window. Its howl broke into a yelp and there was the sound of more glass shattering outside.

Then silence.

The floor swayed as Billi stood. Her muscles burned with pain, and blood streamed down her back from the claw wounds. She leaned her head, eyes closed, against Vasilisa's bedroom door.

'Open the bloody door. Now,' she whispered.

There was a click and a light scurrying of feet.

'Thank you.'

The girl sat in the corner of the unlit bedroom. The house was quiet, and that wasn't good. Billi couldn't let that bother her; she had only one priority and that was getting out of here. But where was Pelleas? Was he still alive? She closed the door and pushed the bolt. Then Billi went to the window overlooking a long front garden. Thick vines covered the wall and a trellis ran from the guttering down to the ground. To the side she saw a greenhouse, the roof broken where the werewolf must have fallen through, but nothing stirring within. In the far distance she saw headlights approaching down the country lane that passed along the farmhouse garden.

Dad's coming, thank God.

'Come here, Vasilisa,' Billi said, grabbing her arm.

'No!' She squirmed and scratched, but Billi just tightened her grip. Vasilisa scurried back, knocking over her bedside table. The lamp broke, but Billi caught sight of something shiny rolling across the floor.

It was one of those Russian dolls: open it up and there would be another inside. Then another inside that and so on. What were they called? Whatever the name, it was beautiful. Delicately painted with a red and gold shawl, flowers on its blouse, its cheeks rosy. So polished it glowed.

'Ow!' Billi cried. Vasilisa hung on to her, her tiny, white teeth sunk deep into Billi's wrist. 'Let go!' She shook Vasilisa off. The bites left a neat arc of red dents. Didn't the girl get it? She was trying to save her!

'Where's my mum –' Billi slapped her free hand over the girl's mouth.

Something was scratching at the door.

'Pelleas?' Billi asked.

It sniffed under the gap at the bottom of the door.

Billi's guts turned cold. Pelleas wasn't coming. Not ever.

'Want grrrl,' it snarled. The wolf voice box mutilated its speech, but Billi heard clearly enough. She glanced back at Vasilisa.

A lot of people were already dead because of this girl. 'You had better be worth it,' Billi muttered.

The door groaned as powerful arms pushed against the wood.

The older werewolf, it had to be. Maybe if she was quick, Billi could shove her sword under and slice it. She reached for her belt.

Bollocks. No sword. She'd dropped it fighting Red. *Big bloody bollocks.*

The door jumped in its frame as the werewolf charged it. It howled as long, vertical cracks broke open on the door.

Billi pressed her bleeding shoulder against a heavy wardrobe and pushed. It slid along the wooden floor until it caught its feet on an unseen edge. Billi pushed harder and it tilted, then crashed down in front of the door, blocking it.

She should stand and fight. That's what a Templar would do. Billi searched the room and picked up a kid's hockey stick. The door jumped again as Old Grey slammed against it and the fallen wardrobe slid a few centimetres.

'Want grrrl!'

Billi gazed at Vasilisa, whimpering in the corner.

There would be no fight. The werewolf would kill Billi and get the girl. The girl seemed to be important. Perhaps she was an Oracle after all.

'C'mon, we're leaving,' said Billi as she smashed the window with the hockey stick. The beast in the corridor howled again and charged the door, each crash sounding like a death-knell.

'Vasilisa!' Billi ordered. Vasilisa screamed as claws dug through a crack in the door and a smouldering green eye peered in.

Billi tossed the stick away and grabbed the child round the waist. She climbed out on to the window sill, resting her right foot on the trellis. It bent, but held.

Wood tore and the wardrobe leapt in the air. The Old Grey ripped the remains of the door off its hinges and threw it at the window. Billi gripped a thick cord of vine. Her left foot scrabbled on the wall, looking for the smallest purchase, but found nothing. A long, hairy arm swiped the air, just missing her face. Billi slipped down the four-metre tangle of vines and trellis, tearing her knees and arms as she tried vainly to grab on to something. They hit the ground hard, Vasilisa landing on top and punching out all her breath. Billi blinked, trying to get the sparks to stop flashing in her eyes. She stood groggily and, on her second attempt, took hold of Vasilisa's sleeve. She heard the car getting closer.

Old Grey, squatting on the window sill, hopped off and landed without a sound. Billi ran, half-dragging, half-carrying Vasilisa. Beyond the hedge the air echoed with the sound of the approaching car, its lights on full beam and spilling across the garden, decorating the ground with a maze of shadows cast by the small, bare apple trees that dotted the lawn.

Billi weaved in and out of the irregular orchard, teeth

snapping behind her. She ducked below a branch and skidded round a trunk, but the werewolf matched every move. Her mad-speed heartbeat filled her ears and her chest burned as she panted in the bitter, cold air. She pulled Vasilisa tight as she saw the gate and barged through it, slipping over an iced-up paving slab. They rolled across the road into the ditch opposite and every bone got a bashing. They lay there, stunned, on the icy ground.

The monster approached, glowing white with victory. Then the Jaguar braked. Its tyres screamed and it smashed the werewolf squarely in the chest, and suddenly the beast was gone. Smoke rose off the rubber burnt on to the road.

The doors crashed open and two men leapt out. Billi's father, Arthur, ran to the front of the car, a heavy sword aloft and his mail armour shimmering silver in the head-lights. He gazed around, but Old Grey had vanished. The second man came up to Billi and Vasilisa.

'Ça va?' said Lance. He hoisted Billi up. 'How are you, Bilqis?' He turned his head slightly sideways so he could look with his right eye; his left was hidden behind a worn leather patch. Billi, too winded to speak, just nodded.

Arthur joined them. His blue eyes shone under his dark brow.

'It's gone,' he said. He glanced at Billi and the small girl. 'Where's Pelleas?'

But before Billi could answer the typically abrupt demand from her dad another vehicle, a van, came up behind them and screeched to a halt. The side panel slid open and out came Gwaine and Bors. Gwaine, the grizzly old warrior, carried his favourite battle axe and Bors a pair of machete-like short-swords.

'There were two,' said Billi. Arthur's deep-blue eyes burned and the others gathered round her.

'Where's the second?' he asked.

'Back there.' Billi pointed back to the farmhouse. 'With Pelleas,' she said.

CHAPTER 3

Billi winced as she straightened up. The claw wounds Red had given her felt like burning oil on her back.

'What's wrong?' asked Arthur.

'Nothing.'

'Doesn't look like nothing. Go and see Elaine.' Arthur tapped Lance's shoulder. 'Lance, you watch 'em both.'

'*Oui*.' Lance smiled at Billi and nodded towards the van. He then held out his hand to Vasilisa. 'Do not be afraid, *ma chérie*.' After a moment's hesitation she took it.

'My mum . . .' started Vasilisa. Lance glanced towards Billi, who shook her head. Vasilisa didn't notice. She was lost, gazing at her home with pale, empty eyes.

'We will look after you,' said Lance. He smiled down at Vasilisa and wiped her cheek. The tears came, but she didn't give in to sobbing. Billi turned away.

She banged on the side of the van. 'Wake up, Elaine!'

The driver's door opened and Elaine sat there, her bony arms resting on the steering wheel. Her slate-grey hair hung like thatch down to her shoulders and she scowled as a stream of cigarette smoke unwound from her nostrils. Billi pointed at her back.

'A Loony.'

Elaine flicked the cigarette past Billi as she climbed in. A mattress lay on the floor with a plastic sheet on it. The wall opposite was lined with compartments of various sizes, all with lockable doors. Two long, fluorescent tubes hummed to life, filling the small van with stark, blue-white light.

'Boots off and lie down,' Elaine ordered.

As Billi lay down on her belly Elaine cut the back off Billi's jacket and began mopping up the blood.

'You're lucky. It was a young wolf. You can tell by the tears: neat and clean,' said Elaine. 'Older werewolves have more jagged claws. Bugger to stitch up.'

'Strange, I don't feel lucky.'

'Well, you are. In more ways than one. The lycanthropy infection is much stronger in older wolves and it takes hold almost immediately. This one –' she poked a raw bit of skin and Billi winced – 'it's barely an adult. You probably aren't infected anyway.'

'Let's be sure, shall we?'

Elaine wiped the wound clean. 'You'll end up with more scars than your dad.'

'As long as they're not all over my face, I don't care.'

'Just lie still.'

Billi shifted around, but Elaine, her hands much stronger than her physique implied, held Billi down firmly on the cold mattress.

Billi couldn't stop thinking about Pelleas. Another Templar gone. Her dad had warned her that the Bataille Ténébreuse, the Templars' war against the Unholy, took its toll. But the price was heavy. Her godfather Percy, Berrant, Father Balin, now Pelleas. Billi closed her eyes, but their faces were there. She could see them, in the mists of the grey shores. But one stood out, closest to her.

Kay.

She could picture the white-blond hair, the albino-pale skin, the secret smile he used to have, like he knew all the answers. They'd grown up and trained side by side. They'd made plans together to go away. To leave the Templars and be like normal people – to be together. It had been a lie, of course. There was only one way out of the Templars.

Kay would welcome Pelleas now.

'Pelleas?' asked Elaine.

'There was nothing I could do. There were two of them.' Billi waited for a response, but Elaine stayed quiet. Her fingers dug into Billi's muscles and Billi gritted her teeth, feeling the blood seeping down her back.

'Saved that girl, though,' said Elaine. She pulled out a box and opened it. The van was suddenly filled with the odour of rotten vegetables and oil.

'They wanted her badly,' Billi said. 'Think she could be one?'

Elaine paused. 'An Oracle?' She pressed a wet flannel over Billi's cuts. 'Maybe.' Elaine used the Templar term too, but once they'd been called witches, or prophets.

The modern secular word was psychic. It was children such as these the werewolves ritually sacrificed to their goddess, believing in return that she would bestow on them a spring season full of good hunting.

Billi winced as Elaine got busy with a pair of silver tweezers, not too gently poking the open wounds to check that no shards of claw remained. She tightened her hands into fists and buried her face further down. *Jesus, that hurts.*

Elaine laid the wet poultice on Billi's bare back, pressing it firmly into the channels of flesh, making sure the medicine soaked in deeply.

'It stinks,' said Billi.

'This, girl, is my own special recipe. Wolfsbane, a dash of holy oil and ground-up werewolf bones. You know how hard it is to get werewolf bones? How much it cost?'

'Bet it cost some Loony an arm or a leg.'

Elaine laughed. 'Too true. An arm, in this case.'

'How long do I have to keep it on?'

'It takes a while for the herbs to soak in and take effect. So, keep it on for a few days – long enough to suck the poison out. You don't want to turn, do you?'

Like she didn't know. Billi had spent the last few months studying nothing but lycanthropy. Anyone could turn into a werewolf if they were scratched or bitten by one. Everyone had the Beast Within. It was the savage part of their soul that revelled in slaughter and violence. It was bloodlust.

If injured by a werewolf, the Beast Within would awaken. First there'd be the dreams, of hunting, of running in the dark forests and howling. Then the appetite would change – the craving for raw meat and red juices. The redder the better. Rage would come. Mindless and psychotic urges to kill and feed. Giving in to it only accelerated the transformation process. So for some the change was swift; others – those with strong wills – held on to their humanity, but the struggle was constant and if they gave in, the change would occur.

And eventually everyone gave in and a new werewolf would howl with joy beneath the moon's ghostly light. Nothing human would remain, except for the eyes. The eyes stayed human. Only Elaine's poultice prevented the infection from taking hold. It had saved more than a few knights in the past.

'You . . . don't think that'll happen? Do you?'

Elaine tore off long strips of tape. 'No, but call me if you have any strange urges.'

'Like what?'

'Like wanting to chase cats.'

Once the bandages were fixed, Elaine handed Billi a fresh shirt and unrolled a blanket. She stepped out for a cigarette break while Billi changed. Billi glanced at her watch: two in the morning. With any luck she'd get four hours' sleep, then up for morning prayers and off to school.

Just great. PE tomorrow. How was she going to explain why she looked like Tutankhamun? The immense

21

weight of tonight's action bore down on her hard, squeezing her into the mattress, and it seemed like her bones weighed as much as lead; she couldn't move for the exhaustion. Just a few hours' sleep . . .

'Well?' came Elaine's voice from outside.

'Too late,' said Arthur wearily. 'Pelleas is dead.'

Even though she'd known it, it still hurt. Billi closed her eyes and tried to blank out the black hole in her stomach.

Arthur continued. 'We'll grab what we can, then get out of here. A bloody balls-up, Elaine. Maybe I shouldn't have sent Billi out so soon.' He shuffled. 'How is she?'

Billi heard the sharp rip of a match swiftly followed by Elaine's wheezing. They were just outside. The van softly tilted as someone, Dad probably, leaned against it.

'She'll be OK.'

'Will she?' Billi heard him kick a stone in frustration. 'She's changed, Elaine.'

Billi's eyes felt hot and watery. She blamed it on the wolfsbane poultices.

He sighed. 'It's been three months but, if anything, she's worse.'

'She loved Kay. You of all people should understand that.'

'But she's just a child.'

'Sixteen in a few months,' Elaine said. 'She's young, Art, but I don't think she's ever been a child. Kay died and she thinks it was her fault. She's taken on a lot of responsibility.'

'She's a Templar.'

Elaine changed the subject. 'What about the girl? Think she could be the one?'

'An Oracle? Lot of effort's been put in if she isn't.' Arthur tapped his sword hilt against the van. 'Were-wolves aren't usually wrong about this sort of thing. They did the same with Kay, remember? The Bodmin pack came looking soon after we found him.' The van rocked slightly as Arthur moved. 'But they've stuck to the Accord ever since.'

'Ever since you chopped their leader's arm off, right?'

'Right.'

'And if she is an Oracle?' asked Elaine. Billi could hear the fear, and excitement, in the old woman's voice.

'Then thank God we got to her first.' Arthur's boots squelched in the slush as he walked away.

CHAPTER 4

Billi slept in the van and only started to stir when the tyres trundled over the cobbles of Temple District.

Home.

She sat up and leaned over the passenger seat. It was still early and the sun wouldn't be up for a few hours yet. The van's engine echoed within the narrow confines of the alleyways that dropped south of Fleet Street and into Temple District. Bors sat slumped in the passenger seat, his twin swords beside him. Billi knocked them on to the floor with a clatter as she climbed up front next to him.

'Oi, watch it,' muttered Bors as he rubbed the sleep out of his face. Blinking blearily, he searched the dashboard until his hand found a sausage roll, which he shoved into his mouth. He caught Billi's stare. 'Sorry,' he said, spitting flakes over his lap. 'Did you want some?'

'God Almighty, d'you have a trough at home or what?'

They entered the main Temple car park on King's Bench Walk and found Father Rowland waiting for them with Mordred, the new squire. The chaplain's thin frame was lost in a huge, black overcoat, his bald head and the tips of his frozen ears the only things visible above his scarf.

Bors jumped out the moment the van halted. He handed his swords over to Mordred.

'Polish these.' He licked the last few crumbs off his fingers. 'And before breakfast, mind.'

The two couldn't be more different. Mordred, an Ethiopian refugee the Order had literally picked up off the streets, was tall and elegant, with jet-black skin and deep, thoughtful eyes. Bors, bigger in girth if not height, was a cannonball of muscle. His neck was non-existent, his jaw comprised of a patch of ginger bristles and his eyes were piggy and close together. But he was a knight and Mordred was a squire.

'Want him to run your bath while he's at it?' said Billi as Mordred left.

Bors laughed.

Father Rowland helped Elaine out and peered in behind her.

'Where's Pelleas?'

Elaine looked at Billi. 'You want to tell him?'

No, not really. But Elaine had already wandered off.

'Dead, Father.'

'Oh.' Rowland touched his crucifix. 'What happened?'

Billi reminded herself this was all new for Rowland. The previous Temple chaplain had just been buried when Rowland had arrived, fresh-faced and eager, all peachy-keen from the seminary. He had thought he'd be running choirs and carrying out christenings. Billi had turned up at the chaplain's house with Arthur and a few of the others. An unofficial welcoming committee. All in all he'd taken it well. Rowland was to manage the day-to-day affairs of the Temple Church except when the Templars themselves required it. He was responsible for disposing of the bodies and managing their library: the remnants of the original library of occult lore the Templars had salvaged from the Inquisition.

Only later did Billi notice the empty wine bottles piling up in the recycling box outside his door. He looked like he could do with a drink right now.

'Werewolves,' Billi said.

Arthur's Jaguar rolled up. Lance lifted the sleeping Vasilisa from the back seat while Arthur and Gwaine joined Billi and Rowland. Over his shoulder Arthur carried his mail shirt, rolled up and held in a bundle by an old leather belt. In his right hand he carried the Templar Sword.

Arthur turned to Gwaine. 'I want a conclave sorted. We need to review what happened tonight.' He inspected his watch. 'Couple of hours' rest, then we'll talk at six thirty, before matins.' Gwaine nodded and left to make arrangements.

Rowland put his hand on Arthur's shoulder, like a good priest should.

'I've just heard about Pelleas, Arthur.' He frowned with concern. 'Is there anything you need?'

'Shovels,' said Arthur. He pointed towards his car. 'Pelleas is in the boot.'

'You're . . . you're joking, of course,' said Rowland.

Arthur did not have his joking face on. He turned to Billi. 'Go with Lance. Put Vasilisa in the spare bedroom.'

'She's staying with us?' Billi asked. She pulled the blanket over her shoulders. The girl had just seen her parents slaughtered and they were leaving Billi to pick up the pieces. She didn't want to be dealing with a hysterical kid first thing in the morning. 'It's not my job to babysit. Give her to Rowland.'

'Your job is to do what I tell you.' Arthur settled the weight of his armour better. '*Now*, Billi.'

Billi headed towards home on Middle Temple Lane, followed by Lance, who carried the sleeping girl in his arms.

The smell of fresh paint still lingered as she entered their house. Billi inspected the limp fern plant beside the door. Their attempt to bring some life into their home was failing miserably. None of the paintings were back up yet, except one. Jacques de Molay, the last Templar Grand Master, gazed down at them as they came in.

'Top of the stairs, Lance. I'll bring some blankets.'

Lance nodded and eased Vasilisa through the doorway and up the steps.

Billi stopped in front of the portrait. As a kid she'd always felt a little scared passing under it.

Now?

These days she didn't feel anything.

A short nap and Billi was up by six. She dressed, checked that the poultice was still in place and she hadn't grown a fur pelt overnight. So far – not hairy. She knew if she was infected, the pain of transformation would come with the moonlight, growing stronger as the moon waxed. She'd known injured knights who'd fought the urge to transform for days, battling their willpower against the Beast Within. Some succeeded for a while, but everyone succumbed under the light of the full moon. Still, she felt no desire to run naked in the woods, howling at the moon quite yet.

She struggled to put her shirt on. Her muscles complained loudly about the treatment they'd received last night. The fragrance of warm bread was rising out of the kitchen as she opened her bedroom door.

'*Bonjour*, Bilqis,' said Lance as she wandered into the kitchen. He slid open the oven and drew out a tray of golden croissants. He emptied them on to a china dish with a shake. 'Breakfast?'

Of course, guard duty. Arthur must have arranged a rotation of knights to protect Vasilisa. The werewolves weren't going to give up their prey that easily. Sooner or later they'd come around here, trying to sniff her out.

Billi sat at the table while Lance stirred up a bowl of hot chocolate. She could only remember being made breakfast once before.

Kay had dished up her usual: muesli and a dollop of honey. Exactly two months and nineteen days ago.

Lance knew his way around a kitchen. The Frenchman had been a patisserie chef in Marseilles. He'd also been a smuggler before getting involved with the Templars. Billi didn't know the full story, but that's how he'd lost his eye.

Billi rocked back on her chair and looked around. The potted plants on either side of the door didn't look good. No matter what she did they just carried on drooping. Her *wakizashi* was leaning against the table. She picked it up and checked the blade: clean and perfect.

'I thought you might like that back,' said Lance. 'I found it in the farmhouse.'

'Thanks, I'm seeing Percy after school. Wasn't looking forward to telling him I'd lost his favourite sword.' She put it down on the table. 'What else did you find?'

'Little of use.'

Billi glanced at yesterday's newspaper that her dad had spread out to soak up the oil he used for weapons' cleaning. The usual blah-blah. Political scandals. More trouble in the Middle East. Football reports and who was wearing what at some charity do last night. Her gaze rested on the image of a smouldering volcano. Out in Italy Vesuvius was rumbling, as it had been on and off for a month. Half of Naples had been evacuated. The other half had decided to stay; rumbles and smoke from the volcano were nothing new.

She was doing Vesuvius as part of her Latin course. It was the one subject she excelled in. There were plans for a school trip in the summer to look at the ruins of Pompeii, the Roman city that had been wiped out by the last big eruption, back in AD 79. It would be cool to go and Billi knew if she asked her dad he'd say yes.

Billi scrunched the paper up. No, she had her Templar duties. Only they mattered.

A plate clattered in front of her. The croissant had been gently torn open and butter lay, molten and puddled, within it. Lance poured out a bowl of hot chocolate and swished a spoon in it. He added a sprinkle of cinnamon.

'*Voilà*.' He leaned against the worktop, waiting. 'Eat, please.'

Billi took a bite and the croissant nearly dissolved in her mouth.

'Wow,' she whispered.

He shrugged like it was nothing; excellence came easily to him. Then he started to set up another meal on a tray: breakfast for Vasilisa.

Billi glanced towards the door and the stairs. The girl felt like an uninvited houseguest, an intruder. Why? She didn't mean anything to Billi, so what was it about her that made Billi so uncomfortable? She should be glad: if Vasilisa was an Oracle, she'd strengthen the Order. But Billi wasn't glad, and couldn't understand why.

'How is she?'

'Still asleep.' Lance glanced up at the clock over the doorway. It was almost half six. 'I will leave some food; you will take it later?'

Billi nodded and popped the last of the croissant in her mouth as she stood.

The conclave was starting.

Billi ran across the ice-covered Temple courtyard. God didn't like to be kept waiting. Neither did her dad.

Her tanned army greatcoat that, despite her own height, swept her ankles. Collar up, chin down, she blinked as the frosty breeze stung her eyes. The Temple Church stood hidden behind towers of scaffolding and sheets of heavy-duty plastic. The repairs were moving slowly – you didn't rush on a nine-hundred-year-old building. The stained-glass windows were all boarded up and it would be another year before they could be replaced.

She paused by the side door, her hand touching the cold stone. The official story was that a forgotten UXB – an unexploded bomb – had gone off in the cata-combs. The building had been bombed during the Second World War, so it was possible that one of the devices had somehow been buried, and sat silent and dormant for all these years until a freak event set it off.

It was logical. It had a basis in reality.

It was a lie.

The truth had a basis in another reality. Had she really met the Devil here? Had he really unleashed his celestial *numina*, his supernatural light, almost blinding her and nearly destroying Temple Church?

Like the thrones of ancient kings, nine high-backed chairs had been arranged in an irregular circle between the effigies of the ancient patrons lying in stone on the floor.

Elaine and Father Rowland sat apart on smaller stools, observing, but not belonging.

The Knights Templar. Arthur, the Templar Master, looked tired and was turning his wedding ring around, never a good sign. Gwaine sat opposite, in his usual position of conflict. In the gloomy light his wrinkles seemed deep crevasses and his eyes were lost in the pits under his lined brow. Gareth, Bors and Mordred watched impassively. Billi looked at the *Sièges Perilous* – two chairs draped in black cloth, commemorating the Order's dead. Kay and now Pelleas. Percy's old position, Marshall, was now Lance's.

Billi kept her head low as she crossed the circle to her seat between Mordred and Bors. Mordred gave her a sympathetic smile as she passed. The church was unheated and Billi's breath puffed out in a great white cloud as she took her seat.

'Now that we're all here maybe we can get down to business,' Arthur said. He stood up and went to the centre of the Round. 'Pelleas's death and the girl: Vasilisa Bulgakov.' He lowered his head. 'Father Rowland will lead a requiem mass for Pelleas tomorrow night. Attendance, it goes without saying, is mandatory.' He beckoned Elaine forward. 'Tell us what you know.'

Elaine came to the edge of the circle. 'While you've

all been catching up on your beauty sleep, I did some sniffing around. Vasilisa and her family came over to England four years ago, when she was five. They're originally from Russia – from Karelia. It's up north on the border with Finland.'

'That's important?' asked Gwaine.

'It's pretty wild. Lots of wolves.' Elaine opened up her folder and handed out a sheet of scanned pictures. 'Of all the packs, they hunt Spring Children most eagerly.'

The photos were of the patio outside Vasilisa's parents' farmhouse. The torch exposed something Billi hadn't noticed last night. The flagstones bore strange carvings.

'These are petroglyphs. Copies of the ones found in Karelia. The original is over five thousand years old. This one.' She pointed at a human figure, little more than a matchstick figure with two circles for breasts and branch-like hands. In one hand was a disc, in the other a crescent. 'It's the goddess image of the Polenitsy.'

'*Eorpata*,' muttered Gwaine. Billi frowned. He would always use Ancient Greek or Latin when English would do just as well. Fortunately she knew Ancient Greek. Unlike Mordred.

'Man-killers,' Billi whispered to him.

Elaine nodded. 'The Polenitsy are an all-female werewolf pack descended from the original Amazons. Out of all the werewolves they follow the ways of the goddess closest. You might call them fundamentalists.'

'They're a long way from home,' said Arthur.

'They could be desperate. Oracles aren't common.

33

The Bodmin pack no longer hunts Spring Children and neither do the Irish wolves, the only other big pack nearby.' Elaine tapped her nails on the top of Gareth's chair. 'I'm convinced they're the ones after Vasilisa, and they are not going to back down quietly. They're old-school.'

'And we'll deal with them the same way we've dealt with all the others,' said Gwaine.

Elaine didn't reply, but Billi could see her doubts. She turned her attention to the photographs. There were markings above the image of the Polenitsy goddess symbol. She could just make out a crucifix. Not like the plain cross of western Christianity, but the Russian Orthodox cross, with three horizontal bars, the lowest one slanted.

'What's this?' She pointed at the cross.

Elaine continued. 'I think the Bulgakovs were, in their own crude way, trying to guard against the goddess. A lot of people believe the crucifix is the perfect defence against all the Unholy.'

'It didn't work,' snorted Bors.

'Believing in something doesn't make it real,' said Arthur. 'So is Vasilisa an Oracle?'

Elaine shook her head. 'I don't know yet. Her parents knew something was up, though. But she's young and even if she *does* have powers, they'll manifest themselves irregularly and she'll have no conscious control of them.'

'But Kay was showing telepathic powers at nine – the same age as this Vasilisa,' said Billi.

Elaine laughed. 'Kay was an extraordinarily powerful psychic. We won't come across his like again. No, if Vasilisa has some talent, it won't be at Kay's level.'

'Don't you have tests or something you could do?' Billi continued.

'You can't just stick a meter in her and get a reading.' Elaine held up her hands, fingers out. 'There are six classes of Oracle: mentalists like Kay – mind-reading and all that telekinetic stuff. Then you've got the mediums, the spirit-talkers. Healers. Elementalists. The fire-starters, and finally the prophets.' Elaine closed her hands into fists. 'Youngsters usually have a bit of ability in each, but that settles down into one or two fields by puberty. Kay was amazing . . .' There was more than a hint of pride when Elaine talked about her last, best pupil. 'He still retained powers in mind-reading, spirit-talking and prophecy well into his teens. But it'll take time to pin Vasilisa down, assuming she is psychic, of course.'

'Well, is she?' interrupted Gwaine. 'Is she an Oracle?'

Elaine scratched her chin. 'The werewolves would call her a Spring Child. They believe that if they sacrifice her to their goddess during the full moon the goddess will reward them with a good spring and bountiful hunting. The spirit of the child is taken by the goddess, renewing her, and the body is eaten by the pack.'

'Good God,' whispered Mordred.

'They're called the Unholy for a reason,' replied Billi. 'But human sacrifice was fairly common in primitive religions.' She'd studied how the followers of the goddess would take their victim, all garlanded in flowers and jewels, to a sacred spot, be it a cave or glade or lake. One priestess, in the guise of the goddess, would then slaughter the body to be passed among the faithful.

'And this goddess? Who is she?' asked Mordred.

'Gaia. Hecate. Morrigan. Isis,' said Elaine with a shrug. 'She's the goddess of nature, the wild and of magic. She's been revered since prehistoric times and each culture had a different name for her. But the Polenitsy call her by her old, old name.' Elaine looked around the circle. 'Baba Yaga.'

'But she's just a name from fairy tales,' said Mordred. 'She's not real.'

'No, she's real all right. An ancient, wise and very evil old witch.' Elaine's eyes narrowed as she observed the young squire. 'And once people worshipped her as much as we do our gods now.'

'The tales must have begun with someone, I suppose,' said Gareth.

Elaine nodded. 'Imagine someone coming to your tribe. She can control the elements. Read minds and speak with the animals. Heal injuries with a touch. What would you think?'

'You'd think she was a god,' agreed Mordred reluctantly.

Elaine pointed at the crucifix on the far wall. 'Is her story so different from his?'

Arthur snorted. 'You're saying Baba Yaga is like

Jesus? You're going to burn in Hell for that one, Elaine.'

'Time passes,' continued Elaine. 'Baba Yaga's powers wane. The new religion rises and Christianity and advancing civilization drives her deeper into the wilderness. Year by year, century by century, people forget. Only a few still remember the old religion and among them are the Polenitsy. They feed her the souls of the Spring Children; she absorbs their powers, memories and lives and is kept going, weak and decrepit, but alive.'

'Is that possible? To be alive for so long?' Billi asked Elaine. If all this was true, then Baba Yaga must have killed thousands, tens of thousands, over her vast life.

'It's called the Ritual of Devouring and is the darkest *maleficia*,' said Elaine, using the Templar term for all black magic. 'A powerful psychic is able to rip the life force from another psychic, which is why Baba Yaga consumes only . . . *gifted* children; a normal one wouldn't benefit her at all.'

'Consumes?' asked Billi.

Elaine opened her mouth wide and mimed putting food in. 'Eats them whole.' She patted her belly. 'That's what a sacrifice ritual is, after all. The soul of the victim goes to renew the life force of the god. In Baba Yaga's case it is literally true.'

'So Vasilisa's food for this Baba Yaga,' muttered Mordred. 'If she's an Oracle.'

'And if she isn't?' snapped Gwaine. 'Pelleas would have died for nothing.'

37

Arthur stood up again. 'We don't leave innocent children to be stolen by werewolves. Pelleas did not die for nothing.' He nodded at Elaine and she sat down. He looked around the circle. 'Vasilisa will stay with us until we find out if she's psychic or not. If she isn't, we'll arrange for her to be adopted somewhere safe. If she is, she'll be recruited into the Order and will begin training.' He looked at Billi. 'If God wills it, Vasilisa will be a Knight Templar.'

'Hold on, Billi!'

Billi had been hurrying out after matins prayers when Elaine dashed across the courtyard, calling to her. She stopped beneath the Templar column, a ten-metre-high stone post topped by the Order's emblem: two knights riding a single horse. Billi checked her watch. An hour before school. She'd drop off breakfast for the girl, then head to the armoury and get some sparring in. Next time she met those Loonies she wanted to be ready.

'Just a sec.' Elaine stopped to catch her breath.

'Those cigarettes will kill you.'

'A lot of things will kill you.' Elaine put her hand on Billi's arm. 'Just wanted to find out how the poultice was holding up.' She glanced over her shoulder to make sure the other Templars had gone. 'Maybe we could have a chat? You had breakfast?'

'A bowl of Pedigree Chum. Delicious.' The wounds still itched, but that meant the herbs were working their magic. A few more days and she'd take them off, fully healed. But Elaine's attention wasn't on Billi's injuries; the old woman had something else on her mind. 'What do you want, Elaine?' Billi cupped her hands and blew into them. 'It's freezing out here.'

Elaine glanced in the direction of Billi's house. 'How's our young guest?'

Billi shrugged. 'How d'you think?'

'Remember when Kay first arrived? It was just like this.'

Billi's eyes narrowed. 'Was it?'

'You and him were as thick as thieves.' Elaine looked deep into Billi's eyes. 'He was a frightened little boy and you looked after him, Billi. It wasn't your job to, but you did. That's what the old Billi did.'

Billi moved Elaine's hand off her arm. 'I am not that child any more.'

'I'm just saying that girl needs a friend, someone who's been where she's been. Things are going to be hard for her.'

'Oh, and they weren't hard for me?'

She'd been forced into the Order at ten. The next five years of her life had been an utter misery of endless training and bruises and lying at school. Her friends had slowly dwindled and when Kay had been sent off to Jerusalem for further training she'd spent all her time alone.

'That's not what I'm saying and you know it. Don't you care what happens to her? Don't you care –'

Billi interrupted. 'No, I don't care.' She couldn't afford to. 'All I care about is the Order now.'

'You cared about Kay.'

'That was a mistake.'

Elaine shook her head. 'I was wrong about you, Billi.' She started across the courtyard. 'I thought Kay's sacrifice meant something.'

'It means I should have been a better Templar.' If she had been, Kay might have lived.

Elaine shuffled away, head lowered and weary. 'You are your father's daughter.'

Billi knew she should feel differently by now. But there was a hollowness inside her that nothing filled. No matter how much she trained, how hard she fought, the emptiness only seemed to grow. She'd cared too much, and only realized how she felt after he'd gone.

Never again.

She sat in the kitchen, looking at the tray Lance had left.

Elaine was too soft. But then she could afford to be; she wasn't a Templar.

Billi had her priorities and looking after a little girl was way, way down the list. Her job was to fight the Bataille Ténébreuse, the Dark Conflict. There was no room for weakness.

She carried the tray up the flight of stairs to the top floor, and stopped outside Vasilisa's bedroom. Billi knocked and went straight in. The quicker this was over and done with, the better. She had no desire to lull the child into a false sense of feeling safe and protected when she would soon find out her true destiny among the Knights Templar.

Vasilisa sat in an old wooden rocking-chair with her back to Billi, gazing out of a small window. They were high in the eaves, overlooking Middle Temple Gardens, so all she could see were bare, black branches against the white winter sky. The chair creaked as she rocked back and forth.

She was wearing Billi's old clothes: a faded brown jumper and pair of blue jeans with sequin flowers stitched round the ankles. Billi had no idea that her dad had kept her old stuff. Vasilisa looked tiny in that big old chair. Her skinny shoulders were slumped, her head low.

She could be me, thought Billi. The girl was so small and alone. For a second Billi felt awkward, seeing Vasilisa so vulnerable. But she flicked her head and reminded herself Vasilisa was safer here than anywhere else. If the Templars hadn't come along, she'd be dog food by now. Still Billi couldn't shake the discomfort. Looking at the child she thought of Kay, how afraid he'd been when he'd first arrived. Vasilisa didn't deserve this.

It was unfair. But since when was life fair? Never.

Billi put the tray down on the table.

'Vasilisa?'

'When can I go?' asked Vasilisa. Brittle twigs scratched the windowpane like a witch's fingers and a low wind moaned through the loft void above.

'Where?'

'Away from here. You're not my family.'

'My dad will sort something out.' Billi began straightening out the bed sheets, doing anything to distract herself. She picked up a plastic rubbish bag and shook the contents out over the bed. Out fell a jumble of stuffed animals: elephants, tigers and a few patched-up bears. Billi rummaged around the bottom of the bag and found something else, curved and solid. She pulled out the Russian doll. She'd first seen it last night in Vasilisa's bedroom.

'That's mine,' said the girl. She held out her hand for the doll. 'Mum said she would protect me from them. But she couldn't.'

As Billi passed the doll to her Vasilisa grabbed her wrist.

'Don't leave,' whispered Vasilisa. 'I'm scared. Please.' Her fingernails dug into Billi's skin and she clung on to her with desperate strength. Billi stood rigid, trapped in the girl's grip, her heart racing. Then she unhooked the girl's fingers and hurried to the door. She couldn't stay here any longer; she had to get to school.

'I'm off now, but I'll look in again later.' Billi fumbled for the door handle. 'You'll be safe here.'

The girl didn't look round, but spoke so softly Billi wondered if she was actually talking to the doll.

'Will I?'

CHAPTER 6

'What do you think, Percy?' Billi asked as she sat beside her godfather's gravestone. It had been a few weeks since she'd visited and the grave needed tending.

Percival. A poor soldier.

That was all his epitaph said. Templars didn't need anything long or melodramatic. 'The others send their regards.' She flicked up the collar of her greatcoat and rewrapped her scarf round the bottom half of her face.

The snow had fallen steadily all week, slowly covering London with a veil of white. Unfortunately school was still open and Billi wasn't looking forward to her midnight patrol. Double thermals would be in order.

'Oh, how's school? Same old same old. You know me, too busy to hang out with the girls.' That hadn't changed. Billi's reputation was already mud, but after Kay's death it had got even worse.

According to the police, Kay's death had been an accident. He'd broken into a building site and fallen. Case closed.

Nothing about the battle that had been fought

against the Unholy, the Dark Angels that had tried to kill them and the firstborn. Nothing about how Billi had slid a sword into Kay's chest, sacrificing him so millions might live.

The nightmares had lasted for weeks. She couldn't close her eyes for seeing Kay's staring at her, wide and empty.

At school people said Billi was bad luck – bad things happened around her. Kay was just an unfortunate soul who'd got too close. Best stay away.

'We might have a new Oracle. Do ask Kay if he's got any advice.' Billi carried on talking to Percy's grave. She wasn't looking forward to getting back home and having to deal with Vasilisa. Why couldn't they move her to Rowland's or Elaine's? The little girl unsettled things. Reminded her too much of Kay. A new Oracle. Would Vasilisa survive longer than the last one?

'I'll come and visit Kay sometime, Percy. Tell him that. I promise I will.' But not yet. She wasn't strong enough to go to Kay's grave.

The icy wind picked up and the hairs along Billi's nape stiffened. The air carried with it a strange, thick smell, damp and cloying, like wet fur.

Two women approached, winding their way through the maze of tombs and gravestones. One, a big girl with hair the colour of flame, was wearing a T-shirt that revealed her wide, muscular torso and long, heavy arms. The other woman was grey-haired and had her hands tucked into the pockets of a hip-length woollen coat, embroidered with petroglyphs much like the ones Elaine had shown the Templars. They walked with a predator's confidence, their movements graceful and economic; a hunter's stride. Billi knew exactly what they were. But even if there had been any doubt, the eyes gave them away. Emerald green.

The old woman raised her palm as she came closer, in a friendly way. 'My name is Olga. This is my grand-daughter Svetlana.' The accent was Russian.

'Polenitsy,' Billi said. The old woman stopped a few metres from her, perhaps surprised that Billi knew who they were. The red-haired girl continued to move, not nearer, but around. She grinned at Billi, revealing teeth that were long and sharp. Her face was a jigsaw of cuts and scratches. The sort you might get if you'd been thrown through a window recently.

Billi took a step back. She should have gone home first and tooled up. Here all she could do was throw snowballs.

'We mean you no harm,' said the old woman.

'Tell that to her,' Billi said, pointing at the prowling girl.

'Svetlana, enough,' snapped Olga. Svetlana snarled, but stopped. 'We merely want the Spring Child, and then we will go.' She glanced down at Percy's gravestone as she stepped closer. 'A poor soldier.' She nodded and looked at Billi, intrigued. 'Now I understand. A Templar. A female within the Order of the Temple of Solomon? Perhaps the knights have acquired some wisdom at last.'

At first Billi thought Olga was taking the piss, but as the old woman raised her head Billi saw she was serious.

'We want no war with the Knights Templar,' said Olga.

'You lay a claw on Vasilisa's head and we'll give you a war you wouldn't believe.'

Olga grinned.

My, what big teeth you have, Granny.

'Templar, you are few. We are many. We would wipe you out.'

'People have tried that before. No one's managed it yet.' Billi clenched her fists, not that she'd last a second if things got hairy. 'Why Vasilisa?'

Svetlana jumped forward, snarling. 'The girl will bring a new spring, one without the foulness of mankind. She has been chosen by Baba Yaga –'

'*Nyet!*' Olga glared at Svetlana, then back at Billi. 'That is none of your concern. She has been chosen by the goddess and that is enough.'

Billi laughed. 'Baba Yaga? Your witch? The one who lives in a hut that walks on chicken legs?'

'You dare insult Mother Russia?' Svetlana growled and talons grew from her fingertips. Olga stepped between them, blocking the younger woman.

'And what of your crucified god?' said Olga, pointing at Billi's crucifix. 'Perhaps in a thousand years his story may be nothing more than a fairy tale. You would do well not to mock what you do not understand.'

'What I understand is that you want to kill a nine-year-old kid. That's not going to happen. Vasilisa is with us now.'

Olga sighed. 'So be it, Templar. Your doom is sealed.'

CHAPTER 7

'So it is the Polenitsy. They're pretty bad news, Art,' said Elaine.

'Now that's a surprise,' replied Arthur. He stood by the window, curtain pulled back as he peered out into the dark. He held the Templar Sword in his fist.

Billi had gone home, checking over her shoulder every thirty seconds or so. If she'd been followed, she hadn't spotted them.

Lance was downstairs, Gwaine and Bors on patrol. Billi, her dad and Elaine sat in the kitchen. It felt like they were under siege. All over a little girl, asleep upstairs.

'And Baba Yaga?' asked Billi. 'What else do you know about her?'

Elaine drummed her fingers on a stack of books. The old Templar diaries. The aged books were a mismatch of leather-bound tomes that were the core of the Order's occult lore. All the knights were meant to have studied them, but nobody knew as much as Elaine – she was practically a walking library.

'Not much. She's been in Russia for thousands of

49

years, but that was never within the Templars' territories.' She gazed into the middle distance. 'The stories of Baba Yaga cast her as an ancient witch, a powerful figure in pre-Christian Russia. Utterly evil, with the ability to command the elements and the beasts, a psychic, just like Kay, but much, much more powerful. She's also called Mother Russia. They say she's part of the soil, the very stones of the country. The stories refer to her having been driven deep into the forests by the Bogatyrs.'

'Bogatyrs?' asked Billi.

'An order of Christian knights, older than the Templars,' interrupted Arthur. 'Last I heard they were being led by Alexei Viktorovich Romanov. A good man by all accounts. That was a few years ago.'

'And now she's after Vasilisa.' Billi leaned back in her chair.

'You got any further with her?' Arthur asked Elaine.

'I'm still testing. These things take time.'

'Make contact with Jerusalem anyway. Once we know for sure we'll send Vasilisa there to start her training.'

'Until then?' Billi asked. She couldn't just sit around, waiting.

Arthur finished inspecting his sword and pushed it into its scabbard. 'Double weapons' training.'

Billi looks down the cave opening, wondering if she can squeeze through the gap. The edges are slick with black mud and she hears the lapping of water. A smell rises up through the hole, a vent, and it's strong, but familiar. It smells of decay and ancient earth, both moist and dusty at the same time. She descends.

She enters the underworld. A vast pool of shimmering black water fills the cavern ahead of her.

The water stirs, and ripples roll out from its centre to Billi's toes on the shore. Then a figure rises. The Stygian waters run off his body, black, oily rivulets sliding down the creases of his pale, bare torso. He rises, smiling at Billi, until he is waist-deep.

He is the ferryman. Billi wants to run into his arms.

'Kay,' she whispers.

'Hello, Billi.' His long, silvery-white hair hangs wet and flat, half-hiding his face. Billi wants to brush it aside so she can see Kay perfectly. Kay's smooth face creases into a smile as he looks in her dark eyes that sparkle in the gloomy cavern. It's a smile she thought she remembered perfectly, but now, in front of him, she sees all the subtle details she missed. The way his lips almost part as they turn upward. How a small frown seems to form in the centre of his eyebrows, just above his nose, like his smile is serious business.

She wades into the freezing water, reaching for him. Her heart beats so rapidly she thinks it'll tear itself apart. She doesn't care. She thinks only of what it would be like to feel him again, to touch him and to kiss those lips, to push back that last breath she stole and fill the hole that opened in her heart when he left her. Billi stretches out, but Kay remains just beyond her trembling fingertips.

'I can't reach you,' she says, despair hanging on her words. If only she can have him back, everything will be OK.

'No, Billi. You can't come.'

She ignores him, ploughing deeper into the water. The cold creeps up her legs, but she keeps struggling towards him.

'Billi, I've come to say goodbye.'

'No!' Billi shivers. The chill rises up her veins, slowing her heart as it drifts into slumber. 'I want to be with you, Kay. Don't you understand?'

'The dead should not linger, Billi. Look to the living now.'

Billi screams as she grabs for him, but Kay's over the far side now, beyond mortal touch.

'Then why are you here?' she shouts.

Kay shakes his head sadly. 'But, Billi, I'm not here. Not any more.' Silent as death, Kay places his hands either side of his face.

His face comes off. He lays it on the water's edge and instead Billi now sees Vasilisa. She's a small girl wading waist-deep in the Styx. Billi reaches to take her hand, but can't.

'Come out, Vasilisa. You're not meant to be here,' Billi says. She sobs. Kay wasn't meant to be here either. Not for a long time.

Vasilisa places her hands either side of her face. Her face comes off.

*

Billi awoke, her blood pounding in her eardrums. She gasped for air and lay there, body damp with sweat.

Was it really Kay?

She'd dreamed about him before, of course she had, but nothing like this. You weren't able to smell anything in dreams, were you? The smell had been the strongest thing about it. She could almost taste the cold water, and goosebumps rose along her arm as she remembered the deep cave she'd entered.

She wiped her face on the sheet. A dream. She wasn't psychic. Her dreams didn't mean anything.

Did they?

Pans and plates clattered noisily from the kitchen. The sound echoed up the stairwell as someone got busy making a midnight snack.

Why couldn't they just shut up? Billi shuffled against the wall, trying to dampen the noise by covering her head with a pillow. No good. She was awake now. Blearily she checked the clock; 3 a.m. Must be Gwaine and Mordred on duty. They did the twelve till four slot. Why didn't they bring sandwiches like everyone else? She sat up and smoothed her hair out of her face.

This constant – and noisy – vigilance was how it was going to be, until the Polenitsy made their move or they got Vasilisa out. Billi thought they should hide her somewhere else, but Arthur said staying in the Temple gave them the home advantage. They would wait and let the werewolves come to them. But waiting wasn't easy. Billi had to do something to keep her mind busy.

She jumped out of bed and dragged out Kay's box. She'd delayed this too long. She carried it upstairs into the study. On the window sill she spotted another one of Arthur's attempts to bring some life into the house, a big, round, glazed flowerpot with God knows what growing in it. Right now it just looked like a few bare twigs stuck in a pile of wet soil. Billi dropped Kay's box down on Arthur's desk. Moonlight shone in through the small windows overlooking Middle Temple Lane. Old bookshelves crowded the walls and above them were ancient portraits of the earlier Templar Grand Masters and paintings of long-ago Templar battles. Acre. Hattin. Hampshire. That had been the last zombie war, back in the nineteenth century.

There was a gentle tapping on the door. 'Billi? Is that you?'

'Vasilisa?'

The girl came in. She'd wrapped herself up in one of Billi's old dressing gowns, which trailed along the floor.

'I couldn't sleep,' she said. Billi had heard her crying earlier. She'd thought about going in and saying something, but what? Nothing would bring her parents back and nothing Billi could say would ease the pain.

'What do you want?' It came out harsher than Billi intended.

Vasilisa stood in the centre of the faded red carpet. 'I want to go home.' She said it in a small, hopeless voice. 'I don't like it here.'

Who does? 'The farmhouse isn't safe.'

'No. Home in Karelia.'

54

'That's not safe either. Don't worry. My dad will sort something out.' Billi shook her head; she wasn't going to get rid of Vasilisa so she pulled up a stool. 'Fine. Sit here, but don't touch anything.'

Billi cut the thick tape that bound the cardboard box and rested her fingers on the lid. This was the last of Kay. She opened the box.

CDs, a pile of books, a copy of *NME* and a couple of paperbacks. Nothing special except it was all Kay's. Billi began emptying the contents, making neat piles on the large desk. Vasilisa sat up and watched.

Billi flicked through a scrapbook of newspaper cuttings. They were all seemingly minor incidents. A grave being defiled. Some wild dog attack in a park. They didn't seem like much, but the Templars kept an eye out for odd events. You never knew if one might lead to a *ghul* or a werewolf. Kay had made notes in his small, neat script in the margins, marking down which he thought worth investigating. He'd even spotted the werewolf attacks, underlining dates and locations. Then there were the cuttings on the mysterious sickness spreading through Britain. The last article was a few days before his death. Billi smiled. He was such a swot. As Billi flicked through Kay's comments she saw Vasilisa reaching into the box.

'No!' Billi slapped the girl's hand and something silver flew across the room and cracked against the wall. Billi stared at Vasilisa. 'I *said* don't touch anything.'

'I was just helping.' She lowered her head and her unkempt blonde hair fell like a veil over her face. 'Sorry.'

Billi got up and picked up the object.

It was Kay's old mobile. Billi turned it in her hand. The screen was cracked now. Billi bit her lip. If Vasilisa had broken it, she'd be furious. Billi dug out a charger from one of the drawers and plugged it in.

The screen glowed and the blood-red Templar cross appeared.

It works, thank God. The logo faded away and Billi stared at the screensaver.

It was her and Kay.

She didn't even remember him taking it. They were outside, somewhere in the gardens, sitting on a bench. Wind caught strands of his platinum-white hair, half-covering his face. He smiled, that smile of his like he knew a big secret. Vasilisa peered over her shoulder and gazed closely at the photo.

Billi looked at Vasilisa. She had a wide, pale face with dimpled cheeks that converged into a small, pointed chin. Her blonde hair was thick and uncombed. She had a young child's nose, a round button, red from sniffing.

Look to the living.

'You've got a pixie face,' Billi said, fighting back a sudden urge to gently tuck Vasilisa's blonde locks behind her ear. *Where had that come from?*

'*Are* there pixies?'

'Not since 1807.'

'I like you with long hair,' Vasilisa said. She pointed to the photo on the wall. 'Like your mum.'

It was a picture of the three of them – Billi, her mum

56

and her dad. It had been taken when she was five. She was being squeezed between her parents. Jamila looked towards the camera, but Arthur just gazed at his wife with open, uninhibited joy. He seemed decades younger, no grey in his hair and his face smooth and worry-free. Billi grinned at her, a five-year-old girl with a small gap in the middle of her baby teeth.

'It's an old picture. She died a long time ago.'

Vasilisa stared at the photo, then back in the box. 'Whose things are these?' she asked, carefully keeping her hands to herself.

'My friend's. His name was Kay.'

'Kay? Was he like you?'

Billi looked into Vasilisa's big, summer-sky-blue expressive eyes. 'No, I think maybe he was like you.'

There were half a dozen folders saved on Kay's mobile. She shouldn't look at them. Kay was dead and she needed to get over him. Quickly. But as she gazed over his belongings she knew that wasn't fair. Not for Kay, and not for her. He'd been the best part of her life.

'Tell me about Karelia.'

'There was a big garden, and my babushka, my granny, she taught me the names of every plant, every flower.' Vasilisa pointed to the pot of twigs and drooping stalks on the window sill. 'Chrysanthemums. You should put those somewhere sunny.'

'When did you leave?'

'I was five. I didn't want to. But someone came.'

'Who?'

Vasilisa closed her eyes and Billi could see she was frightened.

'An old lady. Not nice like my babushka, but horrible, with green eyes. She was looking for me.'

Olga. So the Polenitsy had been after her already.

'My granny made me hide, but she was scared. She said the woman would come back so we had to run. That night we packed our bags and we came here, thinking we would be safe. I miss them. I miss my granny.' Vasilisa swung her feet, idle and wistful. 'They say I'm going to be a Templar.' She looked at the paintings on the wall. 'Are they all Templars? Those old men?'

'I'm a Templar.'

Vasilisa looked at Billi curiously.

'What are they? The Templars.'

Billi took a deep sigh. Where to begin? She had almost a thousand years of history in her head. Short or long version?

Short.

'They were a group of knights who swore to defend the Holy Land from the Muslims, back in the Middle Ages. That's how they started. Just nine men.'

'Like Bogatyrs, yes?'

'You know about the Bogatyrs?' asked Billi.

Vasilisa's eyes brightened. 'Everybody in Russia knows! The Bogatyrs were great knights. My mother used to read me stories about them. They fought dragons, evil witches, the Mongols, the Muslims. All the evil people.'

Billi laughed. 'My mother was a Muslim.'

Vasilisa went red. 'Are you?'

Billi shrugged. She could pray in Latin, Greek, English and Arabic. She knew the direction of Mecca and the psalms. Did God really care?

'Anyway, back to the Templars.' She got up and took a picture off the wall. It was a landscape over Jerusalem, an elaborate medieval woodcut of the Holy City. She pointed to a dome in the centre. 'The knights fought the Muslims for a few hundred years. But then they were betrayed by their fellow Christians, by the pope himself. After that the survivors rejected the Crusades and chose a new war – a war they call the Bataille Ténébreuse. That means the Dark Conflict. Instead of fighting other men, we fight the Unholy – monsters like werewolves. Ghosts. The blood-drinkers. To be a knight you have to face one of those monsters. It's called the Ordeal.'

'Did you have to do it?'

Billi nodded. Alex Weeks. The ghost of a six-year-old boy. Remembering what she'd had to do still turned her stomach.

'You don't like being a Templar, Billi?'

'It's my duty. Like's got nothing to do with it.' She caught the worried expression on Vasilisa's face. She was talking about the girl's future. Her future if she was an Oracle. Billi rummaged around in the drawers and took out a pad and paper.

'Look, Vasilisa, we're going to play a game.' With the pad up, she drew a circle. 'See if you can guess what shape I'm drawing.'

'I've already done this with Elaine.'

'Let's play again.' Elaine had said the powers would be temperamental at this age, but it was worth a shot.

Vasilisa frowned. 'A circle.'

Could just be luck. Billi tore off the sheet and drew a triangle. 'Now?'

'A triangle?'

Now we're getting somewhere. She tore off that sheet and drew a five-pointed star.

'And this?'

'A star.'

'How many points?'

'Five.'

Oh my God. She drew a fish.

'What's on the page? Concentrate.'

'A fish.'

Billi's heart was beating hard and fast. Perhaps the Templars had their new Oracle after all.

'That's amazing, Vasilisa.'

Vasilisa shook her head. 'No. Anyone could do that.'

Billi laughed. 'I don't think so.' But Vasilisa straightened and pointed behind Billi.

The window was right behind her. With the desk lamp on, everything Billi wrote was perfectly reflected in the glass. She blushed.

'Oh, right.' What an idiot. 'Look, Vasilisa. I'd rather you didn't tell anyone what just happened. OK?'

Vasilisa rocked back and forth, laughing until she started hiccuping. 'I tricked you,' she crowed.

'Seriously, it wasn't that funny,' Billi said. Vasilisa laughed harder. Billi smiled. Maybe it was.

Eventually Vasilisa calmed down. She wiped her nose on her sleeve and looked at Kay's belongings.

'What's going to happen now?' she asked.

There was a creak as Billi leaned back into the worn leather of Arthur's chair.

'We'll take you somewhere safe. Then, when things have calmed down, probably send you home to your grandmother.'

Vasilisa nodded. 'I would love to see her garden again.' She stood up and bent over the flowerpot, stroking the bright petals. 'She loves chrysanthemums.'

Billi stared at the plant. Thick, luscious green leaves covered what had been bare twigs minutes ago. Fluffy white flowers bloomed and even as she watched buds rose along the twigs, growing into balls and unfurling into more blossoms. A soft, fresh scent began to fill the room.

Vasilisa plucked a flower and it blossomed open in her hands – she held it out to Billi. Her smile was open and she seemed unaware of what had just happened. Any chance of her living a normal life had just gone forever.

Vasilisa would be the next Templar Oracle.

CHAPTER 8

Mordred jumped up from his chair when Billi rushed into the kitchen. He wiped the ketchup from his mouth and looked guiltily at the half-eaten bacon sandwich.

'Where's Dad?' Billi held the flowerpot in one hand and Vasilisa's wrist in the other.

'On patrol with Gwaine.'

'Get him now.'

A few minutes later Arthur and Gwaine entered. Arthur nodded at Billi as he unbuttoned his coat.

'Tell me,' he said.

Billi put the potted plant on the table. 'Vasilisa did this.'

Arthur touched the large green leaves and plucked a flower. He handed it to Gwaine.

'It was just a bunch of twigs ten minutes ago,' Billi added.

'Vasilisa, I want you to hold this.' Arthur grabbed a wilted African violet from the window sill and put it on Vasilisa's lap.

The leaves began to grow. The stalks lengthened and

the leaves swelled, then buds grew, blossoming into velvety, lavender flowers.

The room was filled with a thick, musty scent – far more powerful than the flowers could have generated. The air was heavy with the smell of damp soil and foliage, like someone had opened a door into a greenhouse. All the other potted plants were in full bloom too, scattering colour over the kitchen.

It had taken a dozen seconds. Vasilisa lowered her hands and looked around at the knights.

'That's amazing,' said Mordred as an ivy plant spread over the floor.

A flower hissed. It turned black and burst into flames.

Within seconds half a dozen of the flowers had combusted and Vasilisa screamed. Billi kicked the flowerpot off the girl's lap and it smashed on the floor. The soil bubbled and spat as smoke rose from the burning bush. Billi grabbed Vasilisa and Mordred ran to the sink as the fire alarm went off. He soaked a hand towel.

The kitchen filled up with smoke as they put the flames out.

'What the hell happened?' Gwaine asked. The alarm shrieked in the background.

Arthur looked at the floor. The heat had melted the lino, which smelled poisonous. He stepped on a still-smouldering flower, grinding it to ash under his boot.

'Get Elaine,' he said.

*

Elaine didn't waste any time racing over. The kitchen still stank of molten plastic and burnt foliage so they crowded in the study, next door to the now-sleeping Vasilisa. Gwaine waited by the window, nervously checking outside every few minutes. Billi sat on the corner of the desk and turned as Arthur came in, having returned Vasilisa to her bed.

Elaine rubbed her eyes as she settled into an armchair in the corner. In the gloomy lamplight her sunken features looked just this side of zombie.

'I spoke to her before she went to sleep,' started Arthur. 'Looks like elementalism runs in the family. Her granny used to do the same – make flowers grow and fruit appear out of season.' He frowned as he gazed at them. 'Vasilisa never really considered it strange. It was just what her family did. It seems they were white witches. The grandmother apparently knew all the tales about Baba Yaga.'

Gwaine spoke. 'You think the gran knew Baba Yaga was real?'

'Yes, but Vasilisa just assumed they were stories.' Elaine smiled to herself. 'I'd like to meet this grandmother. She sounds interesting.'

'What about the other stuff? The fire?' asked Billi.

Elaine sighed. 'Judging by tonight I'd say Vasilisa's psychic powers include fire-starting, pyrokinetics. And elementalism. Not a great combination.'

'Explain.' Arthur took a cigarette from Elaine's packet and lit up. This was the first he'd had in three months. Despite his coolness, tonight's events must have shocked him too.

'Vasilisa's in sympathy with the natural environment.'

'What's that mean? In sympathy?' asked Gwaine. Of all the Templars he was least comfortable with Elaine and the occult knowledge she brought to the Order. He thought she was only one short step from being a witch.

'What happens to the natural world affects her. What happens to her affects the natural world. She could eat an ice cream and then cover the garden with frost. Conversely she could draw heat from a hot summer's day and use it to cook sausages in her bare hands,' said Elaine, like she was explaining something blindingly obvious. 'It's simple Newtonian physics. Every action has an opposite and equal reaction. In this case it's psychic energy being transferred from Vasilisa into the living environment and back again. But she's too in-experienced to control it. The flowers were a victim of that.'

'Great. She'll be so handy if we're ever attacked by demonic daffodils,' said Gwaine.

Elaine ignored Gwaine's not quite veiled insult. 'I brought this.' She took out a necklace from her pocket. It was a thin strip of leather strung with silver plaques.

Billi recognized them. Kay had used them when he'd tried to contact the spirit realms. 'Maqlu?'

The ancient talismans had been found in an archaeo-logical dig in Iraq, on the site of the ancient city of Nineveh. They were a defence against psychic intrusion.

'Someone might try and possess Vasilisa?' Gwaine asked.

'Just to be sure. Vasilisa has no control over her powers. She can't defend herself. It's possible another psychic, someone with telepathy, could access her mind and manipulate her, albeit temporarily.' Elaine handed the necklace to Billi. 'Put this on her when she wakes up. Tell her that she can't take it off, understand?'

Billi inspected the plaques, with their minute cuneiform letters, spells, carefully carved on to each. 'You mean someone like Baba Yaga?'

Elaine nodded. 'If she's been consuming other psychics over the centuries, her telepathic powers would be awesome. She'd be an elementalist, spirit-talker, the whole package. It also means she'd be totally insane. That amount of action in one's head cannot be healthy. I don't want her in Vasilisa's mind, even for a moment.'

'Then the next step is obvious,' said Arthur.

'Jerusalem it is,' agreed Elaine.

'Wait,' Billi interrupted. 'What's to stop the Polenitsy from just heading out to Jerusalem and kidnapping Vasilisa there?'

Elaine smiled. 'Oh, the Holy City has guardians of its own. Guardians who even the Polenitsy might hesitate to cross.'

'Like who?'

Elaine hesitated and shot a wary glance at Arthur. He nodded, but even then Elaine paused.

Eventually she spoke. 'Jerusalem is under the control of the Assassins.'

'Cool.' Who didn't know about the Assassins? The Templars and the Assassins had a secret alliance, going back to the Crusades. The two orders had traded knowledge, allies and enemies. Most of the occult lore the Templars studied was originally gleaned from the Islamic sect of killer mystics. 'What are they like?'

Elaine shrugged. 'Never met one. They operate through a network of middlemen. The Assassins are sleepers. It'll be someone close, a business ally, a best friend you've known for years. Then one day they get the signal. You only meet an Assassin once in your life. At the very end.'

'And that's where we're sending Vasilisa?' Billi asked.

'The Assassins and the Templars have an agreement,' said Arthur. 'The Treaty of Alamut allows us to train among the fakirs and holy men of Jerusalem. The Oracle will be as safe there as anywhere.'

Not Vasilisa any more, but the Oracle.

'I had some friends in Whitechapel make this, just in case.' Arthur took a fake passport out from his desk drawer and tossed it to Elaine. 'Take her to Jerusalem.'

CHAPTER 9

The next afternoon Billi watched Vasilisa building a snowman. Middle Temple Gardens was pretty empty, thanks to the snowfall. The office workers stayed indoors, so Vasilisa had spent most of the afternoon rolling a misshapen ball into the bottom of a snowman, and was now rolling a second ball for the head.

Elaine had been keeping a wary eye out, as had Lance and Bors. They weren't going to let the Oracle out of their sight.

'C'mon, Billi!'

She's happy. Vasilisa patted the small boulder of snow, trying to keep it in shape. Her hair stuck out from under a woollen bobble hat and her bare hands were pink, but she didn't care.

'Let's go inside,' Billi shouted across the garden. 'It's cold.' She felt exposed. Anyone could come wandering by and see them. It wasn't safe. But would Vasilisa ever be safe again? Billi had no idea what happened to Kay out in Jerusalem; he would never talk about it. But he'd come back a changed man, more confident, more detached. More powerful by far. What would happen to Vasilisa? What would she be like, a few years down the line?

Vasilisa strolled over. 'C'mon, come and look! It's almost done.'

'We should start packing.'

'Why?' Vasilisa brushed the snow off her trousers. 'Where are we going?'

No one had told her. The girl was flying to Jerusalem in two days and no one had told her. Damn it!

'Er, somewhere safe.'

'I'm safe here, aren't I? With you?'

Billi looked over for Elaine; she'd be better at explaining this. But the old woman was nowhere to be seen. Typical. Billi frowned.

'Let's play, Billi.' Vasilisa started away, but Billi took her hand. Despite the freezing temperature, her fingers were warm little sausages.

'Look, Vasilisa. About what happened last night.' Billi sat the girl down on the bench. 'This power you have, it could be dangerous.'

Vasilisa rattled her silver necklace. 'No, I'm OK now.'

'That may not be enough. You need to learn how to manage your special gifts. There's a place where you can learn how to do that.'

'Where?'

'Jerusalem.'

Vasilisa sprang up. She stared at Billi. 'Jerusalem? But I want to go home to my granny!'

69

'Vasilisa, try and understand. If you go back to Karelia, they'll catch you. Elaine will go with you. To see you're settled in. It's . . .' Billi lowered her head, unwilling to look at the girl. '. . . It's for the best.'

'No, Billi. Please, I don't want to go.' Vasilisa's fingers tightened round hers. 'Can't I stay with you?'

'No, it wouldn't work. I'm sorry.'

'Liar,' Vasilisa whispered. Her eyes filled with tears. 'You're not sorry.' She closed her eyes. 'I want my mum and dad back. That's all.'

Billi went to put her arm round Vasilisa.

'Don't touch me!' she cried. She dug her fingers into the snowman's head and pushed until the head fell apart and then trembled with silent sobs.

Billi wanted to tell her that she'd do so much good, that she'd be powerful, someone important. But the words felt meaningless. She sighed, knowing the future meant hardship and misery for the nine-year-old, but there was no alternative. It was God's will.

Deus vult.

It wasn't just the Polenitsy who sacrificed children.

CHAPTER 10

Billi awoke to the muted sounds of rattling. Pipes came alive as the old water system gurgled into action. At four in the morning.

What the hell was going on? It sounded like whoever was on guard duty had decided to run a bath.

Every limb demanded that she stay in bed. Three hours of unarmed combat with Bors had left her aching all over. But she forced herself up and looked out of the window. Gareth stood, cold and miserable, in the opposite doorway. He saw the light from her window and waved.

She numbly slid her feet across the bare wooden floorboards until her toes tapped her slippers. She tugged on her dressing gown and wandered on to the landing.

The bathroom door was open and the shower was running.

'Hello?'

'Billi . . .'

'Vasilisa?'

Vasilisa stood in the bath, the dense jet of water

71

bearing down on her. She was still in her pyjamas and her hair lay like a curtain over her face. The shower curtain hadn't been drawn, so water was spraying everywhere. Billi rushed forward and icy-cold droplets hit her bare arms.

'Jesus, Vasilisa,' Billi swore as she twisted the taps shut. The bottom of the bath was half full. Billi grabbed a towel and wrapped Vasilisa in it. The girl's skin was burning.

'So hot,' she said, choking on a half-suppressed sob.

Billi pulled off her dressing gown and swapped it with Vasilisa's sodden clothes.

'What's up?' said Arthur as he came in, dressed in a pair of baggy jogging bottoms and a green T-shirt.

'Vasilisa's sick.'

Arthur laid his hand against her forehead.

'I can't help it,' the little girl murmured. Arthur filled up a glass and got her to take a few gulps.

'Is there a thermometer in these cabinets?' he asked Billi. There were bandages, a box of syringes and tubs of antibiotics, and at the bottom, in a silver case, was the thermometer. Billi handed it to her dad. They both turned to Vasilisa. She was on the stool, sweating, her hands clasped tightly round the glass.

The water in it boiled. It bubbled over and steam rose from the puddles on the floor. Small, red burns marked Vasilisa's hands, but she didn't seem to feel them.

'Bring Elaine up,' ordered Arthur as he put Vasilisa's hands under the tap.

Elaine was on the couch, asleep in front of the muted telly.

Billi shook the old woman. 'Dad wants you. Quickly.'

Elaine nodded and stood up, straightening her shawl. Billi was about to follow when the screen caught her attention.

At first it looked like snow falling, but it was too grey, too dirty. The man's shoulders were covered with it, and long streaks of ash ran down his smart suit. His face too was coated in soot; the ash was everywhere. He stood in a square filled with people and cars, most piled high with suitcases and boxes, all vainly trying to flee.

Nicholas Rhodes – live from Naples, ran the headline on the screen.

Billi paused, caught between the desire to go and help Vasilisa and the apocalyptic scenes on the screen. She turned on the sound.

'. . . it's unbelievable. Even in the poor light, you can see the glow surrounding the edge of the crater. And the column, it just goes up and up . . .' The sound crackled, fading in and out, but there was no mistaking the excitement, and fear, in the broadcaster's voice.

The road signs and advertisements, those not completely lost in the fog of ash, were all in Italian. But behind them Billi saw the burning mountain and gasped.

It climbed like a tidal wave behind the city, a black silhouette crowned by a red-lit cone. Mount Vesuvius. A huge column of black smoke rose straight into the sky. Occasionally a flash of sky-hurled lava would light up the rolling clouds, and lightning stabbed against the rising black tower. The camera shook as a roar broke out of the TV. People started screaming and bumped and pushed past the newsman. He almost fell under a surge of panicking locals. The screen went blank, but the voices carried on.

'Don't lose the camera – there it is!'

The newsman, Nicholas Rhodes, was staring into the camera, close up and coughing. His red eyes ran with tears, but he couldn't speak, the ash was too thick, muting even the cries coming from around them.

The ground shook and again the camera went dark, but then the screen was filled with the blurred image of another eruption. The dense cloud rising out of the cone fattened, then collapsed, rolling down on itself, flooding the mountain top, slipping like overflowing boiling water out of a pan.

'Oh my God,' muttered the cameraman. 'C'mon, Nick. We've got to run.' But he kept filming even as he backed away.

The crater top was gone now as the black cloud dropped down on top of it. Waves of ash and smoke threw newspapers, litter, any loose thing into the air. People fell and were trampled. Cars crashed and their drivers scrambled out of their windows as the square gridlocked.

'What is it?' shouted Nicholas at his cameraman. A howling rose through the streets. People grabbed on to each other as winds shook the white-coated trees. Windows in apartments overlooking the square shattered.

Pyroclastic surge, thought Billi. Hadn't it all been in that Latin book? Superheated poisonous gases travelling at hundreds of miles per hour, incinerating everything in their path. It was the surge that had annihilated Pompeii back in AD 79. The ash fall had merely buried an already extinct city. There was no escape.

'No use, no use,' said the cameraman. The camera lowered to dangle over a pair of boots. 'We're dead.'

The camera swung back and forth. The sound was just screaming and the roaring of the wind. Then the camera went up and Nicholas was back on the screen, his red, tear-filled eyes staring straight at Billi, straight at them all.

'Keep filming,' he said grimly.

He steadied himself and ran his hand through his hair, shaking ash off his hands.

'I love you,' he said. 'I just wanted to say that I love you, Maggie.' He was shouting now as the wailing around them became deafening. 'Tell the girls Daddy's thinking of them.' His voice was hoarse and he cradled the camera with both hands. 'Tell them I love –'

The screen crackled, filled with electronic snow, then went black and silent. The only thing left on it was the headline, *Nicholas Rhodes – live from Naples*, then that too disappeared. The picture went back to the studio. The anchorwoman stared dumbly at her monitor.

Billi raced up the stairs.

Elaine and Arthur held Vasilisa in the half-filled tub. The water steamed and both were using soaking towels to hold the semi-conscious girl; she was too hot to touch.

'What's she doing?' Billi could only think of that eruption.

'She's not doing anything! Something's happening to her!' snapped Elaine.

Vasilisa jerked savagely, almost breaking free. Water splashed everywhere as she fought. Her eyes were squeezed shut. 'This is what she wants!' she screamed. She grabbed Arthur's arm, staring madly at him. Billi held her shoulders and watched the girl's eyes darken, the pale blue melting into black. 'This is what she wants!'

Elaine fumbled for the talismans round Vasilisa's neck. She pressed them against her temples.

'Fight. Fight her,' she whispered.

Vasilisa glared, snapping her teeth in fury. 'Foo*Liis*H.' It was just a word, a curse, but it wasn't Vasilisa. She hissed in a cacophony of dozens of discordant tongues. She clawed at Elaine's face and left red-hot blisters down her cheek. Then Vasilisa's eyes lost focus, glazing over. Her eyelids fluttered, then she slumped into the water.

The water in the bath continued to steam and Arthur pulled back his hand, which was ringed with burns. It was sauna hot in here, and the temperature was still rising.

'Snow,' Billi said. 'Put her in the snow.'

What happens to her affects the natural world. What happens to the natural world affects her.

Arthur wrapped Vasilisa in a wet blanket. The three

76

of them ran into the gardens of Middle Temple, Vasilisa in Arthur's arms. The blanket was smouldering by the time he unrolled her into the snow. Desperately they scooped handfuls over her, and great wet puddles formed as the snow almost instantly melted. But with the three of them at work they managed to get Vasilisa's skin back to a normal temperature. Vasilisa gazed around at the snow.

'Oh. So much snow.' She turned to Billi. 'It's Fimbul-winter . . .' Vasilisa's voice fell into a murmur and she slumped.

Elaine put her hand against the girl's forehead. She waited a minute, then sighed.

'She's OK.'

Arthur lifted Vasilisa, cradling her in his arms. Elaine struggled to her feet.

As they made their way back home they passed a house with the lights still on. Billi paused outside a window.

It was indistinct, but the newscaster was repeating the sentence over and over again, as though eventually she would believe her own words.

The eruption was over, but Naples had been destroyed.

or faith that required a talisman. Maddi shrugged. She had to admit here was no... [faded]

CHAPTER 11

The ash kept falling over Naples. News coverage continued as the scale of the disaster climbed. Towns near Vesuvius had vanished, completely submerged under the millions of tonnes of volcanic detritus.

The pyroclastic blast had petered out as it had smashed into the eastern face of the city, so the western inhabitants had avoided the worst excesses of the eruption. They still streamed out. Huge crowds of terrified people clustered at the bay, all struggling for a space on the flotilla of boats and ships that had gathered as part of the rescue operation.

For a while reports still came out of the city, mostly telephone calls from people who had hidden in their basements as the volcano had raged. But slowly the signals faded as they were buried alive, trapped forever underground.

They'd put Vasilisa back in bed and she was sleeping soundly. Elaine had made sure the talismans were firmly in place before closing the door.

Billi, Arthur and Elaine sat in the kitchen; by mid-morning they'd all had enough of watching the telly. Gwaine arrived, sombre and carrying an armful of newspapers.

'What I want to know is, did Vasilisa do it?' asked Arthur. 'Did she cause that eruption?'

Billi looked up, shocked. Did her dad really think Vasilisa was behind the horrific scenes she'd just watched on TV? Self-igniting pot plants were one thing, but this was on a different scale.

'No . . .' Elaine began, but her tone was ambiguous. 'Vesuvius is an active volcano. Sooner or later something like this was bound to happen.' She stared at the scorch marks on the floor. 'Vasilisa's sympathetic powers meant that she felt the eruption coming – she got worse as it did – but by the same token, as she cooled down so did the volcano. She stopped the eruption. If it hadn't been for Billi's quick thinking, things could have been much, much worse . . .'

'There are *thousands* dead, tens of thousands. How much worse could it have been?' asked Gwaine. 'And in the future?' His hand rested on the day's *Guardian*. 'NAPLES GONE' was the headline and the rest of the front page was black. 'Will Vasilisa be able to cause volcanic eruptions?'

Elaine looked at Arthur, biting her lip. She spoke in a low whisper. 'Yes. It's possible – if she's an avatar.'

Avatar? Wasn't an avatar a computer icon? Somehow Billi got the feeling this was going to be different.

Elaine continued. 'It's a concept I came across in India, during my travelling days.' In the bright overhead light the wrinkles round her mouth were deep, black crevasses. 'A super-Oracle.'

'Christ Almighty,' muttered Gwaine.

'Yes, like him. Don't you get it? Vasilisa stopped a volcanic eruption. To be able to manipulate such energies requires incredible psychic strength; it would be like Kay trying to read the minds of everyone in London at once. The fact that Vasilisa survived and didn't self-combust makes me think she has vast potential. It's all lurking there, deep within her. She's just too young to access it consciously.' Elaine gazed at the stairs that led to Vasilisa. 'But once she learns how to control her abilities she'll be able to create hurricanes with a clap of her hands. Stomp the ground and bring on earthquakes. Manipulate nature to suit her whims.'

'Oh,' said Billi. 'Is that all? I was worried for a minute.'

That was the girl she'd rescued: someone who could destroy cities. Billi struggled to match the image of the frail blonde girl with the destruction that had been wrought in Italy. She had powers and responsibility no human should be burdened with. Billi pitied her. She was a pawn in a game between the Templars and the Polenitsy. Whoever possessed Vasilisa could control nature.

'No wonder the Polenitsy want her so badly,' said Billi. They must have suspected Vasilisa was powerful to have come all this way.

'Not just the werewolves,' added Elaine. 'Can you

imagine what the *ghuls* would give for the blood of so powerful a psychic? Or the devils for her soul? The powers they would gain by devouring her? That girl's just acquired a whole lot of brand-new enemies.'

'And if Baba Yaga finds her, she'll gain all Vasilisa's powers. Not good,' said Arthur. He gazed out at the snow. 'That's who tried to possess her, isn't it?'

The others looked uneasy as Elaine tapped the ash off her cigarette.

'Yes. She obviously made a brief connection with Vasilisa's mind, but the talismans stopped her, thank God. But if she didn't suspect it already, she'll now know that Vasilisa's an avatar. No way is she going to pass up a meal like that.'

Billi shivered. The way Vasilisa had thrashed and screamed. The voices, they had been a major freak-out. How many minds had been in her head? 'But there was more than one voice. I heard a dozen at least. They're all Baba Yaga?'

'Who knows? Baba Yaga's not going to be like anything we've ever encountered before, but even if half the stories about her are true, she must be an avatar too. The voices could be the echoes of all the souls she's consumed over the centuries. Maybe that's what she is – an insane old witch with thousands of spirits trapped inside her. All subservient to her single, awesome will.'

'Careful, Elaine, you sound like you admire her,' warned Arthur.

'I respect her, Art. Like we all should.' Elaine watched

81

her smoke trail rise upwards. 'It's always wise to respect gods, whether they're yours or not.'

'And Fimbulwinter?' Arthur said, grim-faced.

Elaine nodded. 'The Norse legends talk of the long winter that will herald the end of the world.'

'Why would Vasilisa say that Fimbulwinter is coming?'

'Because she told me.' The little girl stood bare-footed in the doorway, the Russian doll in her hand.

Elaine got up. 'You should be in bed. Why don't we –'

'Who told you?' asked Arthur, stopping Elaine.

Vasilisa's small hands rubbed the doll nervously. She winced, apprehensive about speaking. 'Baba Yaga. She told me. Or I heard her.' She bit her lip, staring at them, white with fear. 'I heard her.'

Billi led Vasilisa to a stool, then leaned on the window sill behind her.

Vasilisa had shrunk, or so it seemed. It looked like she'd had her insides drained out. Dark rings circled her eyes, giving her a sunken, haunted look. She bit her lip, glancing at the four of them, and pressed her fist against her temple.

'She was in here, whispering in my head. She wanted more. Much more. She wanted the world to be covered in ice and snow. I could see her dreams,' Vasilisa whispered. 'She wants it all, Billi. She wants it all covered in white. She wants to bury the world.'

Gwaine shook his head. 'That's not possible. How can you freeze the entire planet?'

Billi spoke. 'Eruptions affect the weather.' With her

class studying what had happened in Pompeii she'd picked up a lot on volcanoes. 'The eruption throws up huge volumes of sulphur dioxide into the air. This reacts with the water in the atmosphere and acts like a great big mirror. It reflects the sun's heat back out into space. If the eruption was big enough, it could definitely create a volcanic winter.'

Arthur's eyes narrowed. 'You think Vesuvius will cause Fimbulwinter?'

'Even a medium-sized eruption like Vesuvius will affect temperatures, but for Fimbulwinter something much, much bigger would have to happen.' Billi racked her brains, trying to recall what had come up at school. 'A super-volcano. If one of those blew, we'd have a global temperature drop – cooling, maybe even freezing, much of the planet. Could last ten years.'

'Long enough to obliterate all crops and livestock. Most of humanity would starve to death,' added Elaine.

'A cull,' said Billi. Wasn't that what they did if a species over-populated? Now Baba Yaga wanted to do it to mankind.

Gwaine shook his head. 'But it would wipe out everyone. Polenitsy included.'

'She doesn't care,' said Vasilisa. She sat between Elaine and Arthur, her shoulders hunched and her voice a bare whisper. 'She wants to clean the world. Start it over again.'

Arthur spoke. 'She's near immortal. She could wait a hundred years to allow the planet to slowly repopulate.

That sort of timescale means nothing to her.' He looked at Billi. 'We got any of these super-volcanoes this side of the equator?'

Billi nodded. 'Yellowstone. The entire park is a gigantic one. When that goes it's goodbye for all of us.'

Arthur cleared his throat and squatted down in front of Vasilisa.

'You look tired, child. I think it best you sleep.' He held out his hand. 'C'mon.'

As Arthur took the girl upstairs Billi went to the kettle. She tried to fill it, but her hand wouldn't hold the kettle still enough. She gave up.

Baba Yaga wanted Fimbulwinter. With her and Vasilisa's power combined, could she do it? Wipe out the world?

Arthur returned and stood in the centre of the kitchen. 'I'm moving everything forward.' He glanced at his watch. 'Vasilisa flies out tonight. Elaine and I will go to Jerusalem with her until she's handed over. I want all knights on duty until Vasilisa's on that plane. Gwaine, you're in charge while I'm gone.'

Gwaine nodded.

Arthur put his hand on Billi's shoulder. 'You get some rest, girl. I'll need you later.'

'What about the Polenitsy?' said Billi. 'They'll be coming for her.'

Arthur stood by the window, immobile in the pale winter light. 'Let them come.'

CHAPTER 12

The evening passed with the knights constantly checking in on the house. Billi couldn't rest, painfully aware that things had reached a crunch point, not just for the Templars, but for her personally.

Tonight Vasilisa joined the Order. There would be no ceremony, no all-night vigils or prayers. She couldn't let Vasilisa go to Jerusalem without making peace.

She knocked on the door. 'Vasilisa? Can I come in?'

'No.'

The sun had gone down, but the room was in gloomy darkness. Billi turned on the light. Vasilisa sat on her bed, huddled in the corner, holding her knees.

Billi moved a few stuffed animals aside and sat facing the girl.

Where to begin?

'I'm sorry it's come to this, Vasilisa. But it's the only way you'll be safe.'

'I was safe until you came along.'

'We saved you from the werewolves.'

'I wish they'd got me too.'

85

'Don't say that.' Billi stared hard at the girl. 'You don't mean it.'

'They say I'm going to be the new Oracle. What happened to the old one?'

'I'll tell you about him. Kay was my best friend and I loved him more than anything.' Billi stopped. It had just burst out, this confession. She looked down at her shaking hands and clasped her fingers together, forcing them to be still. 'There's a hole inside that sometimes feels so big I think I'll disappear into it – but he's gone. He's gone and you're here.'

Their eyes met. They'd both already lost people they loved in the Bataille Ténébreuse. Billi joined Vasilisa in the corner.

'When I found you Kay came back. In a way. I dreamed of him and he told me he was saying goodbye.'

'Because of me?'

'The dead should not linger. I should look to the living.' Billi smiled at the girl. 'That seems a fair trade.'

'What will happen to me, in Jerusalem?'

'You'll be taught how to control your powers. Kay was going mad with all the voices in his head. He used to say it was like having a radio in his head and the dial was always moving, but never off. You'll learn how to protect yourself.'

'And become a fighter, like you?'

Billi inspected her calloused hands. All those years of weapons' training and punching wooden boards. Hardly ladylike. She scratched her knuckles, then took

86

the girl's hand. 'There are many ways to fight, Vasilisa.'

The two of them sat beside one another. Outside the window the tree branches scratched at the glass and the old roof beams creaked. Below Billi heard her father and one of the other knights scraping steel against whetstones.

'What is that called?' Billi asked, pointing at Vasilisa's Russian doll.

'A *matryoshka*.'

'Can I look?'

Vasilisa nodded and Billi opened up the doll. The next one was equally exquisite. Each flower was delicately painted into the shawl and the dress's embroidery looked as though it had been done using a single hair. The next doll matched it and within that was a stone figurine, covered in flaking gold leaf.

'It's beautiful,' said Billi. It was a woman, crudely shaped, with a small head and large breasts and hips. She'd seen figures like this in museums. It was a Venus figurine – they were prehistoric religious items, found throughout Europe.

Billi inspected the stone. The gold leaf had fallen off in patches and the stone beneath was highly polished, like black obsidian. Dark veins of iron ran through it.

'Babushka said it was the goddess.'

'Baba Yaga?'

'No, not just Baba Yaga.' Vasilisa took back the statue. 'Baba Yaga is the Dark Goddess, the Winter Crone. But sooner or later winter ends and spring comes.'

Vasilisa kissed the statue gently. 'My babushka's mother made this and the *matryoshka* dolls round it when she lived in Tunguska.'

'Tunguska?'

'Out in Siberia,' she answered, waving at the window. 'She used to say this was magic. That's why she covered it in gold.'

'She sounds an interesting woman,' said Billi. 'What else did she say? Anything about Baba Yaga?'

'Oh yes.' Vasilisa stroked the figurine and whispered, 'Baba Yaga hates us, Billi. For all the damage we've done.'

'What sort of damage?'

'She wants the Earth back to how it was before men came. She feels the Earth; she feels it like it's her. Each time we dig mines we're cutting her skin. When we put our garbage in the sea we're pouring poison in her mouth. We make her sick.' Vasilisa held up the figurine, turning it towards the moonlight.

'You know that, from her mind?' Vasilisa spoke with such simple clarity, Billi could almost see Baba Yaga's point.

Vasilisa didn't answer. She just stared, open-mouthed, at the window.

Bright brown eyes peered through the glass. The hulking black silhouette of a werewolf filled the window frame as it perched on a tree bough.

Billi leapt up, dragging Vasilisa with her. The werewolf smashed its clawed fist through the glass.

Howls filled the darkness outside and Billi heard something crash through the front door below.

Billi pushed Vasilisa out of the door as her father bounded up the stairs, Templar Sword in his fist.

'Out of the way!'

He barged past and Billi glanced back to see the werewolf scrabbling through the broken window. It howled at Arthur, flailing its claws at him, but it was caught in the small frame. Arthur stepped to the side, checked the distance between them and he hacked at the neck twice before the head came off. By the time it had rolled over to the door the head had transformed into that of a woman, not one Billi recognized. Olga and Svetlana had come with friends.

'Let's go,' Arthur said as he flicked the blood off his sword.

With Arthur in front, Vasilisa in the middle and Billi behind, they descended into the basement. More glass smashed, this time in the living room. Gareth, a spiked mace in his hand, went to investigate.

Bors waited in the crowded storeroom. He passed them each a torch, then set about moving a large storage trunk.

Billi found her *wakizashi* and scabbard hanging from the wall. She strapped it to her back and pulled her jacket over it while Bors lifted up a manhole cover. Arthur grabbed his Fairbairn-Sykes dagger, his old Royal Marine weapon, and slid it into a leather forearm sheath that he covered with his sleeve.

'If anyone with a tail comes down here, treat them exceedingly badly,' he said as he handed the Templar Sword to Bors.

'Damn right I will,' said Bors.

They climbed down the shaft, Arthur first. He shone his torch up and down the tunnel before waving the others down. The stink doubled every metre they descended until eventually Billi touched the floor. Rats squeaked in the darkness and Billi pointed the light down the low, circular sewer. The old bricks shone wetly, and foul water seeped through the gaps, collecting into a thin stream that trickled along the lowest point.

A vast labyrinth of underground tunnels and sewers lay under Temple District, and only the Templars knew them all. The old Fleet River had been covered over by the Victorians and turned into a main sewer. One of Billi's earliest training exercises had been to find her way around the system without a map.

'Which way?' Billi asked.

'Exit eleven.'

Holborn. That made sense. They could take the tube straight to Heathrow airport from there.

'Don't tread in anything,' Arthur warned as he led them past colonies of red-eyed rats and pits overflowing with vomit-inducing foulness.

Eventually they reached a flight of steps leading to a steel door. Arthur unlocked it with a large key and they emerged into a white-tiled corridor, Holborn tube station itself. The door said DANGER – HIGH VOLTAGE and had an official-looking London Electricity sign on it, so to the casual observer it was just one of the thousands of substations that covered the city.

Commuters in their winter coats, heads down and iPods in, barely gave them a second glance. It was rush hour and everyone wanted to get home. Billi took Vasilisa's hand and joined the flow.

Buffeted and shoved along by the crowd, Billi locked her fingers round Vasilisa's wrist as the sea of humanity caught her up. She couldn't see anything but the back of the guy in front of her. A Polenitsy could be right there and she'd only know it when the claws went in her back. Someone's elbow went in her ribs and Billi almost lashed out, her senses on hyperdrive. A man barged between Billi and Vasilisa, knocking Billi's grip free.

'Billi!'

Vasilisa screamed as she disappeared in a sudden surge of people heading to the escalator. Billi glanced back and forth. Arthur was gone.

Bloody hell!

'Out of the way!' Billi pushed a man aside, knocking the newspaper out of his hands.

'Oi!'

Billi snarled, then saw Vasilisa turning round and round in a wall of bodies. Billi broke through and Vasilisa ran into her arms. It took a minute for Billi to calm down, her own heart racing harder here in the station than when the werewolves had attacked. She couldn't lose Vasilisa. Billi used her sleeve to wipe the tears from

Vasilisa's face. This time they walked side by side to the westbound platform.

Arthur was waiting at the bottom of the steps. He put away his mobile.

'Elaine will meet us at Heathrow with Vasilisa's passport. She'll take her.'

'You're not going?' Billi asked.

'Not with the Polenitsy on a rampage.'

Together they emerged on to the crowded platform.

HEATHROW – 2 MINUTES

The train pulled in and they pushed onboard. A couple of seats came free and Billi and Vasilisa grabbed them. Arthur stood in the centre of the carriage a few paces away, keeping an eye on the doors.

'We're OK,' said Billi to herself as much as to Vasilisa, who still clutched her hand. People loomed over them, swaying from side to side as the train rattled through the tunnels. 'Just sit tight.'

Billi flicked open her mobile to check the time, but instead stopped to look at the display screen. The photo of her and Kay shone brightly. Billi had transferred it from Kay's old mobile to hers. She knew she shouldn't have, but looking at him felt different now. Only a week ago his smile would have cut her; now she just felt its warmth – its support.

Vasilisa looked up. 'This is all my fault, isn't it?'

'No. This is their fault. The Polenitsy.' Billi wiped her damp hair away from her forehead. 'Don't worry. I won't let them touch you.'

'You promise?'

'Promise.'

Arthur pushed his way through the crowd. His eyes darted left and right, never dropping his guard. 'Once Vasilisa's on her way we'll set up at the Canterbury Preceptory.'

Someone started shouting. Arthur started.

'You two stick together,' he ordered and barged back down the carriage.

Vasilisa tightened her small, cold fingers round Billi's and looked up at her.

'They're here,' she said and her voice was soft and infinitely sad. Tears welled in her eyes.

Then the carriage lights died.

CHAPTER 13

Cries rang out. The carriage was lit by small spots of pearly white as people used their mobiles to see, but all they revealed were other stark faces rigid with fear. Billi tightened her hold on Vasilisa as the mass moved and people buffeted against each other. The air thickened with terror.

'I can't breathe!'

'Get out!'

'It's a bomb!'

'It's terrorists!'

'Open the doors!'

A scuffle broke out as people tried to barge their way through the interconnecting doors while those in the next carriage tried to do the same. The screams multiplied and someone clawed at Billi's leg as they were knocked down.

The howl silenced the entire train.

The second howl unleashed total chaos. The heaving mass of panicked passengers degenerated into pandemonium. They didn't know which way to run – the snarls and predatory growling seemed to come from all around.

Billi heard the tell-tale slash of claws and the ripping of flesh, and someone's scream rose to an ear-splitting screech. Savage barks signalled the attack, then it was all tearing and biting. A black shape with a dripping snout loomed up, framed by the haze of mobile lights. It peered down the carriage and saw them. It shook its ragged head, tossing bloody spittle across the ceiling.

'*Deus vult!*'

Arthur slammed into the beast. He smacked his forearm across its jaw and rammed his dagger into its throat. People screamed around him and suddenly he vanished into the panicking crowd.

'We're leaving,' said Billi.

She jumped up and grabbed hold of the straps dangling over her head. Both feet came up high, then shot out, cracking a window. The glass exploded as she kicked it again. She grabbed Vasilisa round her waist.

'You first. Carefully does it.'

Vasilisa hesitated, then embraced her. 'You did your best,' she said.

'It's not bloody over yet!' exclaimed Billi. She wasn't going to quit. They were getting out. There was no room to fight properly in here. Although the terrified wall of bodies stopped the werewolves from reaching Billi, they only had a few more seconds. She pushed Vasilisa out of the broken window, careful she didn't catch any of the jagged shards stuck in the frame. Billi felt Vasilisa step away and she put her arms through the gap and followed.

Billi landed on a narrow ledge that ran alongside the

train. She reached out and Vasilisa grabbed her hand immediately.

Don't panic. How many times had that been drummed into her? If she just stuck to the tunnel, along the rails, she'd come out at the next platform. Simple. She clicked on her torch and shuffled along the ledge with Vasilisa behind her. They cleared the front of the train and she hopped down on to the tracks.

'Don't touch the rails.'

They followed the curve of the tunnel, slow and steady. They left the train behind and soon the bestial cries and screams were lost and the only sound was Billi's heart thumping in her chest. Her hand found a door handle and tested it: unlocked. She pulled Vasilisa in.

A storeroom. Billi inspected a map of the tube system pinned to the wall; they were halfway towards Knightsbridge station. Two service tunnels branched off nearby and maybe if she took those, she could lose any pursuers. But that was a long detour. Speed or safety? Billi peeled the map off and gave it to Vasilisa while she checked the rest of the small room. Various tools, screws, tape and other engineering tools cluttered the shelves. Billi pulled out her sword and felt better. She smiled at Vasilisa.

Vasilisa put her finger to her lips.

The door was thick, but Billi still heard the scuttling of claws against the concrete. There was a short grunt as something landed on the ledge outside and sniffed. Billi pushed Vasilisa into a corner and gave her the torch. The handle clicked and the door opened slightly.

Billi shoulder-charged the door and there was a yelp as it smashed into the intruder's face. She leapt back into the tunnel, landing squarely on the chest of the fallen werewolf. She slashed twice, each time feeling the blade bite deep. The monster coughed and gurgled and Billi rolled off as two more approached her.

'Behind me!' she shouted. Billi defended the doorway, stopping the werewolves from reaching Vasilisa. The air hissed and Billi ducked as one of the pair swiped its claws in the space where her throat had just been. She stamped on its long toes and kicked out at its legs, but it rolled and was back on all fours, snarling and snapping. Billi slashed and parried furiously with her *wakizashi*, never letting anyone pass. Then she glimpsed lights, torch lights, bouncing along in the darkness. Help was coming. Police, rescue services, transport staff – she didn't care. They may not be able to fight, but they'd give her a chance to escape.

'Here! Here!' Billi screamed. She just needed to hang on a few more seconds. The third werewolf, the one with the bleeding head, got to its feet. Billi swung at it again, but it blocked her blow. Just for a moment she was caught motionless. Then the werewolf swung both its arms into her, catapulting Billi off her feet. She tumbled through the air and crashed down on the ground, banging her head on a ledge. Bright sparks erupted in front of her eyes.

'Billi!'

Billi tried to get up, but was totally lost in the darkness. The floor pitched and tilted and she groped for something to hold on to. She caught sight of a brown-pelted werewolf emerging from the storeroom, Vasilisa trapped in its arms. The light caught its black, oily lips and deadly fangs before Vasilisa dropped the torch, leaving only her terrified screams.

'Vasilisa,' Billi croaked, all the air driven from her lungs. She punched out drunkenly, but there was nothing there. She smelt the raw, damp odour of sweaty fur and spun towards it, hands outstretched. But the werewolf swatted her away and Billi tripped and crashed against the concrete. Then even the distant lights faded and the screams of the small girl fell silent until all Billi had was . . . nothing.

CHAPTER 14

The sky is burning, but it's snowing. People lie around Billi, charcoal statues, slowly accumulating a blanket of snow. The trees are blackened sticks of ash; one has branches that still smoulder.

It's the end of the world and she knows it.

The billboards have burned to nothing and the houses themselves are ruined, black, with their roofs collapsed and all the windows shattered. The cars sit idle, their drivers husks of carbonized flesh and bone.

Billi holds out her hand. The snow is grey.

Ash. The sky is full of ash.

'She will do this, unless you destroy her.'

Billi sees Kay ahead. This time she doesn't go to him, but she feels warm, just seeing him.

Kay walks closer. He's holding hands with two children. One is Vasilisa, dressed in her pyjamas. The other is a small boy, wearing a pair of jeans and a blue and burgundy Crystal Palace football top.

Oh God. No.

'You did it to me, Billi,' says Alex Weeks. He holds a

sword out, hilt first. 'The first time is always the hardest.'
Billi didn't spot it before, but a red stain is spreading
over his chest. His shirt is torn open and his white flesh
is like an empty page. The red is the story of his life. It
wasn't long at all.

Billi takes the sword, her father's sword. She looks to
Kay for help.

'You must decide,' says Kay.

This is wrong. The sword tip is against Vasilisa's heart
now. She looks up at Billi. She trusts Billi.

'No.' Billi tries to drop the weapon, but someone's
holding her hand and arm. She looks around and it's her
dad. The other Templars line up behind him. He grips
Billi's arm and pushes her towards Vasilisa.

'You must.' His mouth is firm. 'It is your duty.'

'Kay, help me!' Billi struggles against her dad, but the
others add their strength to his. An endless line of knights
appears, vague in the gloom, and all their power is being
channelled through Arthur's arm.

'You must. For all our sakes,' says Arthur.

Billi stares down at Vasilisa and sees the girl's shadow.
It is huge, malformed and crooked. The shadow of a
monstrous old crone.

Vasilisa screams as Billi slides the sword into her heart.

'Vasilisa!' Billi jerked awake. She strained against the
straps holding her down while pain pounded behind her
eyes. Bright lights shone all around her and she didn't
know where she was.

'Easy, miss,' said a woman dressed in a green paramedic's uniform. Gas bottles and masks hung off the wall and beside her was a rack neatly stacked with emergency gear: a portable defibrillator and packets of morphine, antiseptics and bandages. Billi was in an ambulance. On the floor beside her lay the torn remains of her backpack. She could see the three deeply carved cuts. Outside she could hear sirens, car horns and the cacophony of hundreds of people.

'I . . . have to leave,' said Billi. She had to save Vasilisa. If she hurried, there might still be a chance. But she couldn't move; the straps across her chest, waist and legs held her firmly on the trolley. 'Please, I'm OK.'

The medic patted her hand. 'I'm sure you are, dear, but you've had a nasty knock. Best we take you in and keep an eye on you, just for tonight.'

The doors swung open and Arthur barged in.

'Hey, you can't just come in here.' The woman stood and held up her hand. For a second Billi thought he was going to break it, but he glanced at Billi and his shoulders slumped. He gave a weak smile, but Billi knew he knew: she'd lost Vasilisa.

'She's my daughter.'

'Oh.' The paramedic looked down at Billi. 'Well, we're taking her into Charing Cross Hospital. Just for the night.'

'Dad, I just want to go home.'

Arthur nodded. 'Fine. The others are waiting.'

The paramedic sighed impatiently. She stood in front of Arthur, blocking him from Billi.

'I'm afraid that's not possible. I'm afraid –'

Arthur put his hand on the woman's wrist. He didn't squeeze, but held it firmly. The woman tried to twist it free, but she was caught. She gazed into his eyes, first angry, then defiant and then away.

'I'm afraid . . .' she whispered.

Yes. She was.

Arthur and Billi made their way through the police cordon, past the row of ambulances treating the injured and past the hordes of sightseers and media. Huge spotlights had been erected along the road and news vans filled the street and thousands of torches bobbed all around her. The news was garbled, but Billi heard one newscaster reporting that some large dogs, Rottweilers or pit bulls, had gone mad when a power failure had plunged the line into complete darkness. Several people had been savaged, but the dogs had escaped down the tunnels.

Arthur waved for a taxi.

'I lost her, Dad.' Billi struggled to keep up, her bones groaning with pain. If she moved too fast, she thought she might crack into a million pieces. But the ache wasn't just because of the beating. She'd failed Vasilisa. But it wasn't just a single girl's life she'd jeopardized – it was the entire planet's.

'It's not over yet.'

Billi stopped. 'You know something?'

Arthur opened the taxi door. 'Bors was mauled and

there are three dead bodies at the Temple. The police are going to have a field day. That's all I know.' He sighed. It had been a long night for them both and there was still a lot to do. 'But Elaine's OK and she has a plan.'

'To find Vasilisa?' Billi gazed at the bedlam outside the tube station. The flashing lights, the crowds and the ambulances. 'And the Polenitsy.'

'By God, yes.' Arthur put his hand on her shoulder and smiled grimly. 'And we will make them pay.'

CHAPTER 15

A few hours later Billi was back in the Temple Church. She peered round at the other knights as they sat patiently in the Council of War. She struggled to keep upright. She'd got back and found that Middle Temple Lane had been cordoned off by the police, who were going house to house, trying to understand how three dead women, one headless, had ended up in an area occupied mainly by lawyers.

Lance leaned over. 'How are you, Bilqis?'

Her head felt like someone was rolling cannonballs in it. Her bones ached and the thwack she'd been given by the werewolf made breathing hard work. She tried to smile, to be stoic and tough, but her grin turned into a grimace.

'You look awful,' said Gwaine as he crossed the circle of chairs and took his own.

Arthur hadn't arrived, but the others waited in the gloomy candlelight of the Round. They'd all got a battering that night. The closed chamber stank of Elaine's poultice concoction, of sour vinegar and acrid herbs.

Each knight had claw and bite wounds, so Elaine had spent half the night patching them up. She'd checked Billi's own injuries and pronounced her fully recovered. It was a relief to get those stinking bandages off her back at last.

The west door opened and a flurry of snow blossomed in, followed by Arthur, Elaine and Father Rowland. Rowland shut the door and took his seat on the pews, turning so he could see the circle of knights. Elaine usually sat with him, but this time she followed Arthur into the circle. The usually cool and sarcastic old woman seemed anxious, and for the first time didn't have a cigarette twitching in her fingers. She looked around the high-backed chairs. She picked an empty one next to Billi and sat down.

Gwaine's mouth dropped open in shock.

'That's Bors's seat,' he said, his voice weak and cracked.

'Not while he's in hospital.' Arthur took his own seat. 'This needs all of us.'

'But, Arthur, she's . . . Jewish,' said Gwaine, still staring in disbelief at the woman in his nephew's seat.

'Right now I really couldn't give a shit,' replied Arthur. He slowly looked each of them in the eye. 'It's been a bad night. Bors was badly wounded, but, God be praised, he's going to live.'

'And the others?' Billi asked. The werewolves had attacked dozens, infecting them all with lycanthropy.

Rowland cleared his throat. 'Elaine and I have been

to Crow Street Hospital, where the injured were taken. We've been able to use our contacts there to make sure they're being treated with Elaine's poultices. They'll recover.'

'But we've no time to rest up and lick our wounds,' said Arthur. 'The Polenitsy have the girl.'

Elaine butted in. 'We've got to get her back. Soon.'

Billi felt flushed and red, like they were all looking at her. She'd lost Vasilisa.

'The last time Vasilisa was with us she spoke of Fimbulwinter, something she believed Baba Yaga would bring about.' Arthur twisted his wedding ring, constantly winding it round his finger. 'Once Baba Yaga performs the Ritual of Devouring, she will be powerful enough to create a global winter that could last for many years.'

'The ritual can only be carried out on the night of the full moon, Saturday,' said Elaine.

'Bloody hell,' said Billi. It was early Wednesday already. 'That's four days from now. How on earth are we going to find her in four days? We've no idea where she is.'

'Oh, Vasilisa's in Russia,' replied Elaine. 'The Polenitsy will take her straight to Baba Yaga and the old witch is *Mother* Russia. She'll be nowhere else.'

'Great. That's going to make it so much easier.' Russia was gigantic. Billi could see everyone was thinking the same. It would be like searching for a snowflake in the Arctic.

Gwaine snorted scornfully. 'And how exactly are we

going to find her?' He spread out his arms. 'Look at us. We've just had our arses whipped by a bunch of hairy freaks and that's with the home advantage. We go into their territory and we're just so much dog food. It'll be suicide.'

'This time we'll have help,' said Arthur. 'We'll go to the Bogatyrs. Romanov is a good man; once he knows what's at stake he'll want to help. Then there's Vasilisa's grandmother, a white witch by all accounts. She could have valuable information for us. Plus there are many wolf packs in the area; the Polenitsy may have come from one.' He stood up and walked slowly round the circle of chairs. 'Two teams, one to Vasilisa's birthplace in Karelia, the other to Moscow, where we'll meet the Bogatyrs. We must stop Baba Yaga.'

'By any means necessary, right?' asked Gwaine. Billi's eyes narrowed.

'We'll rescue Vasilisa if we can.' Arthur looked slowly around, but stopped at Billi. 'But that may not be possible.'

A chill crept up Billi's heart.

'Then?' she asked. She knew the answer, but needed someone to say it out loud.

'If we can't save her, we have to kill her,' replied her father, in his plain, matter-of-fact tone. 'Baba Yaga must not carry out the ritual. That's all that matters.'

'There has to be another way,' said Billi, sickened. 'We can't just kill her.'

Arthur frowned. 'I'm not happy about this either, Billi.

But what's the life of one against the entire population of the planet? With Vasilisa in Baba Yaga's hands, that's the choice we face.'

'But can't we –'

'Enough,' Arthur snapped. 'You will do as you are ordered, squire.'

Billi glared at him, but Arthur's cold, blue eyes were empty. He'd made his decision.

'I will go to Moscow. I have friends there,' said Lance.

'Agreed,' said Arthur. 'Gwaine will lead the Moscow team and contact the Bogatyrs. I will lead the Karelia team.'

'Who goes with you?' asked Billi.

Arthur frowned. 'I take Gareth and Mordred.'

No.

Arthur pointed at Billi. 'You go with Elaine, Lance – and Gwaine.'

'I'm not going with Gwaine,' said Billi the moment she and Arthur left the Temple Church. They couldn't go home – the place was crawling with police – so they crossed the courtyard to Chaplain's House.

'What's wrong with him?'

'Oh, nothing. Except he's a narrow-minded, bigoted religious fundamentalist.'

'You say that like it's a bad thing.'

Oh, he was trying to be funny. That's just what she needed. A funny parent.

'Anyway you'll have Elaine.'

'Gwaine hates Elaine more than anyone. Why don't I swap with Mordred?'

'No. He's too inexperienced. He sticks with me. One squire per team and you're in Gwaine's.' Arthur tapped his watch. 'It's late, Billi. Get some sleep. The flight's at seven.'

'Not until we've finished discussing this.' She stood in the hallway, glowering.

Arthur's eyes narrowed. 'Fine.' He twisted his wedding ring. 'You're even more stubborn than Jamila.'

'You say that like it's a bad thing.'

'Billi, why are you trying to pick a fight with me? Is this really all about Gwaine?'

Billi shook her head and scowled. 'It's not right. We're meant to protect innocent people like Vasilisa. I can't believe her sacrifice is even an option.'

Wearily Arthur took off his coat and Billi saw the slowness in his movements. He'd taken a beating down on the tube and was as bruised and busted as the rest of them. It shocked her to see her dad's moments of frailty. 'Billi, the world's not black and white. The bad guys come bright and beautiful and the good guys might look like monsters. You of all people know that.'

Michael. The commander of the Shining Host. The archangel had tried to kill every firstborn child in Britain. He'd been beautiful right up to the moment she'd destroyed him.

'You know it's not the answer, Dad. If we kill Vasilisa, we stop Baba Yaga. This time. But what about the next

Spring Child she goes after? We kill that one too? And the one after that? What we really need to do is kill Baba Yaga.'

'I don't disagree. That's why I'm going to Karelia. Maybe Vasilisa's grandmother can help us. But it's a long shot. Baba Yaga's very old and very powerful. If she could be destroyed easily, someone would have done it a long time ago.'

'Maybe the right people have never tried.'

Arthur laughed. 'You stick with that attitude.' Then the laughter ended and he got serious. 'Billi, this is important. If you have to choose between saving one life or saving millions, you can't have any doubts. I have to trust you on this. If the time comes, you must kill Vasilisa.'

Billi sat in the hallway well before dawn with her bag packed and ready. Her dad had gone to sort out the last-minute flights and visas for Russia.

She hadn't slept a wink. How could she? The clock on the hall ticked away every second and the noise reminded her of what was at stake. Billi stared at Kay's photo on her mobile, tracing the outline of his face with her fingernail.

Once, a long time ago, she'd believed being a Templar was cool, noble even. No matter how hard it had got in school, the secret that she belonged to something old, important and powerful had kept her going. Her training, her loneliness, her bruises all meant something. She'd hung on to that after Kay's death. The Templars fought the Unholy. They fought the ghosts and the ghouls and all the supernatural evil that preyed on mankind. They protected the innocent.

Billi searched Kay's face, trying to find the answer. He had known his death was coming and had prepared for it. But that hadn't made it any easier for her to be the one left behind. She'd had to close off her heart and her feelings. It had been the only way to protect herself. But now, after the last few days with Vasilisa, Billi felt differently. Despite herself, she cared for the girl. And Vasilisa deserved none of this misery.

Billi had killed Kay and it had almost destroyed her. Now her job was to cross half the world and do the same to a nine-year-old. Billi remembered her last dream. Had Kay been trying to tell her that Vasilisa must die?

It was hopeless to think otherwise. If Baba Yaga got her hands on Vasilisa, she would destroy everything. How could the life of one child compare to that?

There could be no room for pity.

The Knights Templar, from being an ancient order of warriors, was now a death squad.

So be it.

Billi looked at Kay one last time, then deleted him forever.

CHAPTER 16

The eruption had thrown up so much ash that flights throughout Europe had been delayed. Now, two days after the eruption, the backlog of weary and irate travellers still hadn't been cleared. People slept on the seats, on the floors, up against the walls. Long queues of cars and coaches blocked the entrance to Heathrow airport as the passengers were transferred to other airports or hotels, all being managed by forlorn airport staff.

Billi and the other knights picked their way through the groups of abandoned passengers and climbed over piles of waiting luggage. It wasn't yet seven, but the airport was overflowing.

Billi watched the news on one of the big overhead screens. The destruction of Naples dominated everything. Almost ten metres of ash and rock had fallen over the city in the last two days and only now were any rescue vehicles able to even approach the devastated city. Buildings had collapsed under the sheer weight of the falling debris, burying scores of people. Ash had set as hard as concrete and the drills and picks and the desperate hands did little good.

Miracles still occurred. People continued to trickle out of the tunnels. They'd fled into the underground system, then walked out once the eruptions had ended. Thousands were gathered in an ever-growing refugee camp and families pored over long lists plastered to wooden walls, hoping to find a relative or friend among the survivors.

'It seems so hopeless,' said a woman, also watching the coverage.

Hopeless? Maybe. But people still fought on. Billi stared at the small figures moving over the vast, grey city like ants, struggling against the wrath of nature. That's what humanity did, wasn't it? Despite the overwhelming odds, it fought on.

No weapons. Arthur didn't want anyone getting arrested at customs because they'd tried to smuggle in a broadsword. Lance knew an arms dealer in Moscow from his bad old days as a smuggler and that was where Gwaine's team would tool up. Arthur had friends across the waters in Finland and they would deliver the Karelia team their gear. Each Templar had a package of Elaine's wolfsbane poultices.

Billi pulled off her backpack while Elaine arranged the boarding passes. She scratched her shoulder blade. The claw marks had healed up nicely, but she had no plans to get bitten or clawed again. She'd put the roll of stinking brown cloth in an airtight Tupperware sandwich box, but still the smell seemed to linger on everything.

The Knights Templar gathered at the coffee shop on

the other side of passport control. The Karelia flight was just before the Moscow one.

Arthur brought his latte over to Billi.

'How are you feeling?' he asked. He sat down stiffly. The mornings were like that, but since when? Forty-five wasn't that old, not really.

'Better than you, I think.'

'Funny girl.' He stirred in his sugar and the chair creaked as he leaned back. 'It's going to be a bad one, Billi.'

Like she didn't know. They were going in blind. Here in Britain the Templars had secret contacts and hideouts scattered across the country. Russia was the unknown. It was Baba Yaga and the Polenitsy's heartland. They'd be outnumbered ten to one, at least.

'Tell me about the Bogatyrs,' Billi asked. Everything had been so rushed she'd had no time to find out about the Russian knights.

'Christian warriors, set up before the Templars. The Russians never got involved in the Crusades; their enemies weren't the Saracens, but the followers of the old ways, pagans, witches, the werewolves.'

'And what about this Romanov bloke? Alexei-thing-amajig?'

'Alexei Viktorovich Romanov. Please get the pronunciation right – he is royalty. Great-grandson of Tsar Nicholas, if I remember correctly.' Arthur scratched his beard, trying to remember what else he knew. 'The story is that everyone in the royal family was killed at the beginning of the Russian revolution. That much is history. But rumours lingered that one Romanov survived, the princess Anastasia. She was saved by the Bogatyrs. Since then her children and her children's children have served, and led, the Russian order of knights. Stalin tried his best to wipe them out and they went into hiding, like us. But after the collapse of the Soviet Union, the Bogatyrs became active again, under the leadership of Alexei. Tsar Alexei.'

'What's he like?'

Arthur shrugged. 'Never met him. But I hear he's a man of honour.' He glanced up at the overhead display. 'Time to go.' He leaned across the table and kissed Billi's cheek. 'Goodbye.'

The other knights waited. Arthur looked like there was something else he wanted to say. He fidgeted with his wedding ring. 'Listen, Billi. If the worst happens, don't worry about me. Look after yourself.' He patted her arm. It was a pathetic gesture, but neither of them knew what else to do. 'You'll be fine.' Then he turned towards the others.

'Dad, wait.'

Billi wanted to say something. She wanted to say she loved him. That despite how things had turned out, it wasn't his fault. She'd chosen this life.

'*Deus vult*, Dad.'

Arthur smiled and nodded. '*Deus vult*, Billi.'

CHAPTER 17

'What d'you think?' asked Elaine as she leaned over Billi to peer out of the plane window. They were over Russia and would be landing in the next ten minutes.

What did she think? Billi stared out over a world of mutilated white.

They'd left the suburban landscape of south-east England. The blotches of orange-roofed estates and fragmented fields. From up above she'd realized how small, how provincial England was away from the cluster of skyscrapers and parks of London.

Russia was on a different scale entirely. The plane banked over a maze of monolithic housing blocks that seemed dumped at random over the countryside. A huge power station with four hell-hole chimneys belched great clouds of steam into the sky. The snow around it was smeared with soot. Motorways ran like scars across the vast plains, razor-straight and black.

The main roads led to vast expanses of forest, with smaller roads winding to clusters of houses on the edge of a river or a lake.

'Dachas,' said Elaine. 'Once all Russians dreamed of their little hidey-hole in the country. Play peasant during the weekend, then go back to big, bad Moscow.'

'What do they dream of now?'

'Diamonds and caviar, like the rest of us,' Elaine said as she summoned the steward. Her tray table was already overflowing with miniature bottles of Gordon's gin.

Lance appeared. The plane was half empty, giving everyone space to spread out. He and Gwaine were up near the front, while Billi and Elaine had gone to the back.

He grabbed a bottle as it rolled off the small flip-down table. Elaine blushed as he handed it back to her. Was she embarrassed because of her drinking? That would be a first.

Maybe it was Lance. He'd joined the order a week or two after Percy's funeral. The Templars had known about him for years, a loner who stalked *ghuls* and the other Unholy across Europe. Billi had seen him in action a few days after he'd arrived. A trio of blood-drinkers had been feeding on people in a nursing home, safe in the assumption that no one would believe horror stories from the elderly inhabitants. Lance had gone through those undead like a hurricane. Even Arthur had been impressed. The Frenchman had an easy charm and the eyepatch gave him piratical glamour. He was old, maybe in his mid-thirties, but handsome in that Continental way with a long, drooping Gallic moustache. Billi looked at Elaine again. Red as a tomato.

Nah. It couldn't be.

'I've booked us into a small hotel in Arbat. It's central and discreet,' Lance said. 'Vaslav will meet us there with our shopping and some information.'

'Did he get everything?' Billi asked.

'*Oui*. Short-sword, kukri and punch dagger and those heavy steel shuriken you requested.' Lance paused. 'And the knuckledusters, of course.' He focused his good eye on Elaine. 'And for you, Madame Elaine? Is there anything you would like?'

Elaine shook her head awkwardly.

'*C'est bien*.' He stroked his moustache. 'It is Wednesday today. If all goes well, we should make contact with the Bogatyrs later today.'

Leaving them just three days to find Vasilisa. It seemed impossible.

Lance returned to his seat and Elaine watched him go.

'That is so disgusting,' Billi said. 'You're old enough to be his granny.'

Elaine jumped, caught out. 'Oi, none of your lip.' She pressed the call button again. 'Where is that bloody steward? I'm dying of thirst back here.'

The seat-belt sign came on and they descended into Moscow.

Billi's experiences abroad were pretty limited – the odd trip to France and one rain-sodden week in Spain – but Domodedovo airport was just like any other. Huge, glazed facade, modern and plastic with high lobbies and the usual shops. The signs were in Russian and English and so were the announcements.

Beyond the tinted green glass walls of the airport the landscape was obliterated by white. A hazy road crowded with traffic led arrow-straight from the doorways to the horizon. A dense wood of conifers lined it.

They bundled outside and instantly the elements attacked. The cold snatched Billi's breath and her eyes watered as the snow-laden air slapped her face. She'd never experienced anything like it. Despite the gloves, scarf, greatcoat and hat, the blistering wind found and attacked every millimetre of exposed skin. Snowflakes froze on her eyelashes and Billi covered her mouth and breathed through her scarf, just to stop her lips from chafing.

Jesus, how can they live with this weather? An icy gust stung the back of her neck and she shivered from top to toe.

Big, block-busting four-by-fours that looked more like tanks than cars were parked alongside brittle, ancient Trebants and Ladas built back in the days of the Cold War. They bore their winter tyres, the rubber lined with metal studs that sounded like falling pebbles as they rolled over the grit-sprinkled tarmac. Weather like this would have frozen London solid. But the Russians took the metre-deep snowfall and minus-ten temperatures in their fur-wrapped stride.

Russia would manage the volcanic winter better than

others, at least to begin with. The country had vast supplies of gas, coal and oil. Could it make its way through Fimbulwinter? Unlikely – you couldn't eat coal.

Lance pointed at a minivan and the man inside beckoned them. The interior was cloudy with cigarette smoke.

'Let's get a move on,' said Gwaine as he threw his backpack in. The others followed and Billi bagged a window seat.

Huge billboards lined the motorway, hiding much of the estates they passed en route to Moscow. The companies were all big brands Billi recognized – Microsoft, BMW – but the lettering was Cyrillic, a subtle reminder that things were different out here in Russia. The snow was piled chest high along the motorway and wispy clouds were blown off the tops, like the snow itself was steaming.

They had been driving towards the city for an hour when Billi saw a statue in the distance. It was a knight on a horse, with his spear stuck in a writhing dragon.

'Russians follow St George?' she asked.

Lance nodded. 'He's the patron saint of the city. The Russians take their religion seriously. Especially after decades of Communist suppression. The government and a lot of rich patrons paid to have some of the old religious sites restored. No better way to get into Heaven than by building a church. St George is a big man in the city.' Lance pointed at a passing church. 'But he's not the only one.'

The five golden cupolas of the building shone, despite

the dense clouds above. The walls were covered in bright mosaics and the building looked new. Bright as the sun, wreathed in gold, stood a winged warrior. His wings were spread out as though raised to shelter the faithful as they entered the church through the door below him. His long hair was unbound, his eyes sparkled and he seemed to be staring straight at Billi. He held his sword aloft, ready to strike.

St Michael.

The minivan crawled through the winding backstreets of Arbat. They'd come off one of the eight-lane ring roads that encircled central Moscow and were now in the heart of the city's art district. The buildings here were elegant old mansions and apartments from pre-revolutionary Moscow. The buildings bore ornate frescos; some had dark iron plaques beside their entrances bearing the double-headed eagle, the symbol of Imperial Russia.

'There it is, Olimpiyskaya Hotel,' said Lance. The driver manoeuvred the minivan through a pair of tall iron gates into a small courtyard.

The sky, clear now, was a cold white with smudges of red and pink to the south-east. The colours gave a rose-hue tint to the otherwise grey cityscape.

'Pollution from the eruption,' said Elaine. 'We'll have some beautiful sunsets too, thanks to Vesuvius.' She pulled out her backpack and the two of them went in.

A stairway swept up from the marble-tiled lobby to the next floor. Some of the steps had been repaired with coarse concrete. A dusty chandelier hung down on a heavy brass chain. The place had seen better days. Hell, it had seen better centuries.

Beside the entrance was an old sofa of faded red velvet. On it sat a large man with small eyes. He drew his fingers, heavy with gold rings, through his thinning black hair as he watched the new arrivals. One hand rested on a battered old suitcase.

'Nice choice, Lance,' said Billi as he followed her in with Gwaine. Lance looked at the big man and grinned. The two embraced one another and talked rapidly in Russian. Billi didn't understand a word. That is, all but one.

Bogatyrs.

Lance handed over a stuffed envelope. The big man nodded, slid over the suitcase and then left.

'Who was that?' asked Gwaine suspiciously.

'Vaslav.' Lance lifted up the suitcase, straining momentarily. 'Looks like he got everything.'

'You trust him?'

'Of course not. But I pay in dollars.'

'What did he say about the Bogatyrs?' asked Billi. Lance's eyebrow rose at the fact that Billi had cottoned on to the word.

'He's heard they've been at work by the Sparrow Hills, hunting vampires.' Lance raised his hand. 'How you say, *ghuls*?' He still hadn't got his head around the Arabic term the Templars used for blood-drinkers. 'It would be good for us to start there.'

The reception desk was half-hidden in the shadow of the staircase. The bright white bulb of the table lamp shone low over the gleaming bald head of the receptionist. He got up and smiled.

'My friends. American?'

'English,' said Gwaine.

'French,' said Lance.

The receptionist clapped once and the smile broadened to a grin, revealing a row of black teeth. 'Better than Americans. My name is Jorge.' He ducked behind a wall and brought out a stack of cards. 'Fill in, please.'

They doubled up, Billi with Elaine. The only bathroom was at the end of the corridor and they shared it with three other rooms. Billi and Elaine's room looked out on to a brick wall. The beds creaked and the mattresses sagged in the middle. A pile of light-green blankets lay folded at the foot of each bed.

While Elaine went to check the bar downstairs, Billi dropped her backpack on to one of the beds and locked the door. She went to the sink to wash and caught her face in the mirror. The image in the glass looked back at her with cold, dead-black eyes. What was in those eyes? Duty? Kay's had been bright with hope; her father's burned with passion. Hers were dark and unreadable.

She was tired. No, she was exhausted. But she wouldn't rest until they'd saved Vasilisa. Then what? The first plane to Jerusalem for years of training and hardship as a Templar. Fear, pain and most likely an early death. Was that the life she was saving Vasilisa for?

But if she couldn't be rescued? Arthur was right; Billi could not let Baba Yaga have Vasilisa. She would have to die.

What choice did Billi have? None. She doomed Vasilisa if she saved her, and doomed her if she didn't.

CHAPTER 18

Lance swung the old suitcase on to the bed where it landed with a dull thud. Gwaine locked the door and made sure the curtains were fully closed. All four had gathered in Gwaine and Lance's room and stood round the suitcase as Lance threw it open.

'*Et violà*,' said Lance.

There were half a dozen or so packages, all neatly wrapped and taped up. Billi lifted one out and tore off the bubble wrap.

'You like?' asked the Frenchman.

'I like.' She slid the kukri out of its plain sheath. The wicked Gurkha knife was like a machete, with an asymmetrical blade that was wide and heavy towards the tip, creating greater impact with the cut. The handle was bone, a nice touch that meant it wouldn't slip if things got bloody.

The katar was equally plain and very functional. Vaslav knew his knives. The handle was like an 'H' with the cord-wrapped grip along the short crossbar. The blade was shaped like a long isosceles triangle, the tip made of hardened steel and designed for punching through armour. She'd used her dad's once on a sheep's carcass they'd bought for a barbecue. The weapon left deep, wide wounds that didn't heal easily. A few punches with this would upset any Loony. With a bit of modification the sheath would sit nicely on the back of her belt. The kukri she strapped to her left thigh.

The shuriken were black tempered steel and Billi bounced three of them in her palm, listening to the heavy, satisfying clatter. The star-shaped throwing blades were good for short range, and the weight gave excellent penetration. They went in her right coat pocket.

'The sword?' she asked. She wanted a short-sword to replace her *wakizashi*.

Lance shook his head. 'Tomorrow, *ma chérie*.'

Gwaine made do with an axe. Not the tree-chopping size – something that could fit under his coat, but still be hefty enough to take off an arm with the correctly applied violence.

Lance clipped a modern combat knife to his belt.

'That all?' asked Billi.

'Oui.'

Your funeral, mate.

'Oh, one more thing,' said Lance. He handed Billi a chunky knuckleduster.

Billi slipped it into her left pocket. 'What's the plan?'

'We'll head up to Sparrow Hills. Keep our eyes peeled for the Bogatyrs,' said Gwaine. 'Leave the talking to me.'

*

126

It wasn't like the tube back home. Here the station was marble and polished granite. Chandeliers and mosaics. No expense spared.

The escalator sank them deep, deep underground. Ornate lamps from the 1930s lined the walls, their golden light casting long shadows that arched over her. A night reveller sat on the escalator, head sunk between his knees like one of the damned on his way down to Hell.

Billi gripped the rail, her hand damp with sweat. The last time she'd been on the tube she had held Vasilisa.

It was Wednesday evening. Just three days to go.

Art deco chandeliers made of bronze and amber crystal hung along the platform. Puddles of melted snow shone on the polished granite floor. Billi followed Lance and the others to the end. The platform wasn't busy; the few late-night commuters waited quietly, wrapped in heavy fur coats or thick hooded parkas. A cleaner patrolled the platform collecting abandoned cans, bottles and newspapers. Though Billi couldn't read the headlines, she saw that the front pages bore pictures of the still-smoking Vesuvius.

Bronze statues of heroes of the Soviet era lined the platform. Noble soldiers, proud peasant women, handsome engineers and scientists, all striving forward as part of Stalin's great experiment.

A woman rubbed the nose of a bronze guard dog. The sheen had come off, leaving its nose a light golden colour. Obviously she wasn't the first to rub it.

'For good luck,' said Lance.

Couldn't hurt, thought Billi. Taking off her glove, she ran her hand over the Alsatian's muzzle. She could do with all the luck she could get.

A short train ride later and Billi was gazing over Moscow from up on high. Dominated by the gigantic Moscow State University building, Sparrow Hills rose over the south-west of the city and allowed Billi to grasp the enormous scale of Russia's capital. It spread out to the far horizon, full of gothic towers, billboards and bridges whose lights sparkled on the broken ice on the river that wound in huge loops through the city.

Golden towers blazed against the dark blanket of the night sky, marked only by a hazy, waxing half-moon. Below the wide boulevard spread the woods of Vorobyovy Gory Nature Reserve, woven through by lamp-lit paths, descending down the slope to the Moscow River and the vast oval of the Moscow Olympic Stadium.

Engines roared behind her. Cars lined the *ulitsa Kosygina*, bonnets popped and engines screaming for an audience. The wide, curving road in front of the giant university building was the place for road-racing among the bored, rich sons and daughters of the new city elite, the oligarchs. Hundreds milled on the street and snowy square, and music boomed from the open windows of the prowling roadsters. Some even bore flags, gang signs of the various racing teams. Young men in leather jackets crowded round the rumbling cars while their girlfriends, dressed in furs and mini-skirts, huddled in their own cliques.

This was where they'd find the Bogatyrs? What had she expected? A bunch of guys in plate armour, riding warhorses? If they were anything like the Templars, they'd be low-profile and discreet.

A chunky, growling Hummer mounted the pavement. A blazing firebird covered the bonnet. Its feathers were sweeping red and orange flames and its eyes golden drops of lava. The headlights lit the hordes like a super-nova and the crowds backed away reverentially as it lumbered along the pavement.

The passenger door opened and a young man jumped out. He had short-cropped dark hair, wide cheekbones and a broken nose that only enhanced the icy look of his aristocratic face. He swept his hand across a non-existent crease on his black coat, a coat that probably cost more than most of the cars on the street. He spotted one of the posing girls and a smile flickered over his lips, easy, charming and arrogant. Her boyfriend moved instinctively in front of the girl, glowering back. Billi half-expected them to start beating their chests at one another, the rivalry was so animal. Instead he touched the diamond stud in his left ear and turned away, dismissing them both. He had the confidence of a person who'd found life way, way too easy. Gorgeous and didn't he just know it. His driver leaned against the door, lighting up a smoke. Tough and nasty. Definitely a bodyguard.

The young man gazed round the crowds like he owned them. Like he owned Moscow.

Their eyes met and he stopped. Billi must be something new.

She'd noticed that on the train over here. Unlike London with its kaleidoscope of cultures and races, Moscow was pretty white. She'd seen a few oriental faces, mainly Mongolian, but otherwise the population seemed overwhelmingly Caucasian. Maybe he didn't get to meet many Pakistani, or half-Pakistani, girls.

The guy's attention was uncomfortably intense. But Billi wasn't going to flinch. She watched him spread his gloved hand out and he lowered his head to give the slightest of nods, but his eyes never left hers. There wasn't even a hint of a smile, as if that would be too much. Billi's heartbeat went double time as she watched him straighten, hand still out.

'Anything?'

Billi twisted around and Lance peered past her at the young man. Their interaction had lasted a fraction of a second, but Billi was embarrassed. She was here for a reason and it wasn't to check out the local talent. She shot a quick look back; he was gone.

'Nothing.' She turned her attention to the job in hand and inspected the crowd again. How would they spot a werewolf if it was in human form? The single eyebrows and hairy palms were just myths, not that they'd be any use here with everyone wrapped up head to toe.

Billi caught a scuffle on the edge of the square. She

was already crossing the road when a man stumbled out of the dark enclave of trees, clutching his throat. He took a few wobbly steps, and people stepped away, thinking he was just some fool who couldn't handle his vodka, but then he fell to his knees. Someone screamed.

CHAPTER 19

The man thrashed on the ground, blood streaming from his throat, staining the snow scarlet. People crowded round him and a young woman gagged as she tried to staunch the flow.

Billi ran up and scanned the trees, followed closely by Elaine and Lance. Everyone was moving towards the commotion.

Everyone but a bloke in a parka.

'You!' Billi shouted.

He spun and Billi saw the blood-smeared mouth. He snapped his jagged fangs at her. Then he exploded with speed. He shot through the trees and leapt across the road in a blur. Cars screeched to sudden stops and one spun round and round on a patch of ice while people scattered. The *ghul* darted through the chaos with preternatural grace.

A Fang-face. The throat rip was a signature move. Bite and pull for a quick, easy kill. The blood-drinker just couldn't control himself.

All the more reason to kill him.

Billi saw the *ghul* dive over a wall and into the woods that covered the steep slopes of Sparrow Hills. Billi barged through the confusion and, jumping on to the bonnet of a parked car, got the height she needed to clear the wall. She hit the snow and tumbled. Lights whizzed around her and snow crunched in her face. Her heels slammed into a tree trunk and that was enough to halt her chaotic landing. She rose quickly, straight into a run, shaking herself free of the powdery snow.

The noise and chaos of the main drag faded away and the silence deepened. Off the winding path the lamplight was swiftly consumed, and soon she was making her way into the dark woods. Billi pulled off her hat and turned slowly, listening.

She heard a thud and a grunt up ahead, followed by the muffled bang of a gunshot. Something snarled and a man swore in Russian.

Billi flicked back her coat as she ran and drew out her kukri. She reached a clearing and saw two figures wrestling on the ground. She charged forward, surging through the snow as one of the figures revealed himself in a patch of moonlight. The *ghul*. His blood-smeared teeth widened as he twisted the other man's head, exposing his neck.

'*Deus vult!*'

Billi grabbed the *ghul*'s hair and pulled it back, dragging him away. She swung her blade into the monster's neck.

Black blood spurted from the deep gash in the side of

his throat, spraying out over the other man's face. He coughed and shook his head, then kicked the *ghul* backwards, taking Billi with it. The creature screeched and twisted around. He raked his long nails across Billi's stomach, ripping open her coat. He tore away at it, burrowing through the dense material towards her flesh. Billi tightened her grip on the *ghul*'s hair and struck again. A torrent of viscous blood poured from a deep shoulder wound and the *ghul* collapsed.

Billi sank into the snow, chest heaving. The *ghul* twitched beside her, its teeth gnashing in impotent fury for a moment before it went limp, the jaw hanging slack. The young man stood over them both.

'*Chort!*' he cursed.

Billi looked up at him. She was shocked to see the face of the flash young man that had got out of the Hummer. 'No, I'll get up by myself, thanks,' she said.

'I didn't need your help,' the man said. He glared at Billi, then back at the corpse. He held a pistol and his face was splashed with the *ghul*'s blood. 'I had him.'

'What you had was your arse kicked by that *ghul*.' Billi got up and shook off the worst of the snow. Her coat hung in tatters, nothing more than long, ragged strips of wool barely held together by the stitching.

'*Ghul?*' The guy stopped. His fingers tightened round the pistol grip. He looked at Billi, his grey eyes darkening. 'You called it a *ghul*?'

'Vampire. *Ghul*. Fang-face. Whatever. It was about to rip your throat out.' Billi watched warily as he pointed the pistol in her direction. 'Easy, Tiger. In case you hadn't noticed, I did just save your life.'

'Tsarevich Ivan!'

They both turned as a huge man lumbered through the snow like a buffalo with maybe half a dozen others following. The way they fanned out meant military.

'Easy,' said the big man as he approached, hands half-raised. 'Put the pistol away, Tsarevich.' The accent was Russian, but his English was perfect. He stepped into the moonlit clearing.

The pale light gleamed on his polished bald head and red cheeks. He had a red beard and moustache that was curled and turned up. His thick red eyebrows were as bushy as a fox's tail and he grinned like the Cheshire cat.

Tsarevich? That meant 'prince', didn't it? Billi gave Ivan an appraising look. He didn't look like a prince. Not with the broken nose, the crew cut and diamond stud.

But there was something strangely out-of-time about Ivan. An archaic elegance, even as he wiped the snow off his shoulders and straightened his black leather gloves. He reloaded his pistol, checking each round with the same methodical care he gave his clothes. He flicked back his coat and clipped the weapon away. Then he smoothed out the folds, making sure the weapon didn't leave any tell-tale lumps. He could be getting ready for the opera, if it wasn't for the blood covering his face.

The other men wore discreet body armour that covered the torso. No one would notice it under a coat, especially in this weather. The trousers weren't too obviously military, but the boots were shin-high with tripled-knotted laces. One man carried a modern crossbow, all pulleys and matt-black carbon fibre, another a pistol, complete with suppressor. Crucifixes dangled from their necks and Billi suspected they had holy oil and all the other mystical accessories in their utility pouches.

They were just like the Templars, upgraded for the twenty-first century.

'Bogatyrs, are you?' Billi asked.

'It looks like you've done our work for us,' said the man with the red beard, avoiding the question. 'I am Koshchey.'

'He was trying to take it alone,' said Billi. *Stupid idiot*, she thought. Then she remembered she'd been trying to take it alone too.

Koshchey huffed with disapproval. 'Foolish. You should have waited, Ivan.'

Ivan scowled. 'She's lucky I didn't kill her.'

Billi wiped her kukri clean. 'As if.'

Koshchey inspected the dead monster. He looked at Billi with a hint of admiration. 'You have obviously done this before, *da*?'

'She called it a *ghul*,' said Ivan. His hand hadn't strayed from his holster by much.

'There are only two people who use that term, Assassins and Templars,' said Koshchey. 'Which are you, child?'

'My name is Billi SanGreal.'

Koshchey paused. He drew his beard into a point as he pondered. 'Daughter of Arthur SanGreal?' He bowed. 'We are honoured.'

Billi began to laugh, but stifled it when she realized he was sincere. The other men didn't follow suit, but she could feel all their eyes on her.

Lance came charging down the slope, Gwaine and Elaine behind. Two of Koshchey's men raised their guns, but Koshchey waved them through. He waited until all four were gathered together.

'Which of you is the Templar Master, Arthur?'

Gwaine shook his head. 'The Master isn't here. He sent us. My name is Gwaine, this is Lance and her –' he jerked his thumb at the old woman puffing for breath beside him – 'her name is Elaine.' He looked round the group, taking in the weapons, the men, the attitude. 'You are the Bogatyrs.' It wasn't a question, more a confirmation. He turned his attention to Koshchey. 'Am I addressing Tsar Alexei Viktorovich Romanov?'

Ivan flinched and there was a brief flash of pain as his mouth hardened into a thin line.

The big man shook his head sadly. 'I am Koshchey.'

Lance stepped forward. 'I have heard of Koshchey the Undying.' He stood between Koshchey and the other Templars. The move was subtle, but clear. Whatever Lance knew wasn't all good.

Koshchey jutted out his chest proudly. 'That is I. The Undying. The Afghans tried. The Chechens. So did the Bosnians. All tried and failed. This is Tsarevich Ivan

Alexeivich Romanov.' He slapped Ivan on the back so hard he stumbled forward.

Ivan straightened his coat and gave a stiff nod. 'At your service.'

Gwaine turned his attention to Ivan. 'And where is your father, Tsarevich Ivan?'

Ivan lifted his head, just enough for Billi to see the fury in his storm-grey eyes. 'My father is dead.' With that he left abruptly to join one of the other Bogatyrs. Billi recognized him as the driver of Ivan's Hummer. She'd been right: the older man had bodyguard written all over him. He spoke with Ivan quietly, his hands resting comfortably on the Heckler & Koch submachine gun strapped across his chest.

Tsar Alexei is dead. And now it seemed Koshchey was the new man in charge.

'What brings the Poor Fellow Soldiers of Jesus Christ and of the Temple of Solomon to Moscow?' asked Koshchey, swiftly breaking the silence that had followed Ivan's pronouncement.

One of the Bogatyrs opened up a small silver bottle and poured its oily contents over the *ghul*. Puddles of blue flame erupted wherever the oil touched. In seconds the small clearing filled with sharp, sickly-sweet-smelling smoke.

'We're hunting the Polenitsy,' said Gwaine. 'We could do with your help, Koshchey.'

Koshchey thrust out his hand, completely covering Gwaine's in his massive palm. 'You have it, Sir Gwaine.'

Well, that was easy. If Billi was of a paranoid nature, she'd think it was almost too easy.

Koshchey summoned one of his men. 'You will be my guests. I will have Nikolai collect your belongings. Where did you say you were staying?'

'We didn't,' replied Lance a mite aggressively. Koshchey stopped.

'You're a long way from home, Templars, and Moscow is not London,' he said. 'It is a bad place to be without friends.' The big Russian, his hand still gripping Gwaine's, frowned. 'We know much of the Polenitsy; who would know more? We Bogatyrs have fought them for centuries. Come, friend Gwaine. Let us help you.' He winked. 'The Cold War is over, *da*?'

'It makes sense,' Elaine whispered, barely moving her lips. 'And we're running out of time.'

What did Lance know that made him so wary of Koshchey?

Gwaine nodded – ignoring Lance's glare. The Templars fell in together a few paces behind the Bogatyrs.

'Let's just keep our mouths shut and leave the talking to me,' said Gwaine. 'And that means you, Lance.'

Lance peered at the back of the big Bogatyr. If looks could kill, then Koshchey would have been a corpse.

'What is it?' asked Billi. 'What d'you know about him?'

'Ex-Spetnaz colonel. Did some work for the KGB. Last thing I heard was that he'd joined the Russian mafia. Nothing about the Bogatyrs.' Lance's voice sank into a whisper. 'He is very dangerous.'

'Sounds like just the man we need,' replied Gwaine.

'Nothing about Vasilisa being an avatar, understand?' ordered Lance. Gwaine bristled; he didn't like his authority questioned, but relented.

'Nothing about avatars.'

They plodded silently down the slope until they approached a line of cars. Ivan headed to his big Hummer, doing his best to ignore them. He unholstered his pistol and put it on the dashboard. But just before he shut the door he looked back at Billi. He'd cleaned the worst of the blood off his face, but a single dark line smeared his cheek, underlining his startling pale eyes.

Beautiful and dangerous. Billi knew all about that sort of boy.

She needed to watch out for Ivan Alexeivich Romanov.

CHAPTER 20

Billi and Gwaine rode in the rear seat of the limousine with Koshchey, who sat opposite, silently watching her. Lance and Elaine were in the car behind.

She gazed out at Moscow as they sped along the wide lanes that ringed the city. Despite the cold, people were out. Wrapped in furs and fuelled with vodka, they made their way across slush-swamped pavements to cafes, bars and restaurants that seemed to glow with a magical, golden light. All around her shone bright skyscrapers, huge hotels and vast apartment blocks, relics of the city's Soviet past. Power cables criss-crossed the roads like the broken webs of giant spiders and chunky trams rattled by on the old cobbled pathways that still ran through the city's older districts.

'You have come a long way to hunt, Sir Gwaine,' said Koshchey. 'While the Polenitsy are the enemy of the Bogatyrs, that doesn't mean I'll send my men to battle without a good reason.'

'The Polenitsy have taken someone from us. We wish to recover her,' replied Gwaine.

Koshchey smiled. 'A Spring Child, is she? Who else would the werewolves be after?'

Gwaine's eyelid twitched, then he nodded. 'Yes. Her name is Vasilisa Bulgakov.' Despite Gwaine's initial reaction, Billi could hear the caution in his answers. He wasn't going to tell Koshchey any more than was absolutely necessary, certainly nothing about her being an avatar. Lance had put all of them on guard.

Koshchey nodded. 'We cannot allow the werewolves to murder innocent children. I will put all my men on it.' He looked out of the window. 'If she is here, I will find her.'

'I thank you.'

'What's Ivan's story?' asked Billi. Not that she was interested in any way. But if they were going to work together, it would be useful to know a little more about him. That's all.

Koshchey sighed. The leather of the seat creaked as he leaned into it. 'It is sad. His father, the great Alexei, was killed six months ago by the Polenitsy. So you see, your enemies are ours.'

'Did you find the ones that did it?'

'Alas, no. We suspect it was their leader, the Old Grey. She is a dangerous one.'

Olga. The dates tied up. They must have come to Britain via Moscow. Did that mean they'd returned by the same route? Could they be here right now?

'We are in a rush to find our kidnapped friend,' added Gwaine. 'The Polenitsy will sacrifice her on the full moon, three days from tonight.'

'I will put all my men on it,' repeated Koshchey.

They crossed a bridge and came to an immense structure that dominated a whole block on the river. The building comprised three towers, the highest one bearing a shining red star on its spire. No light shone from any of the windows, and as they approached Billi saw that the entire block was protected by a tall wire-mesh fence. For a building so extravagant, it bore an ominous ambience.

'Stalin's Ministry,' said Gwaine. 'I thought it was sold off during the collapse of Communism.'

'To me,' said Koshchey. 'You will treat it as your own home during your stay here. You will want for nothing.'

The gates opened up and the cavalcade of cars rolled down a ramp into the car park. Only small patches of the underground chamber were lit, but the distant reflections of light on metal gave Billi a sense of its size. It had to be as big as a football field.

Koshchey owned all of this?

While the Bogatyrs got busy unloading their kit, Koshchey directed the Templars towards the row of lifts.

'Ivan.' He summoned the young man over. 'Escort Billi to her room. I have business to discuss with the Seneschal.'

Billi stepped between them. 'We don't have any time to waste. I think we –'

'Enough, squire,' snapped Gwaine. He glowered at

her and for a second Billi was tempted to ignore him. The full moon was only days away. But slowly she shut her mouth. Ivan, close by, cleared his throat.

'Which one?' he asked.

'The Morevna suite.'

'Shall we?' Ivan gave a mock bow and led her to a polished bronze door. A lift. The door slid open and they entered.

The lift car was panelled with dark wood and inlaid with an abstract pattern of mother-of-pearl that glimmered in the hazy lamplight. Ivan pulled a small key from his pocket and inserted it into a brightly polished plaque in the wall.

As the lift ascended Billi took a long look at Ivan. He had typically Slavic features: pale skin, wide, high cheekbones and deep-set eyes of storm-cloud grey. Ivan sensed her studying him and his hand rose to awkwardly cover his face as he drew his fingers through his bristling black hair.

'The thirteenth floor?' asked Billi. 'Isn't that unlucky?'

'Only for a Templar.' The lift settled gently to a halt, and the door opened into darkness. The light from the lift illuminated just the first few metres of an emerald-veined marble floor. Then, one by one, like night constellations, huge chandeliers came to life, their light caught and amplified a thousand-fold through a sparkling cosmos of brilliant crystal.

Tall columns like flutes rose to support the huge, multi-vaulted ceiling, and Billi peered at the sky-filled mosaics of gods, heroes and demons. Warriors clad in gold battled monstrous bears and wolves. Castles floated among the clouds, and wolves flew from the towers. In a vast battlefield stood a shining warrior woman, sword aloft and long blonde hair swirling. She wore a deep-red coat and its sleeves and front were embroidered with golden designs of flaming phoenixes.

'Maria Morevna,' said Ivan. 'A great princess. A Bogatyr.'

'Who made all this?' It was unreal.

'The Soviets.'

'No expense spared, eh?'

Ivan marched onwards. 'Follow me.'

Ahead was a double door decorated with gilt filigree. Ivan pushed it open.

The bedroom was dominated by a canopied bed, the wood as pale as pearl. Sheer white curtains hung from the bed's frame, while thick, red drapes half-covered gilt-framed mirrors on the walls. They reflected the room infinitely upon itself; it was difficult to see where the room ended and the illusion began. Through a curtain Billi saw a free-standing marble bath on curling, clawed legs, with steam rising from the water.

'How do you like my home?' asked Ivan.

'Yours? Koshchey said it was his.'

Ivan's eyes flashed angrily. He was a strange mix of coolness and anger. The two emotions played out just under the surface. He acted the aristocrat, in control and in command. But underneath was a young man

145

who'd just lost his father. And from the way he spoke to Koshchey, all was not well on that front either.

Ivan peered round the vast suite. 'Bought with Romanov money. Koshchey is . . . safeguarding it for me, until I'm old enough to inherit, when I'm eighteen.' He smiled ruefully. 'I need to make sure I stay healthy for two more years.'

'Then just avoid fighting *ghuls* one-to-one,' said Billi. She wandered around the room in a daze. Its ceiling was higher than her whole house.

'It is like a fairy tale, yes?' Ivan tossed a key on to the bed. 'Do you remember the way to the lift?'

'Straight down, through the double doors.'

'The other Templars are on the twelfth floor. Koshchey is on the thirtieth; he has temporarily requisitioned my father's suite. I am on the floor below him.' It was clear he wasn't happy with this arrangement. 'There is a swimming pool in the sub-basement.'

He turned to leave, then stopped.

'What did you mean earlier, "we don't have time to waste"?' His forehead crumpled into a crinkled frown and Billi had a sudden and overwhelming urge to smooth it away. She flushed and shifted her attention awkwardly to the mural above her. It wasn't as if she could trust him with the information about what Vasilisa really was just yet. She didn't know who to trust in this place.

'I just mean that an innocent girl will die unless we find her,' she mumbled. When she dared to look back at Ivan, he was watching her, amused.

He knows I'm hiding something.

'*Da*, that is true. We will help you find her, as we promised. We will talk tomorrow.'

'Well, thank you very much,' she managed stiffly. 'So . . . goodnight, Ivan.'

He smirked. 'Goodnight, Billi SanGreal.'

Billi lay, wide awake, staring up at the firebird mosaic over her head. Her body begged for rest, but her mind kept turning over.

It had gone perfectly. Koshchey wanted to help. He hated the Polenitsy as much as they did. Gwaine had called by and told her Koshchey had all his men out already. He should have news by tomorrow morning.

If Vasilisa was here, Koshchey would find her. Billi had been up over twenty-four hours and without some sleep she'd be useless to anyone. The best thing she could do was rest and be ready in the morning.

Then why did she feel something was so terribly wrong?

The previous Tsar's death? People died in her line of business. The Templars had counted on Tsar Alexei's aid, but Koshchey seemed just as willing. Almost too willing.

Paranoid. Maybe that was all it was. For once things were going her way and she wasn't used to it. Maybe Koshchey's past wasn't a good one. Maybe he did have a bad reputation for the things he'd done long ago, but who didn't? Her dad had been accused of her mother's

147

death and Billi had blood on her own hands; she had no right to pass judgement on others.

No, Koshchey didn't bother her.

Ivan bothered her.

She couldn't get those grey eyes out of her mind. He looked at you like he was looking right into your soul. A lot of girls might fall for that sort of thing.

But not her.

CHAPTER 21

Billi had slept badly. It was still an hour or so before breakfast and she needed to clear her head.

Thursday and another day gone. She checked her mobile for news from Karelia. Nothing. Maybe she should find Koshchey, see if he'd discovered anything. Or Ivan. Someone had to know where Vasilisa was. They only had three days left to find her. Three days before Fimbulwinter.

Billi paced the room, full of nervous energy, constantly flicking her mobile open and shut. Eventually she threw the phone on the bed. She needed to get herself together. Some hard exercise to clear out some of that buzz in her head.

There was a wardrobe of brand-new clothes waiting for her in the suite lobby and she slipped into a dark-blue swimsuit, then grabbed a thick, white cotton bathrobe and towel on her way out.

The route to the swimming pool was simple, out on level minus five, then follow the smell of chlorine and moisture.

Dim, blue pool-lights shone from under the water. The pool itself was Olympic-sized, the roof a ribbed, curving barrel hung with brass lamps. The only sound was the water lapping against the pool edge.

Billi took off her robe and stood, arms raised, at the head of the pool. She watched her reflection quiver on the water's surface for a second, then dived in.

The cold stunned Billi and her chest clenched as she sliced through the dull blueness of the pool. The lights were large, circular plates, their frames bonded stainless steel. Billi's eyes adjusted swiftly to the hazy underwater world and she was surprised by the water's clarity. She thrust herself deeper and skimmed across the white-tiled floor. Then, with a kick, she rose and started attacking the water with long, chopping strokes.

What was she doing here? She had three days to save Vasilisa. She hated the idea of relying on others, but the Bogatyrs were the experts on the Polenitsy. Her hands cut into the water as she pumped her legs, letting her frustration fuel her strokes. The far wall was approaching so Billi dropped her head and turned underwater, sensing the distance before she pushed off again.

A loud splash made Billi stop a quarter-way along the pool's length. Someone was coming up, fast. Muscular arms drove a long, torpedo-swift body through the cold water. Billi kicked off again, aiming at the far wall, some twenty-five metres away. The first few strokes lacked rhythm, but soon she was steaming. But no matter how quick she was, the guy behind her was catching up.

Suddenly he was at her shoulder and she could see the wall a few metres away. She pounded harder, but he was too strong. His big arms pulled him forward and Billi felt herself caught in his wake. Then Ivan slapped his palms on the wall and stopped.

Billi bobbed up behind him.

He hung on to the brass railings running just above the water's surface. His hair was loose and the dappled light lit the sharp angles of his face.

'I'm not disturbing you, am I?' he asked.

Billi said nothing. He'd easily outswum her and she didn't like it. Maybe he was pissed off with her having saved his life and just wanted to boost his ego.

Ivan slid along the railing towards her. He was a few centimetres away. The ripples splashed against Billi and she tried to retreat.

'You have many scars,' he said.

'Not that many.' Well, not compared to the other Templars.

'This one?' Ivan's gaze lingered on Billi's neck.

'Sword cut.' Her hand went to the scar Michael had given her. 'It could have been worse.'

Ivan smiled. Billi paddled back a bit more. It was hotter in here than she'd thought. 'You have an interesting face, SanGreal. Not quite beautiful.' He lifted his hand as if to touch exactly where he'd been gazing.

Billi quickly wiped her hair from her face. 'Is that meant to be a compliment?'

'An observation.' He splashed back into the water, not

more than a metre. 'Koshchey says you're here looking for a Spring Child.'

'Yes, she was kidnapped by the Polenitsy.'

Ivan was trying to find out more. She could feel the pressure of his questions – nothing direct, but the guy just got under her skin. She found it hard to think clearly with him around. But she'd let her guard down before – with Michael – and look what had happened. She had to take a more objective view, follow Gwaine's lead. She must be careful to tell him only what was necessary.

She kept her eyes down, but couldn't help but see his reflection wavering in the water. The pale-blue under-water lights cast rippling shadows over his athletic body. She remembered Michael, built of marble and nothing but hard surfaces and edges. Ivan wasn't anything like that. He wasn't chunky like a warrior, more like a dancer, graceful. But he and Michael were similar. Both had that mixture of pain and threat, of beauty masking the anger beneath. That's why she had to be careful. She needed to get his attention off her.

'I'm sorry about your father,' she said.

Ivan's lips thinned. Though he tried to hide it, the pain was obvious. 'He was a great man. A great leader.'

'And Koshchey? What's he like?'

'He is adequate. No, that is not fair. He has done well. He has made Moscow safe from the blood-drinkers and other *vrolock*. A few, like the one last night, escaped the net, but not for long. He acts as regent until I reach my majority.'

'You hope.' Koshchey made it seem as though all this was his. He didn't look like the sort of man who'd just hand over his wealth and power just because Ivan turned eighteen.

'I do more than hope,' said Ivan. He wiped the water from his face and put his hand on Billi's. Her instinct was to pull away, but Ivan's intense gaze held her. 'They say a Templar's word is their bond. Is that true?'

'It is.' Billi smiled wryly. 'Are you going to get me to promise something I'll regret?'

'Can I trust you, Billi SanGreal?' Instead of waiting for an answer he decided for himself with a frown. 'The Bogatyrs are not the men they were,' said Ivan. 'Once they were noblemen who knew their duty was to serve Russia.' He gazed into Billi's eyes, moving closer and lowering his voice to a whisper. 'Now they serve only themselves. Many are Russian mafia, recruited by Koshchey after my father's death. They are good fighters, but they are not . . . good men. That will change when I am their master.'

'You think Koshchey will allow you to take charge?' Billi was doubtful.

Ivan bit his lip; he must have had his doubts about Koshchey too. 'I have a legacy to uphold, Billi. Do you understand that?'

'Tsarevich!'

The name echoed loudly off the curving walls and undulating water. Ivan's bodyguard, Dimitri, stood by the door, all tooled up in his combat gear.

Ivan looked once at Billi, then reached up and drew himself out of the water with a single, smooth pull. Rivulets of water ran off his skin and through the chasms of his muscular back. He took a deep breath, his chest rising then sinking, as he turned to face her. Then he bent down and held out his hand.

Billi took it, and he pulled her out effortlessly.

'Yes?' asked Ivan as he began drying himself. Dimitri whispered in his ear.

Ivan stopped. He turned to Dimitri, his brow furrowed. 'Are you sure?'

Billi's heartbeat quickened.

Ivan handed her a towel. Billi's hand shook as she took it.

'Koshchey has found your friend Vasilisa,' he said.

CHAPTER 22

Ten minutes later Billi came running down the stairs into the main lobby. She'd whipped on her combat trousers and black T-shirt and her boots hadn't been laced yet. She'd banged on Elaine's door and left her to get Gwaine and Lance.

Sixteen men had gathered under the huge crystal chandeliers that lit the marble-clad lobby. All wore body armour and carried guns. One man shook out a box of cartridges on to the top of a grand piano and one by one loaded them into his shotgun.

Koshchey leaned over a set of floorplans. Unlike the rest, he wore a smart suit, a big red rose tucked into the buttonhole.

'You've found her?' said Billi. She pushed her way through the men to Koshchey. The big man nodded to one of his guys, who made space for her round the table and the papers scattered across it.

'Some tea for Lady SanGreal,' he ordered. The Bogatyr beside him went over to the china samovar standing at the end of the long table. The tall, vase-like container was, like everything in the Ministry, a beautiful work of art, the china painted with weaving vines and bursting red flowers. The Bogatyr turned the dainty gold tap and filled a small cup.

'You've found Vasilisa?' Billi demanded. If it was true, then Vasilisa could be safe in their hands within hours. They'd have her on a plane to Jerusalem by the end of the day.

'My men report that a girl matching the description of the Spring Child has been seen in this apartment block. It is known to be occupied by the Polenitsy.' He handed over a blown-up photo.

It wasn't clear, but a young girl with untidy blonde hair stood at a half-frosted window. Snow blurred the lens, so the photo must have been taken from some distance. The girl had turned her head, obscuring her face, but it had to be Vasilisa. It had to be. Billi stared at the photo, as if the girl might suddenly turn round and look back at her. Oh God, she was here, in Moscow.

'Then we'd better get her. Now.'

Koshchey's fist tightened. 'This is a delicate operation, Lady SanGreal. I think it best you let my men handle it.'

Ivan stood at the top of the stairs. 'Koshchey!' he shouted. 'Why did you not inform me of this?'

The prince wore his own combat armour and had his utility belt slung over his shoulder. He marched up to them and dropped the belt on to the table, banging the wooden surface hard with the holstered pistol.

For a second a blaze of rage crossed Koshchey's face.

Only Billi saw it, but his face went livid red. Then he puffed out his cheeks and rotated on his heels to face the prince.

'My prince, I did not want to disturb you. Especially after last night's unfortunate incident. It was only through the intervention of young SanGreal that you were not killed.' He put his hand on his heart. 'I swore to your father that I would protect you. Leave this to me. You should wait here, where it is safe.'

That is so much bullshit. Billi kept her thoughts to herself, but Koshchey couldn't have been more patronizing. Everything he said was intended to undermine Ivan. Ivan's jaw went rigid. He buckled on his belt and his hand rested on the pistol a moment longer than necessary. Billi noticed and so did Koshchey.

'Thank you for your concern, Koshchey.' Ivan stared at one of the men and he stepped away from the table. 'But I decide what is best for me.'

Ouch.

Koshchey wasn't going to let that one go. She could see he was parking that insult. The rivalry between them bubbled just below the surface, but Billi could see it would erupt, sooner rather than later.

'Tsarevich, until you are a man, upon your father's wishes I am afraid it is my duty to lead. But by all means come, look.'

Ivan missed the cold contempt in the response; his attention was on what was in front of him, the floorplans of a block of flats. Koshchey stood behind him.

That's where Ivan should be keeping his attention. On his back.

'A Khrushchev block?' asked Ivan.

'What's that?' Billi peered at the drawings. The yellowed paper was held together with tape. The floor-plans showed a five-storey building with four separate staircases. Four apartments ran off each landing on each floor. Each apartment was identical to the next.

Ivan drew his finger along the outline of the building. 'They were built in the sixties. There are thousands of them all over Moscow, all built exactly the same way.'

Gwaine and Lance appeared. Without a word, they came up and joined them.

Ivan stood up and looked around. 'Four teams. Four men per team.'

Koshchey tapped the staircases on the drawings. 'One team per staircase. We will sweep up the building and clear each floor.' He looked up at the clock – just after seven. 'The sun will be up in an hour.'

Ivan nodded. 'And you, Koshchey?'

He laughed. 'Tsarevich, can you see me creeping up those steps? I doubt I could fit through the front door. Andrei will lead the attack.'

Ivan turned to the Templars. 'There are four of you. I suggest one be attached to each squad. You know what this girl looks like.'

'Fair enough.'

'Tsarevich, that is not wise.' Koshchey put his hands on the drawings as he leaned over towards Ivan. 'The

Bogatyrs are trained for this – the Templars are not. Their style is archaic; they will only get in the way.'

Ivan paused, tapping the handle of his pistol. 'Then perhaps it would be best if you remained behind. Mistakes can happen.'

Billi shook her head. 'Forget it. We're coming.'

'Billi, this will be dangerous.'

'Damn right. All the more reason I come and watch your back.'

'Fine. Just stay out of the way. Understood?'

'Understood, *Tsarevich*.'

Ivan opened his mouth to reply, well aware of Billi's not-quite-respectful tone, but let it pass.

Koshchey tapped his watch. 'We leave in ten minutes.'

Lance handed Billi her armour. The Kevlar jacket went on like a waistcoat and zipped up high. The collar covered her to her chin, but was wide enough to allow Billi to turn her head. The jacket had been modified to hold Billi's katar and kukri; each sat comfortably when strapped in. Then Lance grinned as he showed Billi a slim-bladed straight-sword, similar in length to Percy's *wakizashi*. This he slid into a sheath clipped to her back.

Billi promised herself an outfit just like this for her next birthday.

Gwaine came over. 'Leave the rough stuff to the Russians. If they're right and this place is crawling with Polenitsy, they won't give Vasilisa up without a fight. Not that I'm complaining.'

'We get her alive, understand?' said Billi. This was

their chance and she wanted everyone to be of the same mind. Vasilisa could be saved.

'I don't need you to tell me my job, squire,' was Gwaine's reply.

Billi glanced at Lance, who nodded. 'We save the *petite fille*.'

They were set.

'Where's Elaine?' Billi asked.

Lance gestured upstairs. 'Koshchey showed her the Bogatyrs' library. It is like she's gone to librarian heaven. Maybe she might find something on Baba Yaga, *oui*?'

As Lance and Gwaine discussed tactics Billi went into the corner of the lobby and took out her mobile.

'Dad. You there?'

The line crackled, but then she heard the familiar voice of her father.

'Billi?'

'Dad? We found her. We found Vasilisa.' She couldn't keep the excitement from her voice.

'You sure? How?'

'The Bogatyrs found her. She's being held not far from here by the Polenitsy. We're heading over there right now.'

'I don't need to tell you to be careful, do I?'

Billi looked around at the soldiers armed to the teeth. There was enough firepower here to conquer a small country. 'I think we've got that covered.'

'Praise be to God,' said Arthur. 'We've drawn a blank here.'

'Did you find Vasilisa's granny?'

'She's gone into hiding. I suspect the Polenitsy have come looking for her. We're still looking, but Karelia's a big place. But we've picked up some interesting legends about Baba Yaga.'

'Like what?' Billi's attention was pricked.

'Baba Yaga vanished a hundred years ago. There were no more hunts for Spring Children – the werewolves just stopped. The local wise women say that's because Baba Yaga was hurt in the early twentieth century, and went to sleep deep in the Earth to recover. Now she's back and she's hungry. That's why the Polenitsy have returned.'

'How was she injured?'

'Wish I knew.' Arthur coughed. 'You just get Vasilisa to Jerusalem.'

'Bilqis.' Lance came up. 'They are waiting.'

'Dad . . .'

'I heard.' Arthur's tone deepened as he drew the mobile close to his lips. 'Give them hell.'

'Come,' Ivan said to Billi as they stepped out of the lift into the car park. 'You will stick close to me, Dimitri and Yuri.' Another Bogatyr fell in step with them. Two beady black eyes glistened from beneath a thick, bushy eyebrow that ran straight across from ear to ear. Tattoos covered his arm, neck and ears. His tattoos had tattoos.

'Pleased to meet you,' said Billi.

Yuri smiled, exposing a fortune in gold teeth.

A silver BMW growled as it crept along the snow-covered drive, leading a line of big, shiny four-by-fours.

Billi and Ivan took this car, with Yuri up front with Dimitri. Lance and Gwaine took the next.

The car slipped out on to a main road. Snow trucks rolled along the roadside, but otherwise the traffic was pretty light. Billi settled herself into the soft leather seat.

'Oh, I almost forgot,' said Ivan as he sat in the deep, tan-coloured leather. He held out a lacquered wooden box. 'A present.'

It was made from dark-red wood, and had a lid decorated with an inlaid pattern of silver.

Billi's fingers touched the case, then she raised the lid slowly.

A pistol lay on a white cushion. A fan of silver bullets had been arranged around it. It was a matt black colour, simple-looking and plain, but as Billi put her hand on the cold surface, she could see that the gun was elegant in its simplicity. The best weapons always were.

'You do know how to shoot?'

'Point and click.'

'Glock 26,' Ivan said. He held one of the silver bullets between his thumb and forefinger. 'Ninety-nine per cent pure. Just in case.'

Despite the three bladed weapons buckled to her armour, Billi picked it up. It was light, and not much bigger than her palm, with a stubby light fixed to the underside of the barrel. Ivan took the magazine and, one by one, clicked in the rounds.

'Fashion is all about the accessories,' said Ivan.

Billi turned the pistol over. She'd used one for target

practice, but this was very different. Despite the contempt the Templars had for such weapons, she couldn't stop herself from wrapping her fingers round the butt and lightly touching the trigger. Her thumb felt along the safety catch.

So small a thing. But there was something compelling in the object. A sword could be played with. There was pleasure in the physical act of wielding it, learning the moves, the cuts, the way it shone and flashed. There was art, beauty, in the sword.

But gunpowder was pure destruction. The gun's simple functionality made it want to be used ... carnage called to it. Despite herself, despite the prejudices against such weapons, Billi wanted it. She slipped it into her pocket.

'Is it true you don't use guns?' asked Ivan.

'I live in London, not Baghdad. Gunfights tend to attract a lot of unwanted attention,' Billi said. 'Anyway nothing says serious body trauma like an axe to the head.'

Despite the advances in military technology over the centuries, old-fashioned swords and axes still did the job best. Besides, many of the Unholy needed beheading to be truly destroyed.

The car slowed to a halt.

'We're here,' said Ivan.

CHAPTER 23

They were in a derelict part of the suburbs, out past the huge, wild Izmaylovsky Park. They drove through a ghost town of empty garages, abandoned factories and lonely, single-storey shops. All the buildings around them had been demolished, except for one old housing block that sat like a squat brick in the centre of a wasteland of mud and concrete. The only thing that broke its shape was a tall, faintly smoking chimney. Otherwise it was five storeys of identical windows, with a few satellite dishes to break the monotony of the design.

Snow flurries tumbled chaotically around them as they stood outside the car. They'd parked down a side alley. Large, industrial-sized bins lined the wall, stuffed with broken furniture, bits of carpet and snow-sprinkled bin bags. Ivan walked to the mouth of the narrow corridor and waited, watching the building opposite. His two companions were making last-minute checks to their gear. Yuri reloaded three times before finally leaving his pistol alone. Everyone had their own way of dealing with their pre-battle nerves.

'Come on,' Billi urged. 'What are we waiting for?' For God's sake, Vasilisa was just across the road! Billi fought the urge to simply run over there and shout out her name.

'Hush,' ordered Ivan.

Two policemen crossed the street towards them. They'd been under the shelter of a boarded-up shop. One flicked his cigarette into the slushy snow and shook Ivan's hand.

The three men conversed and Ivan passed over a stuffed envelope. The two cops tapped their caps in thanks and wandered away.

Yuri popped the boot open and inside sat a neatly stacked row of very new-looking Heckler & Koch submachine guns, all with built-in silencers. Just the thing for house clearance. Dimitri took one and handed another to Ivan, who slung it over his shoulder. He blew across the laser targeter, wiping the lens with his gloved finger, then switched the beam on. The red spot of laser light slid across the white snow, up the wall and on to the building across from them. 'Three families. All are Polenitsy.' He spat the last word.

How he hates them. Billi almost winced at the intensity of his anger.

Ivan checked his clip and slotted it in. 'Are you ready?'

'Lead on, Macduff.'

Billi watched the first team of men sneak into the lonely building.

Ivan nodded and the four of them, him leading, then

Dimitri, Yuri and Billi at the back, ran across the snow-covered street.

Billi pulled out her pistol as she came through the entrance.

The front door had been replaced with a hardboard panel and Dimitri unscrewed the landing light, leaving the place dark. There was a small lift in front of them: the doors wedged open with a steel bin. The stairs up were bare concrete. A rag of carpet lay at the entrance, sticky with filth. Old cigarette butts littered the tiled floor.

This is where they're keeping her? They were scum. Billi realized how tightly she was clutching her pistol and slowly loosened her grip. Getting mad now wouldn't help anyone, least of all Vasilisa. She sighed and put her hand on the door in the side wall.

It opened to reveal a man wearing a thick woollen dressing gown, yawning. He straightened his spectacles and stared at Billi. Yuri stepped past her and put the barrel of his pistol against the man's chest. There was a muffled click and the man stepped back. Then he lowered his eyes to the wet stain spreading on his chest. He shook his head, confused, then sank to his knees. He put his hands on the floor, coughed, and finally collapsed, face down. Blood seeped out from under him, spreading to the newspaper on the floor, staining the white pages red.

Yuri blew the smoke out of the end of his silencer.

Billi clenched her teeth hard, holding in the scream. The man had just stepped out to get his paper. The burnt gunpowder stung her eyes, raising tears. Ivan nudged the dead man's head with his boot.

'Clean up,' he whispered and instantly Dimitri and Yuri swept past him into the flat.

Cold blood. That man had been killed in cold blood. She shoved Ivan aside.

'What are you doing?' he hissed, grabbing her arm.

Three families were in this building. Billi had only been thinking of getting Vasilisa, not about the other people here. It seemed like the Bogatyrs were going to slaughter them all.

'The Polenitsy are monsters, Billi,' said Ivan. The hate in his eyes transformed his face into something dark and ugly.

'Let go of me.' This was not how Templars did things. She pulled her arm free.

'Shh!' he hissed. Moving slowly, Ivan walked up to the half-landing, gun pointing up.

Billi listened.

Something sharp was scraping the wall on the floor above like nails on a chalkboard. Billi gritted her teeth. She took the pistol in a two-handed grip and tripped the safety.

A sharp edge clicked on the concrete above her. Then another. A light cloud of dust trembled off the staircase over her head. Billi held her breath and concentrated on the minutest of noises.

There was a brief grunt and a black beast launched itself from the floor above, diving across the stairwell and crashing on to the landing in front of Ivan. It grabbed the long silencer of the gun and twisted it away. Ivan instinctively pulled the trigger, but the trio of bullet holes popped the plaster. They wrestled for control of the submachine gun and Ivan charged forward, sending them both over the banister.

Howls and screams erupted from everywhere, swiftly followed by gunfire as Yuri and Dimitri came into the lobby. Sparks of light blazed above Billi. She saw a momentary tangle of Ivan and the werewolf wrestling on the floor. For a second she moved towards Ivan to help, then stopped. Vasilisa was what was most important here. Billi had to find her. The stairs were a dangerous place to be caught so she rushed up to the next floor. She switched on her pistol light and swept it down the short unlit corridor that led off the staircase.

Jesus, this is insane. Billi fought to control her breathing, and to try and hold the pistol steady; the light was jumping all over the place. Panic rose up in her chest. Vasilisa could be behind any one of these doors, and if she didn't find her now, she may never get the chance again. She peered down the corridor and made out four doors. The stairs continued upwards.

Search or keep climbing?

A door ahead of her creaked open.

Billi booted it hard and there was a yelp and a thud as someone fell backwards. She pointed her light through the open door and a werewolf leapt to its feet. Billi fired, but the beast was already gone, and all she shot was a curtained window. She heard screaming from one of the rooms in the apartment. A child's scream.

'Vasilisa?' Billi shouted. *Oh my God, she's in here. She's here!*

Clawed feet scuttled across the tiled floor and the were-wolf darted in and out of sight. There had to be interconnecting doors. She should go back, wait for the others.

But Vasilisa. She was so close. Billi couldn't risk leaving her. She took another step into the apartment.

The smell of damp heat permeated the air. A girl's dress lay steaming on the radiator. The small spotlight from Billi's torch showed her peeling wallpaper, spots of mould and flaking paint on the doors. The furniture looked like it had been collected from a skip, a patchy sofa with threadbare seats and half-untangled wicker chairs. She checked the light switch. Nothing. The Bogatyrs must have cut the electricity.

Billi squinted, trying to penetrate the darkness ahead. The torch beam was nearly useless; it was so narrow that it lit only a hand's width of space.

Billi could hear a child's sniffling coming from somewhere ahead. Vasilisa was so close. Billi wanted to run towards the sound, but had to fight to keep herself focused on the job at hand. Her search was almost over. But almost wasn't good enough.

A floorboard creaked next to her and Billi spun, but a thick forearm crashed across hers and her pistol flew away. The bestial roar was by her ear and hot, offal-scented breath hissed across her face as she grabbed the black snout to stop it from tearing out her throat. Her fingers dug deep into the werewolf's muzzle as she held it away and the long fangs snapped only centimetres from her face. It lifted her high up against the wall, its claws slashing at her body armour while she kneed it in the stomach. But even as it cried out, it pushed its head steadily closer to her. Billi's arms quivered and hot spittle dripped on her cheek. She had her kukri, but needed to let go with one hand to grab it. The monster hissed; Billi couldn't resist its primordial strength for much longer and it knew it.

So close. So close. Vasilisa was on the other side of that door and she had to save her. Billi's teeth locked into a feral snarl and she dragged up every ounce of strength she had, burying her nails into the fleshy snout, grinding them in. The beast flinched as she drew blood, but it wasn't going to let its prize escape. She felt its body stiffen as it focused all its own power on tearing out her throat.

'No,' Billi whispered. It couldn't end like this.

But it would. Her arms ached and she couldn't hold it back any more. She buckled under the relentless force and the werewolf's jaws opened wide as it shook itself free of Billi's grip. It opened its jaws and –

screamed. The knife went in through its jaw and slammed it shut as the blade buried itself in its upper palette. Blood frothed through its black lips and a snort of red foam burst from its nostrils. Ivan wrapped his arm round the monster's neck and twisted his knife deeper. The werewolf tried clawing at him, but Ivan bent it backwards, almost lifting the huge creature off its feet, so its attacks were wild and weak. Ivan pulled the knife out and plunged it back in. The werewolf's scream rose into a high-pitched wail and it went slack. Ivan stood and slowly released the body. The werewolf slid to the floor, its body shedding fur second by second. Billi stumbled across the room and snatched up her pistol. Then she turned back to the monster.

It was gone. In its place lay a young woman. Her body was stone-white except for the scarf of crimson blood that ran from her jaw and down her chest. Ivan stood over her, panting hard. Then he straightened up and slowly wiped the sweat off his forehead, dragging his hand over his short, dark bristles and leaving them spiky with blood. The red fingerprints left a long trail over his face.

'You are a fool, coming in here alone like this,' he said. 'But now we are even, *da*?'

Still trying to catch her breath, Billi looked up into Ivan's serious grey eyes and nodded. She would have been dead without him.

A child's whimper pulled Billi suddenly away from her thoughts.

Vasilisa. Billi jumped to her feet. 'Vasilisa?' She went to the far door. There was a clown painted on it. Billi twisted the handle and heard a cry from inside. Locked. Ivan came up beside her. He hoisted the gun up and smashed the brass knob off with the butt.

The bedroom was basic, but clean. A chest of drawers stood in the corner, and next to it, under the window, was a child's bed, the quilt patchy and faded. Someone huddled beneath it.

Oh thank God. She'd made it. It had been worth it. Billi moved forward and gently pulled the cover away.

'Vasilisa, I'm here.' She could take her back; it would all be OK. Billi's eyes blurred and the pistol torch wouldn't lie straight. The cover fell from the child's face.

The girl sobbed, clutching a clown doll. Her blonde hair was bristly and unkempt, much like the woman's who lay dead in the corridor. Her eyes were light brown; her teeth were an even row of ivory needle-points. She growled.

No. It wasn't Vasilisa.

'Stand aside,' ordered Yuri. Billi spun around as he raised his gun and she jumped in front of him. The smallest squeeze of the trigger and Billi's guts would be decorating the wall. At this range her body armour would be as useful as tissue paper.

'Polenitsy,' he insisted.

'It doesn't matter.' Billi turned her back to him and looked at the girl, her heart tripping with fear. She put the Glock on the table and held out her hand. 'Come with me.'

The girl didn't understand what Billi was saying, but she looked at her hand, then reached out. Her fingers were thin and cold, but her grip fierce. She stepped off the bed and Billi held her close. She may not have found

172

Vasilisa, but she wasn't going to be responsible for this girl's death.

Yuri blocked the doorway. He raised his pistol and Billi blinked as the red laser spot rose to the centre of her forehead. She looked at the Glock on the table. It was only a metre away, but it might as well have been on the other side of the planet.

I'll never reach it.

Ivan took a step in front of Yuri.

'*Polozhi pistolet,*' he said.

Yuri didn't lower his weapon. '*Nu ona zhe odna iz nix, ona oboroten.*'

'*Ya skazal poloshi pistolet!*' Ivan pulled out his own pistol and pointed it at Yuri.

Any second now this is going to go all Tarantino. Maybe she could just sneak out while they were busy?

Yuri scowled. Sweat formed on his forehead. Billi held her breath, her hand slowly moved towards her Glock, just in case.

'*Chort!*' shouted Yuri, dropping his pistol to his side.

Ivan lowered his own weapon, but never took his eyes off the Bogatyr. 'Now what?'

'Get her out of here.' Billi's hands were still shaking. That had been too bloody close. She picked up the pistol and shoved it back in her pocket. She came to the door and Yuri stepped aside, tapping his pistol against his leg impatiently. She looked down the corridor. No one. 'Well, are you going to help or what?'

'Billi . . .'

'What, Ivan? What?' Billi wrapped her arm round the girl. 'Is this what the Bogatyrs do? You think this is noble?'

Conflicting emotions fought in Ivan's eyes. Frustration and rage. Against his desire to be better. To be a true Bogatyr. Nobility wasn't in the blood, it was in the deed.

'Follow me.' He headed upstairs.

The floor above was no different, rundown and damp. Ivan went to the furthest door and rammed his boot into the lock, shattering it out of its frame.

A young woman cowered behind a cupboard. She wore a rough woollen coat and had been putting on her shoes when they'd burst in. An old-fashioned paisley scarf covered her head. She fell to her knees, hands raised, cowering.

Ivan spoke rapidly and helped her up.

The girl in Billi's arms whimpered and struggled when she saw the young woman. Billi let her go and she ran into her arms.

Men shouted from below. The Bogatyrs must have gathered in the lobby. They wanted to know if Ivan was OK.

'I'll deal with them,' he said and left.

'Do you speak English?' Billi asked. The young woman nodded.

'Good. We're getting you two out of here.' She inspected the apartment for a way out, but found none. She pulled back the curtains.

The back of the block overlooked a wide field of

derelict buildings. The nearest abutted the back of theirs. Billi opened the window and reckoned the drop was about four metres. The young woman stood beside her and peered out.

Billi heard footsteps banging on the stairs.

The paisley woman jumped first. Despite her human appearance, she landed softly on all fours. She twitched her head, then stood up, arms reaching towards the window.

Billi took the girl and dangled her out over the edge, lowering her slowly down the wall. Her back strained and she bent double over the window sill, the stiff Kevlar jacket now a hindrance and restricting her movements.

'Billi!' Someone, Lance, shouted for her. But there were more men, more voices, behind him.

Sod it!

Billi let go.

The girl cried as she fell, but then there was a grunt as Paisley caught her. Billi struggled back in – she was half-fallen out of the window – just as Lance and two other Bogatyrs burst in. Billi blocked the window from their view.

'*D'accord?*' Lance asked.

Billi took a deep breath and straightened her armour. 'Yes, I'm OK.' She followed Lance and the other men downstairs.

Back in the lobby it was clear the battle was over. The air was tainted with the metallic sting of gunpowder, and fresh bullet holes decorated the walls. A half-dozen

Bogatyrs had gathered in the ground-floor lobby. Three more lay against the wall, unmoving. The man who'd come out to collect his paper lay by the door and there were four other bullet-ridden corpses, women, their bodies bleached white.

Ivan stood by the door with Dimitri. Billi gave him a small nod.

'No Vasilisa?' asked Gwaine. His axe had been cleaned, but blood still smeared the bright steel.

Billi shook her head and gestured to the bodies. 'All this bloodshed for nothing.'

'They were the Unholy,' he said.

Billi just thought of the frightened girl cowering under a quilt, her mother dead in the corridor. 'Yeah, course they were.'

CHAPTER 24

What a bloody disaster!

Billi hurled her body armour across her bedroom. It crashed into an elegant antique chair, sending both across the floor, then she slumped down on to her bed.

She glanced at the satellite phone; her dad had left a message. No doubt eager for the good news.

How many dead? Three Bogatyrs and nine Polenitsy. A couple of the werewolves had escaped in the confusion, but there had been no other children. It was clear that Vasilisa hadn't been there. That photo that Billi had convinced herself was Vasilisa had been the werewolf child. Some news.

Maybe Elaine had found something in the library. But if she came up blank, Billi had no idea how they could find Vasilisa before it was too late. It was Thursday lunchtime already, and the full moon was coming up on Saturday.

She grabbed the phone and took the lift down to report in to her dad outside – you never knew who was listening here.

The lift halted on one of the other floors. The doors opened and Koshchey stood waiting.

His massive frame blocked the elevator doors, and he was so tall he'd have to lower his head to get in. His suit rustled softly as he brushed it and adjusted his cuffs. Billi caught the brilliant crimson sparkle of rubies in the cufflinks. The guy was vain and flash. It was as though he'd modelled himself on Ivan: debonair outfits and cool looks. But Ivan carried himself with a seamless, casual elegance. Koshchey was a million miles away from that. Billi wasn't sure what suited Koshchey except a butcher's apron.

'Are you well, Lady SanGreal?'

'I'm fine.'

He stepped into the lift and Billi could have sworn it dropped a few centimetres under his weight.

'I am sorry about today. Very unpleasant. But do not worry, we will find your friend.' He straightened the fat knot of his tie, checking himself, admiring himself, in the mirrored panelling. 'We moved too quickly, without confirming our intelligence. Such operations carry a large risk of . . .'

'Failure?'

'Disappointment. We will find her. I promise you the Polenitsy won't get her.' He spoke with hard certainty. 'You will have my best men to help you.'

'And Ivan? Will he help?'

'Alas, no. I cannot permit it. He is best here, where I can protect him.'

Where you can keep an eye on him, you mean.

Koshchey made a broad sweep with his hand. 'Come with me. I have a gift.'

'Really, it's not necessary.'

'Oh, but it is.'

The lift took them up and up. Billi shifted as far away from Koshchey as she could, but the lift was small and Koshchey was huge. As they passed each floor a bell chimed and illuminated the floor numbers above the door.

The lift stopped at the thirtieth floor and the doors slid open.

'My suite,' said Koshchey.

'Which used to be Ivan's father's, right?'

'And now it is mine. You like Ivan, do you not?' He raised an eyebrow, interested in Billi's response. 'All the young women do. He has charm, that boy.'

'And guts.'

'Yes, yes. The Romanovs never lacked for courage.' Koshchey shook his massive head. 'But the boy is an idealist. He does not understand that there are no rules in war.' He smiled, like he was sharing a secret joke with Billi. 'Unlike you, SanGreal. I think you understand that all too well.'

'What do you mean?'

'Is there anything you wouldn't do to get the job done?' He drew his red beard into a neat point as he talked, tugging it as he watched her.

Billi couldn't answer. She couldn't say, 'But I don't go

around killing innocent children,' because she might have to do exactly that before the week was through. Billi lowered her head in shame.

'I thought as much,' said Koshchey. 'If Ivan was more like you, I would gladly hand the Bogatyrs over to him.' He stepped out of the lift and strode across into a large reception, tall windows along one wall, the morning sunlight sweeping across the lofty space. 'Magnificent, isn't it?'

Morning mist hung over Moscow. Only the tallest towers pierced the white veil, so they looked like the palaces of angels, floating on clouds. The hazy morning sun shone across the sky, staining it with scarlet and pink. Billi followed Koshchey along the row of windows towards a pair of doors, each bearing the Imperial double-headed eagle in dark bronze.

The doors opened into a long gallery, grander and more opulent than Billi's. Thick, black marble columns rose up twenty metres to support a domed roof that was covered in mosaic art. A trio of valiant knights on horse-back fought in a circle of wolves, their swords deep red with blood and their bodies slashed and torn by claws. The battle was in a snowbound forest and within the darker recesses a figure stood, half-emerging from a cave. All Billi could see were the shining black eyes and matted grey hair. Long, bony fingers clutched a tall staff decorated with bones.

'Baba Yaga,' Billi said.

'Very good. The greatest foe of the Bogatyrs.' Koshchey

gazed up at the ceiling. 'The Bogatyrs were the first to face Baba Yaga. Many times the old knights came close to defeating her, but she would always retreat into the deepest woods and darkest caves to hide. Places even the bravest knight would not dare to venture. And there she lurks, even now. But she is old and weak, I think, and we have heard nothing from her in a hundred years.'

'The knights almost defeated her? How?'

'The men of the past were great and blessed heroes, capable of extraordinary things. Such men do not exist any more.'

Billi walked along the exhibits, inspecting the golden cups, bejewelled icons, crowns and other ancient treasures arranged on plinths, pedestals or suspended from the ceiling by chains. Then one made her stop.

A heavy gilt frame was suspended from the ceiling by two golden chains. Within it was a flattened shirt with the arms spread out and embroidered with flowers. The white cotton was splattered with blood. Punctures covered the chest and crimson stained the sleeves and collar.

Somebody had wanted the wearer very dead.

'The shirt of the *vurodivyi*, Rasputin.'

'The what?'

'It means Holy Fool. A mystic, a shaman.' He looked up at the bloodstained garment. 'Grigori Efimovich Rasputin was all these things.' Koshchey pointed to the shadowy image of the old crone in the cave. 'Did you know, as a young man he was taken by the Polenitsy, as food for their goddess?'

So Rasputin had been a Spring Child. That didn't surprise her. It was common knowledge that he could read minds and had cured the Tsar's son of haemophilia by the laying on of hands. What surprised Billi was that he'd met Baba Yaga and lived.

'He got away? How?' If Rasputin had escaped Baba Yaga, maybe there was a chance to save Vasilisa. Maybe the ancient witch wasn't as powerful as they'd feared. Maybe if Rasputin had beaten her, they might too. This would change everything if they could take the battle to Baba Yaga.

'Baba Yaga was injured, very badly, for the first time in thousands of years. Rasputin got away in the confusion. He trekked all the way to Moscow and offered his services to the Tsar. In exchange the Tsar ordered the Bogatyrs to keep him safe.' Koshchey laughed. 'At least from Baba Yaga.'

'Was Rasputin the one who hurt Baba Yaga?' Billi struggled to keep the desperation from her voice. They had so little time!

'No. Rasputin was not that powerful. All he knew was something had happened to the planet, to the land, and that Baba Yaga had suffered as a consequence.'

'Sympathetic magic. Baba Yaga's psychic connection to the Earth.'

'Yes,' Koshchey said. 'But the knowledge of Baba Yaga's weakness is buried with him.'

So close, so close! She wanted to scream. If only she knew just a little bit more, but hope was fading fast.

Three more days until Fimbulwinter. Billi looked at the blood-soaked shirt and her blood chilled. The tears in the cloth, the stains. All she knew was how to fight. If you fought, there was always a chance, no matter how small and what the odds, that you might win. Hope lived in the fight. But this was different. You couldn't fight Baba Yaga. Billi felt a sickening void swelling in her stomach, a great hole of despair. Without Vasilisa, without a clue of how to defeat Baba Yaga, they were all going to die.

For the first time ever Billi stared at true and final defeat. The Templars had faced countless enemies in battle. They'd never been defeated, only killed. The Order had survived and the Bataille Ténébreuse continued. But not after this. The battle would be over for everyone.

'Lady SanGreal?'

Billi shook her head, freeing herself from the black feelings of hopelessness. Three days. A lot could happen in three days.

Just give me one shot. That's all I ask for.

'Come, I have something to show you.' Koshchey led Billi away from the shirt and brought her to a corner of the hall.

'For you,' he said.

A mannequin wearing a long, red coat stood in the shadows. Golden embroidery ran along its sleeves; flaming wings and emerald peacock eyes stared out, mysterious and alien. Billi brushed her fingertips along the material, and it rippled like feathers. The collar was high and stiff and lined with gold thread. It was something from another age.

'Beautiful, is it not?' He carefully unfastened the silk-covered buttons.

Billi couldn't take her eyes off it – the way its colour seemed to change as Koshchey unwrapped it from the mannequin and slung it over his arm. The golden wings stretched out gracefully and the unblinking green eyes turned to watch her. A warm breath passed across her carrying a subtle perfume; it was as if the coat was alive. The scent seeped down into her lungs and made her tingle.

He handed the coat to her. 'Try it.'

Billi hesitated. She'd only just changed out of her fighting clothes, but her usual outfits weren't much different: tough leather boots, combat trousers with lots of pouches and a black T-shirt. The cuffs on her hoodie were frayed and the only jewellery she wore was a small silver crucifix. The coat was too beautiful for her. And *could* she accept a gift like this from him?

'What do you want for it?'

'You are my guest. It is a gift.'

Billi couldn't remember when she'd ever had a new outfit that wasn't from the Army Surplus store. God, did she even have a dress at home? The cloth was warm and feather-soft. She pressed a sleeve against her cheek and inhaled the delicate scent, a smell of dreams.

It fitted like a glove. Buttons open, Billi stepped into the light.

'More beautiful than a Tsarina,' said Koshchey. He put his hands on her shoulders and turned Billi to face a mirror. 'Look.'

It wasn't her. It wasn't the Billi she knew, or thought she knew. She barely recognized herself. The coat looked darker in the glass, bloody. The collar forced her to raise her head, to hold up her chin. It was an imperial look.

Billi could imagine what sort of person would wear such a coat. Someone who knew they were important, more special than others. Wear the blood-red coat too long and she might start believing in its promise.

'It suits you.' Koshchey leaned into the reflection, pleased at what he saw. 'It suits you indeed.'

Billi called in and Arthur had real news; there had been massive wolf migrations in the north. Dozens of packs were making their way into the deep forests of the Kronos National Park. The region had a volcano. Arthur believed that's where they'd find Vasilisa. He had also found Vasilisa's granny and was on his way to talk with her.

Billi had passed the information on to Gwaine immediately and he'd spoken to Koshchey. They were flying north first thing tomorrow, with extra men and weapons, courtesy of Koshchey. The Bogatyrs might be cruel, but the Templars needed them.

At last the hope she'd been looking for. Billi had her gear packed and ready by her suite door. The red coat lay across the bed and she inspected her weapons, deciding to pack the Glock alongside her blades.

She checked and rechecked the array of weapons, hardly able to contain her excitement, picking up her knife to give it an extra polish. Moscow had been a dead end, but now they had a lead, a real one.

Less than three days to find Vasilisa.

'Billi?' Ivan knocked on the door and came in.

He looked pretty rough, his white shirt hanging out of his trousers and held closed by one button. He swayed slightly and held aloft a small bottle. She'd only ever seen him dressed to the nines, but Ivan probably looked good even when lying in the gutter.

'Why aren't you celebrating?' he slurred. 'Our great victory over the werewolves.'

'Didn't think that was worth celebrating.' She leaned back as he swayed over her. 'You're drunk.'

'I'm Russian.' He stopped as he saw the backpack beside the door. 'You're leaving? Already?' He nodded slowly. His hands dropped and he sank into an armchair. 'So it's true. The wolves are in Kronos.'

'I've no more business in Moscow.' Billi put down the knife she'd been cleaning. 'But thank you. Thank you for helping me when you didn't have to.' Billi knew Ivan had risked a lot – including his loyalties as a Bogatyr. Let alone overcoming a personal vendetta in order to help the young Polenitsy child escape. Her heart beat faster as she looked at him sitting there. She needed to remind herself why she was here in the first place.

Ivan's frown slowly mellowed into a smile. He put

the bottle on the floor and stood up. He offered his hand.

'Let me show you Moscow before you leave.'

'I really don't have time. There's still a lot to do before tomorrow morning.'

'Please. We won't be long.' Ivan's hand hadn't moved. Maybe he wasn't arrogant, but he was certainly stubborn.

'Ivan Alexeivich Romanov!' Billi exclaimed, frustrated. He straightened some more, head up and proud. His black hair with its military crop contrasted with his pale, wintery skin. Deep shadows formed under the cliff-like high cheekbones and those grey eyes lost their weary drunkenness as she spoke his name.

It was already six and this was her last evening here. She had no idea what lay ahead except hard fighting and doomsday. She could spend it pondering and worrying about things she couldn't control, just waiting for tomorrow. Or she could spend it with Ivan. There he stood, his wide chest heaving under the half-open shirt as he took a deep breath to steady himself. Despite the vodka flowing through his veins, his hand was steady.

Billi took it.

Dimitri drove them into the heart of the city. Unlike London with its labyrinth of narrow streets and buildings all cramped together, Moscow was wide and broad. The boulevards gave Billi endless panoramas, especially along the river. Ice shone on the roads and a fresh cloud of snow was beginning to descend.

The tyres rumbled on the cobbles of Red Square. Ahead stood the multicoloured onion domes of St Basil's Cathedral. The composite building was actually interconnected churches, each with their individual spire and dome. Veiled in snow, the cathedral looked as though it had been snatched from a fairy tale. Moscow had an ethereal magic when it was cloaked in winter. To one side stood GUM, the gigantic department store, its walls and windows outlined by thousands of golden bulbs. Opposite that were the immense, dark-red walls of the Kremlin fortress.

'Once this was all ours,' said Ivan. His eyes shone with the reflection of the lights and dazzling colours. 'My ancestors were crowned there.' He pointed to a series of golden roofs behind the red fortress walls. 'Archangel Cathedral. St Michael was said to be the protector of our family.' He leaned back in his seat. 'I heard a strange story about him recently.'

Billi kept her attention on the scenery, but her voice went soft and quiet. 'Oh? What story?'

'Do you believe in God? In His archangels?'

'You're asking a Templar that?'

'The Patriarch of Moscow is a close personal friend of the Romanovs,' said Ivan, referring to the head of the Russian Orthodox Church. 'He told me Michael had fallen; it came to him in a dream. That he had been cast down.'

Billi didn't move, but sweat trickled down her back. Did he know? That she had cast the archangel down?

'I wonder what the other archangels must think, knowing that their brother has been sent to Hell.'

Billi could feel how close he was to her.

'What do you think, Billi?'

'I think you should be careful what you read into the dreams of an old man.'

Ivan laughed. Billi liked the sound of his laugh. His guard was down and the imperious barrier he usually put up had fallen away.

'You are a difficult person to understand,' he said. 'You have many secrets, I think.'

'No more than most.'

Ivan watched her thoughtfully. 'Perhaps that is true – we all have things we are frightened of telling others.'

They drove along *Kremlevskaya nab*, the broad road that ran beside the riverbank. Billi watched the broken platforms of ice drift slowly down the Moscow River.

They were rolling along beside a park when Billi caught a flash of fire from beyond the trees.

'What's that?' There were more flames. Streaks of light wove and spun in the darkness.

'Dimitri, stop,' said Ivan.

The car pulled up by the kerb and Ivan jumped out and opened Billi's door.

'Bolotnaya Square.' He held out Billi's new coat for her to put on.

'You're quite the gentleman, Ivan,' Billi laughed.

'We do things differently in Russia.' His hands lightly

brushed her shoulders as he placed it round her. Then he turned her so that they were face to face.

'Are you warm enough?' he asked, straightening her collar, his fingers resting on the top button, next to her neck.

Billi flushed. Despite the snowflakes, she was suddenly more than warm enough.

Ivan took a step back and collected his own coat from Dimitri. Then he offered Billi his arm.

'Shall we?'

They moved down the path towards the flames. Music beat across the night sky, a cacophony of clashing beats and drums and guitars, and slowly Billi started to make out groups of people, collected like tribes round the open centre of the park.

Firedancers spun long chains with fireballs attached to the ends round their bodies in a seamless path of golden light. There were dozens of them: some competing, others showing off or egging one another on. Large steel bins were placed round the park, each a firepit that one of the tribes gathered around.

Despite the sub-zero temperatures, some of the men were bare-chested and the orbiting fireballs threw ever-changing patterns of light and shadow over the contours of their bodies.

'Koshchey doesn't like me coming here,' said Ivan. 'He says I shouldn't mix with "peasants".'

'Is that what you think?' She'd never met a bona fide member of a royal family before. Her own ancestors

190

were thoroughly anti-monarchy. The SanGreals had taken part in the French Revolution. The closest they'd come to royalty was when they'd operated the guillotine.

'Nobility isn't about coats of arms or titles, Billi.' He nodded in the direction of more dancers. 'I'll never be free, like them. Every moment of my life has been dedicated to one purpose. To lead the Bogatyrs. To protect those under me. And as a Romanov that means Russia.' He sighed. 'That's why I like it here. Just for a short while I can forget what it is to be Ivan Alexeivich Romanov.'

Billi touched his hand. Ivan took it all so seriously. When she'd met him she'd thought he was just about fancy clothes and plush living, but he was more than that. She knew how he felt. Didn't she feel the same about being a Templar? They were both dedicated to their lives of duty, and nothing else.

'For what it's worth,' said Billi, 'I think you'll do a great job.'

'If Koshchey lets me.' Ivan gripped her hand. 'I'm not so naive as to think he'll just hand it all over when I turn eighteen. He's just waiting for me to slip up.'

'Look, if you'll get in trouble here, we can go.'

'I'm in enough trouble already.' He waved at one of the dancers. The girl smiled as she whirled a pair of burning chains round her body, wrapping herself in an incandescent pattern.

'For helping me?' Billi should have known that there were always going to be consequences for Ivan. 'I'm sorry.'

Ivan frowned. 'Don't apologize. You stepped up to protect that girl. It's what I should have done.'

'You defied the Bogatyrs.' She thought about that talk she'd had in the lift, about how Ivan was a naive idealist. 'You defied Koshchey.'

'Only because I followed you.' Ivan raised his hand to her cheek. 'You have that effect on people. Haven't you noticed?'

Billi laughed, trying to cover how unsettled she felt from the heat of his touch on her face. But she didn't move. 'Don't follow me. I have a *bad* effect on people.'

'Do you know what it is to be a noble?' he said, more to himself than to her. He peered into the fire, the orange glow of the flames casting him in gold. 'It is to have an ideal and to strive towards it. No matter what the cost. To believe in something more important than yourself.'

'I had a friend who thought the same.' A coarse, thick lump, a stifled sob, rose to Billi's throat as she recalled Kay. Ivan was so like him, but so different. Tears rose and she tried to stop them. What would Kay think, her being with Ivan? Ivan, the prince, the nobleman. Kay had been a noble man too.

Ivan moved his gaze away from the flames and looked at her. 'What happened to him?' He moved his hand from her cheek, cupping her chin, and gently lifted her face.

Billi blinked, but the tears still fell. 'He died.'

'I hope his killer suffered.'

'Yes.' Billi held it in by biting her lips. She had done

what she had to do, but she'd regretted it ever since. Eyes closed, she tried to hold back the misery she'd fought down for the last three months. Kay's death by her hand. 'I suffer every day.'

'I am sorry,' said Ivan. He leaned closer, until she could hear him whisper. 'Chekhov said to begin to live in the present, we must atone for our past. But we can only atone by suffering extraordinarily.' He drew her nearer and as he spoke her eyes were drawn to his lips. 'But then the suffering has to end.'

Billi could hardly breathe as the distance between them slowly closed. She didn't want to betray the memory of Kay – she never thought she'd meet anyone as good as him. But Ivan was good; he was like her, trapped in duty and responsibilities beyond his years, yet he still cared.

She paused – just for a second. Ivan waited, sensing her uncertainty. But Billi realized she didn't want to move away. She leaned forward, grazing his mouth with hers ever so lightly. She felt dizzy with the sensation. With his arm around her, supporting her, Ivan kissed her and for that moment Billi forgot everything else.

Now was the time to look to the living – to Ivan.

Billi held Ivan's hand as they walked back to the car, silent. There wasn't anything to say now. They knew how they felt – but she was leaving tomorrow. Billi felt the calluses along his fingers, which, like her, he'd gained through years of sword practice. One indent on the forefinger she didn't have: trigger time. He'd spent as long on the firing range as he had on the duelling deck.

His grip was firm and secure, warm and soft.

Then his fingers tightened.

A woman stepped out from the cover of the trees. The flames swayed in the large steel drum in front of her. She wore a paisley scarf over her hair. Billi recognized her. She was the Polenitsy they'd helped escape out of the apartment block earlier that day.

Three other women stalked the darkness on the edge of the firelight, moving like the wolves they truly were.

Billi shot a look at the car and saw Dimitri lying on the ground, a heavily bearded man leaning on his back, knife to his throat. Her hand dropped to her hip, feeling the edge of her kukri strapped to her belt.

'We come under a flag of truce,' said the woman with the scarf. She kept her distance and her hands open.

'What do you want?' asked Ivan, backing away from the four approaching women, keeping Billi behind him.

'To thank you for allowing us to escape.' She looked up at Billi, eyes narrowed. 'And to deliver a message from our pack leader, Olga.'

Old Grey. The fact they hadn't been torn to pieces already boded well. Billi moved to Ivan's side. His fist trembled as he struggled to control his rage. He flipped back the corner of his coat and a moment later his pistol was in his hand.

'Old Grey killed my father.' He whispered it, his grip tightening on the pistol.

'He died well, young Romanov. She honoured him with single combat, after Koshchey had abandoned him.'

'You are wrong,' hissed Ivan. 'He was trapped, betrayed. I was told so.'

The woman shrugged. 'He was, as you say, betrayed, but not by the Polenitsy.'

'What do you mean?'

The Paisley woman glanced down at Ivan's gun, then spoke. 'People have been disappearing, Tsarevich. Your father knew. We had information regarding who was behind these disappearances. We had agreed to meet. He would allow us to live in the cities, provided we did not hunt humans, and we would tell him who was responsible for the missing people. I'm sure it will come as no shock to you to know who this man is.'

'Koshchey,' Ivan croaked.

Paisley nodded. 'Your father trusted him. That was a mistake. He told Koshchey of the meeting, and Koshchey followed secretly. We discovered this and thought your father planned a double-cross, so he was killed. Just what Koshchey wanted.' She shrugged. 'Only too late did we discover we too had been used. We regret your father's death. He was a noble man.'

Ivan stared dumbly at them. But it all made sense. He closed his eyes and Billi watched the rage build in him. He pressed his fists against his head, teeth clenched together as he held in the anger, letting it swell.

'*Nyet, nyet, nyet,*' he repeated. Billi touched his hand and a cracked sob came from deep in his chest.

'Who knew?' asked Ivan.

'Many of the Bogatyrs. We have watched how Koshchey has built his army of loyal followers. Once he controlled your father's wealth he bought all the men he needed. Many have become rich with your father's demise.'

'What is the message you've brought?' Billi snapped.

'Go home, Templar. The Spring Child is where she should be. Olga warns you to come no further: she would be honour-bound to fight you, and that is something she does not wish.'

'And what of Fimbulwinter?' Billi asked. 'Wolves freeze as well as men.'

'Fimbulwinter?' repeated Ivan, looking at her, confused. She'd kept this from him and now Billi realized she'd made a mistake; she should have trusted him. She had a lot of explaining to do.

The woman scowled. 'That is a lie. The goddess has promised us a great spring. She would not betray the wolves, who have served her loyally since the earliest times.'

'It is not like the gods to care for mortals,' said Billi. She'd seen enough horror from Michael, and knew that lesser beings were always sacrificed to the ambitions of the divine. 'Fimbulwinter is coming and Baba Yaga won't care if the packs starve. The Spring Child learnt this directly from your goddess.'

'She is mistaken, and afraid. Her death will be a glorious sacrifice, far better than what Koshchey has planned for her.'

'What do you mean?' asked Ivan. 'If what you say is true, why is Koshchey even helping the Knights Templar find the Spring Child? Saving her serves no purpose. There is no profit in it for him.'

'You are wrong. There is profit.' The woman turned away. 'We will show you what he has planned for the Spring Child.'

CHAPTER 25

'Follow us,' said Paisley.

The man with the big beard let Dimitri get to his feet and tucked away his knife.

The Polenitsy got into their own car, a plain, non-descript white Volvo. Paisley motioned to them to follow as they started their engine.

'And what else have you been hiding?' snapped Ivan the moment he sat down.

'Please, Ivan, we need their help.'

Ivan crossed his arms. 'Tell me. Everything.'

'I will. But let's go.' The Polenitsy car rolled away into the light traffic.

Ivan gave a single, curt nod to Dimitri and the car started up.

'What do you mean about Fimbulwinter?' He sank his head in his hands. He looked shattered. The news of Koshchey's betrayal threatened to overwhelm him. That and how the Bogatyrs had become so swiftly corrupted. His father's legacy, everything he was striving for, was in tatters.

So, as they trailed behind the Polenitsy, Billi explained. She told Ivan how they'd found Vasilisa, how they'd discovered she was not just a psychically gifted child but an avatar, a being with the power to control nature. Ivan listened, not moving, his eyes barely blinking. Eventually Billi finished. They sat silently for a minute. Ivan had a lot to take in.

'You really think Vasilisa can cause such a huge cataclysm?' said Ivan.

'She felt the eruption of Vesuvius and was able to damp it down, so she's certainly got a psychic link with volcanoes. Beyond that we don't truly know. But we have to assume the worst case that Vasilisa has the power to cause a super-volcanic eruption.'

'And why didn't you tell me this at the beginning?'

'I didn't know if I could trust you to begin with, but Ivan, I've messed up before, trusting someone, because I cared about them too much, trusted them too early.' Billi touched the scar on her neck. 'Only I was betrayed and a lot of people died. I couldn't make that mistake again.'

'Who was this person?'

'Michael. Your Michael.'

Ivan gasped. 'So it is true. Michael was cast down.'

'Believe me, he deserved it.' Billi took his hand. 'That should change nothing between us. I trust you, Ivan. I need your help.'

Ivan slowly nodded. But he still pulled back his hand. 'Nothing that I thought I knew about my father or even this situation is as I imagined it – you are not the only one who needs some time to trust now, Billi.'

They drove for an hour, not really speaking much, before the Volvo stopped and Paisley got out. Dimitri drew their own car up beside the Volvo. As soon as they'd stopped, Ivan got out and confronted Paisley.

'Come and see,' she said.

They'd parked in the wasteground beneath a massive, rumbling motorway flyover. The cars roared overhead and graffiti covered the concrete supports. Three large lorry containers sat gathering rust and the shell of a burnt-out car lay among the weeds and piles of rubbish. A tall wire fence lined the far side, isolating this derelict area from another equally derelict zone.

'Have you ever wondered why the vampires no longer hunt in Moscow?' asked the woman.

'Koshchey has driven most of them out,' said Ivan.

'No. Koshchey made a *deal* with the blood-drinkers.' The woman walked up to one of the containers. It was ten metres long, about three high and four wide. The corners were deeply pitted with rust and the paint flaked, exposing the dull brown and orange panels beneath. Someone had tried to set fire to it, leaving black scorch marks along the doors.

The chain and lock holding the doors shut were brand-new.

One of the Polenitsy hauled a large pair of steel-cutters from the back seat of their car and after a few grunts of effort snapped the shiny chrome chain, then tossed it into the undergrowth.

Paisley stepped back, indicating for Billi and Ivan to go before her.

'I'm not here to play games,' Billi said.

'This is anything but a game. Look inside.'

Ivan looked at the door, testing the handle. He nodded at Billi. He wanted to know how far Koshchey had gone.

Together she and Ivan heaved the door lever up. The smell warned her before her eyes were able to penetrate the darkness within. She'd smelt the putrid odour of death enough times to recognize it without being sickened. But this time she covered her mouth as she looked into the dark chamber.

Naked, emaciated bodies lay piled within. Billi's head swam with nausea as she saw the broken teeth sprinkled across the steel floor. She saw the hands of one man who lay closer than the others. The flesh on the fingers had fused together. Billi stepped forward and saw his face. She closed her eyes too late. The image had burned itself into her.

It was like his face had been wax and put against a fire. No facial features remained, just rivulets of skin.

The man's face had been melted with acid.

There were dozens of them. They didn't look human, more like malformed wax statues, failed human shapes that had been abandoned. Then Billi saw the bites. Along the arms. Along the thighs and necks. Chunks had been bitten off where the *ghuls* had frenzied and gnawed the flesh.

'No fingerprints, no features. No way of finding out who they were,' said the woman. 'Every month Koshchey delivers a container of fresh ones to the vampires. They pay him and he keeps them fat and off the streets. A few decide they would rather hunt than pay. Those Koshchey eliminates.'

'Koshchey arranged this?' Billi asked. Even for him this seemed beyond inhuman.

'Yes. That is why the vampires no longer hunt. They do not need to. Koshchey delivers them all the fresh blood they could want. They pay him well. And think of what the vampires have offered him for a Spring Child.'

'Just for money? All this just for money?' Billi had thought, despite their brutality, that the Bogatyrs fought for the same cause as the Templars. But she knew that *ghuls*, vampires, supped on the soul of their victim. That's why they couldn't survive on blood from animals or blood-bags. It was those last few drops of blood, the drops that carried the last heartbeat and with it the soul, that strengthened *ghuls*. And the soul of a Spring Child, an avatar, would be richest of all.

The woman closed the container door. 'You call us evil, when all we do is defend what is ours. You call the sacrifice of the Spring Child evil when she will renew the world.' The woman waved her three companions away. 'I have seen what evil is, and it is mankind. You do this for paper.' She spat on the ground. 'Perhaps you are right and Baba Yaga *will* bring Fimbulwinter. But she will save us from it. My goddess is old and wise and if she thinks that the world will be purged and born anew, I will not question her wisdom. All I care is that mankind be destroyed.'

'No. Not all of us are like that.' Billi grabbed the woman's wrist. 'You came here to thank me for saving you and the girl, but I haven't. Not her, not anyone, if Baba Yaga gets her way. We will *all* die! Tell me where Vasilisa is, please.'

Doubt briefly crossed the Paisley woman's eyes. She could see that Billi believed what she was telling her.

'Please,' Billi begged. 'Just because Koshchey is a monster doesn't mean we all are. You know that, otherwise you wouldn't be here. Tell me where they've taken Vasilisa.'

'I'm sorry. I cannot defy the will of the goddess.' She waited for Billi to release her.

'You're making a big mistake.' Billi dropped her grip. She turned away and looked at Ivan. He stood as rigid as a statue, eyes fixed on the contents of the rusty container.

'Let's go, Ivan.' The smell of decaying flesh clung to her and fogged her brain.

'Look at what he's done, Billi.'

'We'll deal with him later,' she promised. She'd never seen anything so horrific. The Unholy had done the killing, but it had taken a human's capacity for cold, heartless logic to make it happen, month in, month out.

Ivan shook his head. 'No. I will deal with him.' There was a conviction in his voice that Billi found chilling. 'I will kill Koshchey.'

CHAPTER 26

'I'm calling the others. We're leaving.' Billi started dialling her father's number. The Templars had to get out, tonight, and meet up with Arthur. Vasilisa's granny was the only lead they had now. There was no way they could trust the Bogatyrs. The moment Koshchey had Vasilisa, he'd no longer need the Templars. Billi had no illusions of what would happen then: they'd be eliminated without a thought.

Ivan put his hand on hers. 'Koshchey is monitoring your phones.' He took it and switched it off. 'It is standard KGB procedure.'

'And you talk about trust?' Billi snapped. The moment she said it she regretted it. Ivan was in a bad place right now and she needed him. She could see it in his eyes; his whole world teetered on the brink of destruction. Koshchey had betrayed his father. The Bogatyrs were involved in the vilest trade with the *ghuls*. Everything he knew was a lie.

Billi held his hand. 'We'll get through this.'

Ivan gritted his teeth, holding down the rage that must be like a tidal wave inside him.

'How shall we proceed?' he asked. Obviously he didn't trust himself to keep his head, not right now.

'Act like nothing's happened. Let's get back to the Ministry and get Gwaine and the other Templars.' Billi walked back towards the waiting car. 'Who else in the Bogatyrs can you trust? Really trust?'

Ivan pointed to his bodyguard. 'Dimitri.'

'Anyone else?'

'No one for certain.'

Billi thought about it. Ivan had to come with them. A look from Ivan confirmed he knew that too. Koshchey had already tried to kill him; it was obvious now. He'd rushed off to fight that *ghul*, assuming the Bogatyrs were right behind him. If Billi hadn't saved him, Ivan would have been murdered by Koshchey's vampire and Koshchey would have got shot of him without getting his hands dirty. No blame. No suspicions. Sooner or later Koshchey would get rid of him, especially if he got a hint that Ivan had uncovered his trade with the *ghuls*. He would throw caution to the wind and there'd be a straight and simple killing.

'You'd better stick with us,' Billi said.

Ivan stopped by the car door and looked down at the pistol clipped to his belt. Billi knew exactly what he was thinking. How he wanted to take that pistol and put the barrel against Koshchey's head and pull the trigger.

'Ivan, you'll get your chance. But we've got to get Vasilisa. She has to be our priority.'

Ivan nodded, his honour as a Bogatyr guiding his decision.

Billi respected him even more then than she ever had before. She touched his arm. 'Don't pack. Just find out what you can – if Koshchey has any leads he's not sharing. We'll call my dad on an outside phone and plan our next step.'

'Which is?'

'Buggered if I know.' She needed a phone. 'Dad was looking for Vasilisa's grandmother. The woman knew a lot about Baba Yaga. He's hoping she might point him in the right direction. He thinks the witch is near; the area's got lots of wolves. But it's all just guesswork. We don't know anything for sure.'

Billi looked up at the moon. Almost full. They only had a couple of days left.

'We must stop her, Ivan.'

Ivan opened the car door and squeezed Billi's hand. 'I will help you, Billi SanGreal.'

A crash on the motorway meant it took them almost three hours to get back to the Ministry, and Billi couldn't think for the turmoil her emotions were in.

How could they have known that Koshchey was a monster? That the Bogatyrs had become human traffickers? Lance had suspected Koshchey was no good, but never that the entire order had been corrupted so swiftly.

Ivan was right; Koshchey had to die.

But not today.

As they entered the lobby they passed two of the Bogatyrs, who each nodded to Ivan.

'You get Lance and Gwaine. I'll get Elaine,' Billi murmured, glancing at the large clock above the main staircase. It was just gone ten. 'I'll meet you in the car park in ten minutes.'

Minutes later Billi banged on the library door.

'Elaine, you in there?'

A book slammed on to the floor and Elaine, glasses resting on her forehead, stared at Billi, rubbing her eyes.

'Where the hell have you been?' she demanded. She took hold of Billi's sleeve and dragged her in, shutting the door behind her. 'You have got to see this.'

'We don't have time.' Billi tried to resist, but the old woman wouldn't let her go.

Books from the Bogatyr library filled the entire floor. A long dining table covered with old books and scrolls faced a row of windows. Lance was right: Elaine was in research heaven. A mattress and blanket lay on the polished wooden floor. So this was where Elaine slept. Billi had guessed as much. She glanced over the endless cabinets and rows of stuffed bookshelves, then rested her eyes on a large portrait above the fireplace, and on a face she recognized.

That could be Ivan.

Tsar Nicholas II gazed at her with imperious indifference. He stood behind a chair on which his wife, the

Tsarina, sat. Beside him were three young women. Billi didn't need to guess which was Anastasia. Ivan had inherited more than just her beauty. He even stood the same way she did, straight, relaxed, regal.

Elaine grinned. 'I know what happened to Baba Yaga.' She slapped her head. 'Obvious really. She's an elementalist. Whatever affects the Earth affects her. And something did affect her, the Earth, a hundred years ago.' Elaine smacked her fist into her palm. 'Right here, in Russia.'

'What, Elaine?'

Elaine began searching through the scattered books, opening and slamming them as she tried to find what she was looking for. 'I'll show you. I'll show you . . .'

Billi sighed impatiently and leaned up against the table. Arms folded, she caught a glimpse of movement. A shadow moved in the gap between the bottom of the doorframe and the floor. She heard a man take a deep breath, followed by the click of a catch. She grabbed Elaine and dived behind the sofa as the door exploded open and the darkness screamed with gunfire.

CHAPTER 27

Billi threw her arms over her head as shards of glass from the long line of windows around her exploded like crystal shrapnel. The sofa pulsed as bullets thumped into the dense wood. The wind pulled savagely at the long curtains and Billi felt the snow-carrying cold blast her. In a matter of seconds the world had gone to hell.

Her ears rang with the echoing gunfire that bounced back and forth off the heavy marble walls. The air carried the acrid, metallic flavour of gunpowder.

Petrified, Elaine hung on to Billi, her eyes shut tight. She shook so badly that Billi had to wrap her arms round her, even though she herself could do nothing but pray.

The echoes lasted longer than the gunfire. Snow blew in from the line of now-demolished windows, and the city beyond sparkled.

'Hello? Are you still alive?' a mocking voice boomed, deep with amusement. Koshchey.

'Of course!' shouted Billi, sounding a hell of a lot braver than she felt. 'Were you shooting at us? I didn't realize.'

Two Bogatyrs poked their guns over the sofa. One

dragged Elaine out by the hair and the other went for Billi. She slapped his hands away and stood up.

Billi casually brushed the splinters from her coat. She couldn't let Koshchey see how frightened she was. The Bogatyrs gathered round them. The Bogatyr released his hold on Elaine and she stood beside Billi, staring at the devastation.

Koshchey strolled into the library, wiping his hands on a rag. His collar was loose and his shirt stained with sweat. Red droplets decorated his white cuffs. He pressed the rag against the back of his neck, drawing it over his bald head. Then, carefully folding the cloth, he tucked it into his shirt pocket.

There were now ten Bogatyrs in the library. They all wore casual clothing, but carried guns. Two held Ivan between them. He struggled, but the men had his arms bent behind his back.

Where were Lance and Gwaine?

Koshchey glared at the portrait of the royal family and held out his hand. One of his men put a pistol in it.

Koshchey shot Tsar Nicholas between the eyes. The hole in the canvas flickered with flame, then turned into wispy smoke.

'I've wanted to do that for a long time,' said Koshchey.

Koshchey put another hole between Anastasia's eyes.

'And that,' he said, handing the pistol back. With one sweep of his trunk-wide arms he hurled the books off the table. Elaine flinched as the priceless, one-of-a-kind tomes and scrolls scattered.

'You can't –' Elaine started as she scrabbled among the discarded books. One of the Bogatyrs knocked them out of her hands and pushed her back against Billi.

Koshchey glanced at the man. 'Andrei, if the old woman speaks again, break her jaw.'

'Is something wrong?' Billi asked. If Gwaine and Lance were anywhere close, they would have heard the gunfire. She needed to play for time. Give them a chance to get away.

'I offered you hospitality, my aid,' said Koshchey. 'My men's lives, Templar, and you betray my trust. Sneaking off behind my back. Aiding the enemy. Yuri saw you and Ivan talking with the Polenitsy tonight. Did you not think I would find out? Is that gratitude?'

'All you've ever done has been for yourself.' Ivan glared, trying to break free.

'Ah, Romanov.' Koshchey waved at the men on either side of Ivan. 'All this you owe to me. If your father had been left in charge, we'd be as poor as the Templars.' He slapped his chest. 'I have made the Bogatyrs strong. I have made them powerful, feared. And you dare to think I would hand this over to a whelp like you? It is my destiny to rule the Bogatyrs. Your father had to go.'

'You don't even deny it? That you are a traitor?'

Koshchey looked round at his men and laughed. They laughed too. 'Deny it? I deny nothing. I led him to the Polenitsy and left him there. He was weak. The grey werewolf made short work of him, I hear. He died, begging on his knees. I still celebrate your father's death.'

Ivan roared and charged. Koshchey's right fist snapped forward and the blow took Ivan off the ground. Billi caught him as he stumbled backwards, amazed he wasn't unconscious, or dead, from the blow.

'No, Ivan –'

He threw himself forward, but, still reeling from Koshchey's blow, his punch was off target. Koshchey took it on his chest without a reaction. Then he grabbed Ivan's collar and slammed his knee into the young man's belly.

The young Romanov slumped down. His chest heaved and his fingers scraped the floor as he searched for a grip that would help him get up again.

'It would have been better if the vampire had killed you, as planned,' said Koshchey. 'But Lady SanGreal had to save you.'

Slowly Ivan rose to his feet, his rage and defiance undiminished.

'Fight me, fight me like a man of honour,' he snarled, staring hatefully at the huge Bogatyr.

'Honour is for old men and young fools.' Koshchey, dripping with sweat, pulled out a rag and shook it open. Up close, Billi saw it bore a green pattern, one she recognized.

Paisley.

Koshchey spotted Billi's look of horror as he wiped his face.

'Oh yes, Templar. The woman told me everything.

Eventually.' Then he straightened and pulled the pistol from his waistband. 'I will find Vasilisa – you can take comfort in that. I will make sure Baba Yaga does not get her hands on her. And I will make sure Fimbulwinter never happens. That is what you all want, yes? She is much too valuable to be left to the Polenitsy and their insane goddess. You cannot imagine how much the vampires would pay for a Spring Child.'

He drew back the slide of his gun, chambering a round. Then he pointed it at Ivan's head.

'I've dreamed of killing a Romanov,' he said.

'Drop it, fat man.'

Koshchey's jaw fell open. Gwaine stood right behind him, the barrel of his pistol pressed against the back of Koshchey's head.

The other Bogatyrs reacted in different ways. Some turned to point their guns at Gwaine, but Koshchey was so large he practically formed a human shield. Lance appeared from behind a shot-up column and motioned Billi and Elaine towards him and the door. He held a pistol in his hand and had a backpack slung over his shoulder. They'd come in a hurry. They'd come in the nick of time.

Gwaine turned Koshchey around so the big Russian covered him. 'We're leaving now. Thanks for your hospitality.'

Billi and Ivan gathered all the men's guns, took two each, then tossed the rest out of the nearest window.

They backed slowly towards the lift, Gwaine holding Koshchey in front of him as a shield.

They got in and Lance pressed the bottom button for the car park.

'You won't get away with this,' snarled Koshchey.

'Now that's original,' replied Gwaine.

Billi used her sleeve to wipe Ivan's face, as gently as she could. She knew how much it would be hurting right now.

'You all right?'

'I'll live.' He faced Koshchey. 'Unlike this pig.' He shoved his pistol under Koshchey's chin. Koshchey's face drained of all colour.

'*Alors*, Tsarevich,' said Lance. 'He is our hostage, *oui*?'

Ivan pushed the pistol further into the man's jaw. Billi leaned back, expecting scattered brains any second. Ivan saw her and hung his head in frustration. He nodded and lowered his weapon.

'What's the plan?' asked Billi.

'First we get out of here. After you.' Gwaine pushed Koshchey forward as the doors opened. Men spilled out of the doorway from the stairs in the far corner of the car park, but they could do nothing but glower; no one dared approach while Koshchey was their hostage. A few had grabbed more weapons, but no one was going to risk a shot in the poor light.

Elaine and Billi bundled into the front seat of a big seven-seater four-by-four, the others got in the back. It took Elaine only seconds to hot-wire the vehicle.

'When did you learn that?' asked Billi.

'During my misspent youth.'

'They had cars back then?'

Elaine flattened the accelerator and twisted the wheel without commenting. The large vehicle spun around to face the exit. Billi could see that many of the Bogatyrs were starting up their own cars. They weren't going to let their boss out of their sight.

The four-by-four rolled up the ramp and on to *ulitsa Bolshaya Polyanka*, the main road that headed away from the city.

Behind them three vehicles rose out of the Ministry car park. At this time of the morning there were hardly any other cars on the road.

'Where to?' Billi asked.

'There's a private airfield to the south,' said Ivan. 'We can leave Moscow, but my plane is too small for all of us.' He gazed coldly at their prisoner. 'Where is Dimitri?'

'Where do you think, Tsarevich?'

Ivan sank into his seat, head bowed. Billi saw him close his eyes and bite his lips. Dimitri must have meant a lot to him. 'He was loyal, Koshchey.'

'To you. I had no need of such men.'

'So, Ivan, what about this bloke?' asked Gwaine. They all looked at Koshchey. No one leapt to his defence.

With Billi and Elaine up front, the rear two rows faced each other. Gwaine and Ivan were opposite Koshchey, with Lance wedged up beside him.

'Too bad for you, fat man,' said Gwaine. He looked at Lance. 'What do you think?'

Koshchey's eyes widened as he got it: they were going to execute him.

Billi couldn't help glancing at the reflection of the four men in the back. Despite the crowded car, she felt cold and put up her hood, casting her face into shadow.

'*Oui*, kill him,' said Lance with little feeling. He could have been ordering a baguette.

'Billi?' asked Gwaine.

She turned around and looked at the big man. Koshchey was ashen, frozen stiff in his seat. He raised his hands in a futile gesture.

This was not how they did things, Billi knew that. Templars were warriors, not executioners. Killing a defenceless man went against the Templar Rules, their code.

But as Billi peered out from under her black hood she knew even Arthur would make an exception in this case.

'Yes, kill him.'

'Wait,' said Koshchey. His eyes darted between them, desperate. 'I can help you.'

Gwaine found a strip of cloth and began wrapping it round the barrel to use as a crude silencer. 'We don't need your help.' He pointed the pistol at Koshchey's face.

'No, no, you don't understand.' Koshchey's voice rose an octave, almost screeching in fear.

Lance slapped him. 'Hush now,' he said. 'At least die like a man.'

The big, bad Bogatyr. He could torture and murder. Melt people in acid. He'd killed so many, but couldn't face death himself. There he sat, white with terror, sweat pouring off his face, legs trembling. Billi reached back and put her hand on Ivan's shoulder. He hadn't moved throughout the discussion. He put his fingers through hers. Gwaine creaked in his seat, slightly shifting to half-face the young man.

'Tsarevich?' Ivan should have the right to issue the command.

'No!' Koshchey screamed. 'I know where Vasilisa is!'

Gwaine tutted. 'Sorry, mate, but I don't believe you.'

'Lady SanGreal, let me help you save your friend.'

'Wait,' said Billi. Gwaine lowered the pistol.

'How do you know where she is?'

Koshchey looked down. 'The Polenitsy woman. She told me.'

'The woman you tortured to death. Right?'

Koshchey didn't respond.

Blow his brains out. That's what he deserves. But Billi realized that if he knew where Vasilisa was, well, the execution would have to wait.

Billi pulled down her hood and drew her hair behind her ear. 'Where is she?'

He shook his head. 'Your word, as a Templar, that you will not kill me if I tell you.'

Gwaine looked at Billi; this was her play.

'I swear neither I, nor any Templar here, will kill you,' she said. 'Now where is Vasilisa?'

Koshchey smiled. 'She is to the south. In the old forest.'

'The *Belovezhskaya Puscha*,' said Ivan. 'It is the oldest

remaining forest in Europe. It stretches from Poland, through Belarus, into Ukraine.'

Billi cursed. 'Better call Dad and tell him he's at the totally wrong end of the country.'

'I am telling the truth, I swear it,' said Koshchey, his old arrogance slowly returning.

He was, she could tell. They had found Vasilisa. Billi's heart surged, but she couldn't let it show. After days of stumbling in the dark, hope glimmered inside her. They had their chance. Koshchey smirked, knowing she believed him and thinking he had saved himself. A Templar's word was their bond and Billi would not break hers.

Billi looked at Ivan and nodded slowly. 'He's all yours.'

'W-w-wait!' Koshchey stuttered, his face ghost-white. 'You gave your word.'

'And I'm keeping it,' Billi answered in a flat, pitiless tone. She drew the collar of her red coat tighter. 'Ivan's not a Templar.'

Ivan pulled his own pistol from his waistband.

'Please, Tsarevich.' Koshchey clasped his hands together. 'Where is the honour in this? To murder a defenceless man?'

Ivan paused. The pistol was in his grip and his finger rested in the trigger, but he looked up at the big man opposite. 'Honour? I thought you said honour was for fools.'

'I am the fool, Tsarevich.' Koshchey leaned forward, his knuckles whitening as he squeezed his hands together. 'You are Tsarevich Ivan Alexeivich Romanov,

I am nothing. Think what your father would have done. He would not have permitted this . . . execution.'

'I . . .' Ivan hesitated, just for a moment.

Koshchey bellowed incoherently and sprang forward, barrelling into Ivan. Lance grabbed at the huge man, but Koshchey swung the Frenchman against Gwaine, who crashed into the back of Elaine. The car swerved as she momentarily lost control and Koshchey kicked the side door open. Lance grabbed him as he jumped and both of them tumbled out.

Elaine slammed on the brakes and Gwaine leapt out, Billi a second behind him.

The three cars behind accelerated.

Koshchey and Lance tumbled down the high verge, taking a small avalanche of snow with them. Gwaine glanced back at the cars, then grabbed Billi.

'Go back! Now!' He pushed her towards the van, then leapt off the road after Lance and Koshchey.

Bogatyrs rushed out of their vehicles and made their way down to the two struggling men.

One of the cars swung around and came towards Billi, blinding her with its headlights.

Gunfire deafened her left ear as Ivan shot at the approaching car. It swerved savagely and skidded to a halt. Ivan took a few steps forward, his black coat swirling around him, as he coolly fired the entire magazine into the car's engine and lights, oblivious to the gunfire coming at him. The pistol empty, he tossed it away and took Billi's hand.

'Come on,' he ordered, pulling her away from the verge.

Billi glanced down, hesitating, hoping that Lance and Gwaine were clambering back up. But all she saw were indistinct shadows fighting in the snow, and she was unable to tell Templar from Bogatyr.

Billi ran into the car, slamming the doors shut just as they were raked by gunfire. Billi and Ivan huddled together on the floor as the four-by-four accelerated under the hailstorm of bullets. She buried herself against him and didn't look up until they were far away.

CHAPTER 28

The ring of Soviet-era tower blocks gave way to snow-cloaked fields and after an hour Ivan directed Elaine down a side road through the woods. Billi saw a light two-seater aircraft rise from behind the shield of trees and moments later they came to the gates of a small airfield.

Ivan's window rolled down as he greeted the security guard, who took more than a little interest in the bullet-punctured vehicle. They talked briefly, then Ivan took off his Rolex and handed it over. The guard pocketed the watch and waved them through.

'We fly south from here,' he said.

'You know how to fly?' Ivan obviously took his James Bond pills every morning.

'Doesn't everyone?' He pointed at a single-storey concrete building to the left. 'Canteen. Fill yourself up with something hot. The goulash is good.' He headed towards the hangar. 'Let me freshen up and then I will sort out a plane.'

The canteen was rough and ready. Posters of aircraft

and old Soviet airshows hid the majority of the awful brown and yellow wallpaper. There were four chipped Formica tables with plastic fold-out chairs stacked up against each. Two men – mechanics judging by their greasy overalls – sat at a table, smoking and reading the paper. On the side of the counter was a large jar filled with loose change. On it was stuck the word 'Vesuvius'. The whole world was joining in with mourning the loss of the Italian city, little realizing what was still to come if the Templars failed.

Billi and Elaine each ordered a bowl of goulash and a cup of tea and sat by the window. Billi faced the doorway, keeping her eyes peeled.

'What are we going to do?' asked Elaine. She was busy trying, and failing, to light her breakfast cigarette. Billi took the lighter from her shaking hands and applied it.

Elaine took a long drag of her cigarette and closed her eyes.

'We'll be OK, Elaine,' Billi reassured her. She reminded herself that Elaine was mostly back-of-house research, a glorified librarian really. This sort of fieldwork was way out of her comfort zone.

'Yes, just give me a minute,' said Elaine. She nodded, like she was agreeing with herself.

Above the door was a clock, just coming up to eleven thirty. Billi wanted her bed, but it looked like that wasn't going to happen. She got up. She needed to splash some water on her face and get thinking about their next step. She found the washroom and went in.

223

Ivan was leaning over a steel basin in front of a mirror. His shirt hung over a radiator and his wet back shone like marble under the stark, white fluorescent lights. He ran his hands over his bristling hair, sighing wearily. Then he raised his arms and turned slowly, looking at the marks Koshchey had given him. He gently pushed his finger against the row of bruised stomach muscles. Then he saw Billi, watching him in the mirror.

'Er . . .' said Billi, mortified at being caught out.

Ivan said nothing and turned his attention back to his bruises. He leaned closer to the mirror, checking the swelling on his cheek. Water dripped off his chin; small, sparkling droplets glistened on the surface of his neck.

'What do you think?' he asked. He struck a pose, flexing his biceps like a body builder. 'You can touch me, if you like.'

Billi laughed, grateful to Ivan for breaking the tension. She handed him his shirt, finding it hard to keep her attention on his shoes. 'You'd look great even in a body bag.'

'Let us hope we never need to find out. And it's not what you wear that's important,' said Ivan as he slipped the shirt over his head. He then picked up his pistol. It was a Glock 19, one of the pair of guns he'd grabbed off the Bogatyrs. He tucked it into his waistband and patted it.

'It's all about the accessories,' said Billi.

Ivan smirked at her and left.

A few minutes later Billi returned to the canteen and joined Elaine.

'I called Arthur. He'll be on the next flight south,' said Elaine, still lost in her own thoughts. She smiled, but it was stiff and forced. 'Should be in Kiev by morning. He'll get local transport from there into the forest.'

'You OK?' Billi asked as she sat down.

Three cigarette stubs smouldered in the ashtray and Elaine lit up a fourth. 'I just needed my vitamins.'

'I didn't realize nicotine counted as a food group these days.' Billi took a sip of her tea and shifted her chair nearer. 'What was it you found out about Baba Yaga that you were going to tell me in the library before we were so rudely interrupted?'

Elaine grimaced at the memory.

'You remember how Baba Yaga had been injured?' Elaine said. 'Apparently she'd vanished at the beginning of the twentieth century, after suffering some terrible injury. That first made me suspicious. I looked up events around that time, natural disasters mainly.' Her eyes brightened. 'And I found a *big* one. The Tunguska blast.'

Tunguska? Why did that ring a bell? Hadn't Vasilisa said her great-grandmother had been there?

'What was it?' Billi asked.

Elaine spread out her arms. 'A meteor. Just ten metres across. It hit the forest region of Tunguska in 1908 and wiped it out. If the rock had hit London, the entire city would have been obliterated.' Elaine leaned closer, whispering but excited. 'Baba Yaga *is* Russia. What happens to the land happens to her. That meteorite impact must have sent shockwaves, psychic shockwaves, into the old crone, nearly killing her. I believe she's spent the last hundred years healing.'

'So we need to stand Baba Yaga under the next meteorite strike? There's going to be one in the next two days? And you know where?'

Elaine screwed the cigarette into extinction. 'This is sympathetic magic, Billi. That meteor injured Baba Yaga once. A connection has been established between her and that meteor. Now if I'm right, any piece of that rock, however small, will have the same effect on her as the whole meteor.'

Billi laughed. 'It's just like homeopathy. You dilute the medicinal mixture in more and more water, but the potency remains. That's it, isn't it?'

Elaine frowned. 'That's not the comparison I would have chosen, but yes, that's it. The rock injured Russia; it will injure Baba Yaga.'

'So we need to go to Tunguska and find a lump of space rock? Fat chance of that, Elaine.' Billi shoved her bowl away. 'Bloody hell, that's worse than useless. We've two days, Elaine, just two.'

Elaine took a picture from her back pocket and unfolded it. 'After the blast locals explored the crater and picked out bits of the meteor. Made carvings with it and sold them to tourists and scientists who'd come to investigate. I'd hoped, by staying in Moscow just for another day, I might have been able to get to some museum or antiquities shop and buy one. Or steal one.' She slid the picture, torn from a book, over to Billi. 'That is how we *could have* defeated Baba Yaga. It was taken at a market in Tunguska.'

The photo was a grainy black and white that showed a couple of well-dressed men standing either side of a simple, wooden-framed bazaar stall. The table was half-hidden in shade, but one of the men held out a small stone carving. A carving of a crude, big-hipped woman.

'Oh God. A Venus figurine,' Billi gasped. She held the photo in her quivering fingertips.

Vasilisa's great-grandmother had *made* one. She'd put it into the heart of the *matryoshka* doll.

'I had one, Elaine, in my hand.'

'What?'

Billi stared at her palm, remembering the small stone statue lying there, maybe hoping by some magic, by her own desperate desire, that it would suddenly appear.

'Where is it now?' Elaine dug her fingers into Billi's arm. 'We've got to get it.'

Where was it? The last time she'd seen it was with Vasilisa, just before the Polenitsy attack.

'At home. It's probably lying under Vasilisa's bed.' Billi had literally let the means to defeating Baba Yaga slip through her fingers.

'We could call Rowland. Get him to search for it.'

'Even if he finds it right now, what good would that do? No way he'll get it to us in time.' Billi slapped the table. 'And send it where? The Knights Templar, care of Baba Yaga, the big cave, deep forest, Russia?'

Billi couldn't duck it any longer. It had been the default

plan from the very beginning, but she'd hoped there'd be some way out. 'We're not going to be able to save her, are we?' she said, but not to Elaine, to herself. 'Poor Vasilisa.' There was only one way to stop Fimbulwinter. But the price was Vasilisa's life.

Billi peered out of the window, her body weary and her heart heavy. Somewhere out there was a frightened nine-year-old girl, held hostage by monsters and a cannibal witch, hoping that someone, that Billi, would keep her promise and rescue her.

Perhaps there were times when Templars had to break their promises.

Ivan entered, Lance's backpack slung over one shoulder, and with some food supplies. 'The plane is ready. We should leave now, before the others find us.'

He then pulled out a brand-new mobile phone and gave it to Billi. 'Full satellite function and GPS – useful where we are going. If Lance and Gwaine escaped, you could contact them with this.'

'What's next, boss?' Elaine asked, looking to Billi.

Boss. What did she know? Billi felt like she was stumbling from one disaster to another. God, she wished her dad was here. She didn't want this responsibility. But being a Templar – this was her life. And she had chosen it.

'We take the plane south and try and find Baba Yaga's camp. Simple really.'

Elaine put her cup down. 'No time to lose then.'

'You can't come, Elaine,' said Billi. 'I'm sorry, but we

won't be needing you here any more. From now on it'll just be fighting and the Templars need you alive.'

My kind of work, not yours.

Billi addressed Ivan. 'Elaine needs to get back to London. Can you sort that out?'

'I'll make a few calls.'

Elaine started forward, wanting to say something. But she couldn't; Billi was right.

Billi held out her hand. '*Deus vult*, Elaine.'

Elaine sprang forward and crushed Billi against her chest. She had a lot of power in those scrawny limbs. She held on to her and squeezed tightly. Billi squeezed the old woman back. When Elaine eventually let go her eyes were red and watery.

'Good luck, girl.'

CHAPTER 29

Ten minutes later and it was done. Elaine would go straight to the airport and get on the next plane to London.

Billi went through Lance's backpack while Ivan took Elaine to find a taxi.

She could smell the poultices for wolf bites as soon as she opened the zipper. They were tucked tidily into sandwich bags. There was also a box of silver bullets, 9mm calibre and perfect for their pistols.

Ivan returned and led Billi out on to the airfield. The deep night sky was littered with stars, not a cloud in the sky.

'You can sleep on the plane,' Ivan said.

Billi looked at him guiltily. Even though she hadn't been thinking about it, she was exhausted. Ivan must have been feeling even worse than her; she hadn't been used as a punchbag recently. The bruise on his cheek was coming up big and shiny, but it didn't mar his good looks in any way. She glanced sideways as they walked across the airstrip. His hard jaw was fixed, his grey eyes focused on the job ahead.

Everything about Ivan radiated iron discipline. She'd seen how he'd entered the gunfight, unflinching as the bullets had whizzed around him. Then he turned and smiled, and the almost machine-like persona vanished. Another Ivan appeared. One warm and thoughtful towards others. The true noble. He took her hand.

'Here we are, Billi.'

They stopped by a small, white propeller plane. It was about six metres long, its wingspan ten. The cockpit looked like it had been built for hobbits.

'This it?' said Billi. The two-seater seemed pretty fragile.

'They were out of MiG jet fighters. This will do the job.' He patted the fuselage. 'I like to think of it as . . . cosy.'

The instrument panel was basic, just two small electronic screens and a couple of switches. The mobile phone had more functions. Ivan unhooked the headphones and started the engine. The propellers turned slowly twice, then the engine sparked. Billi felt the aircraft wanting to surge forward. The displays came on and Ivan scrolled down a series of options on one of the screens. He tapped it.

'This is the EFIS: the Electronic Flight Information System. Most of the key data is on this nowadays. Altimeter, compass, the artificial horizon, stuff like that.' He pointed at the screen next to it. 'That's the GPS. Combined with the EFIS, the thing practically flies itself.'

'How long's the trip?' Billi straightened out her coat as she settled into the cramped seat. The dark-red cloth rippled with shades of purple through to pink as she smoothed her hands over it.

I'm becoming as vain as Ivan. She found the seat belt and clipped herself in over the shoulders and across the waist.

'Depending on the tailwind, three to four hours.'

The plane started to accelerate down the runway. It lurched upward and Billi's stomach lurched downward. Wind buffeted the plane sideways and Ivan swore, both hands fast round the control column, fighting to bring the plane level. Billi's heart pounded, but then suddenly the fight was over and the plane rose smoothly away from the ground and towards the clouds.

Ivan's bruised cheek was big and shiny now, and he winced as he adjusted his headset.

'That hurt much?'

'You want to kiss it better?'

Billi smirked. 'I do that and we'll crash.'

'You have a lot of confidence in your kissing.'

'No. I just don't have much confidence in your flying,' Billi replied, looking out at the black horizon. 'So, where are we going on our first date? Somewhere special, I hope.'

'Due south to the Ukrainian border. From there we'll turn west. Then we'll find somewhere to land,' said Ivan.

'There's no airfield where we're going?'

'Don't need one for an aircraft like this. Just a straight bit of road. It'll take a few hours so why don't you get some sleep?'

They settled into silence. The engine drone filled the small cockpit, but Billi couldn't sleep. She just stared out of the window.

'So, what is the plan, Billi SanGreal?' asked Ivan, his eyes never leaving the distant horizon.

Billi almost laughed – first Elaine and now Ivan presuming she would be the one to lead.

'Don't *you* have one?'

'Me? I'm the good-looking one. You're the brains.'

'You mean the smart but ugly one?'

Ivan glanced out the corner of his eye, amused. 'I never said you were ugly. I said you were interesting-looking.'

'And I suppose you usually date supermodels?'

'I've not really thought about it, but yes. I suppose I do.'

Great. Interesting-looking versus long-legged glamazons. Not much of a contest.

'But one can get tired even of perfection.' Ivan took a hand from the control panel to brush back a strand of Billi's hair which had fallen loose. 'I like a little . . . battle-damage in a girl.'

'You think I'm battle-damaged?' Billi huffed and shoved herself further into her seat, arms crossed. 'You really know how to woo a girl.'

'Billi . . .'

'No, don't apologize. Good thing we're only looking

233

at the short term then.' Exceedingly short term. It had just ticked into Friday. Tomorrow was the full moon. No Vasilisa, no future.

'Yes. I know. That's if we fail.' Ivan's eyes turned steely certain. 'We won't.'

'I wish I had your faith.'

'Tell me what you're planning.'

'We find Vasilisa.'

'And then?' Ivan didn't look at her, but he wasn't stupid. He knew what Billi would have to do – the sacrifice she would have to make to save everyone else.

'If only we'd had a few more days . . .' Billi wondered aloud.

'What difference would that have made?'

'Baba Yaga has a weakness. The trouble is, the weapon we could use against her is back in London.'

She explained about the Venus figurine and everything Elaine had told her.

'We've got no way to kill Baba Yaga – you know that, don't you?' Billi said.

Ivan gestured at the backpack. 'Don't you have some Templar superweapon in there? I thought your Order had all these holy relics. Don't you have the Holy Grail?'

Billi's face flushed. 'Er, we did. Sort of.'

'Sort of?'

'I don't want to talk about it.'

Ivan smiled slowly, intrigued by Billi's apparent embarrassment. 'Tell me.'

Billi huffed. 'It's in Jerusalem now, but we did have it,

all safely locked away in our reliquary. We took it out once a year, at Easter.' She waved dismissively. 'Y'know, to celebrate the Resurrection and all that.'

'And?'

'And I dropped it.'

Ivan coughed loudly. 'What happened?'

'What do you think happened? It broke.'

Ivan coughed again, but struggled. 'What did your father say?'

Billi could picture it so clearly. The knights stood at the altar in Temple Church; Gwaine had gone white, still holding the velvet cushion Billi had lifted the clay cup from. She'd been so nervous. Arthur had picked up a few of the pieces.

'He said, "Better get some glue."'

Billi waited while Ivan gathered himself. He didn't say anything, but sat there, biting his lip. 'Ow,' he said.

'Still leaks a bit,' added Billi.

Ivan roared with laughter.

'Well, I'm glad you find it funn–'

The plane shook violently.

Lightning flashed in the distant cloud banks. Ivan frowned.

'Didn't see that coming,' he muttered. The clouds were heavy and angry and the winds buffeted the small plane.

'We OK?' asked Billi nervously. Ivan checked his controls.

'It's meant to be clear skies the whole way.' He studied

the storm clouds ahead. 'We don't have enough fuel to go around them.'

The plane shook from a sudden gust. The elements were making their threat known. Billi tightened her harness.

Ivan's knuckles whitened round the control column and Billi sat silently, focused on the rolling horizon. The cockpit blazed white as sheet lightning struck, and Billi saw Ivan's face, his jaw locked and sweat dripping off his ivory skin, his concentration total. She saw him breathe slowly through his clenched teeth.

Maybe we'll make it.

Then the plane plummeted as thunder exploded around them.

It didn't glide; it fell with all the aerodynamics of a brick. Ivan groaned as he fought with the control column.

'Downdraught! The winds are driving us down!' Ivan shouted. 'Hold on!' He'd lost it. The plane spun wildly. Billi's head was bashed against the side window and all she could see through the spinning haze were black clouds. Another curtain of white light broke around them and the next roar of thunder nearly blew out their windows. Through her blurred vision Billi saw treetops rapidly approaching, an endless mass of snow and a silver line – a river – glistening in the distance. Branches scratched the undercarriage and the fragile shell of the plane bucked and jolted as it skated through the treetops. A thick bough caught a wing, which sheared off, the sudden impact throwing Billi forward in her harness.

She grabbed hold of the straps and hung on with all her strength.

No! Not like this! It can't end like –

The plane spun horizontally and in the scream of crumpling metal and splintering glass, Billi's world shattered.

CHAPTER 30

CHAPTER 30

Blinking hurt. Billi tried to move, but spasms of sharp pain shot through her; it was as if she'd spent all week at the armoury, losing. Billi opened her eyes, then shook the broken glass out of her hair.

Dirt and snow filled half the cockpit. The safety harnesses had done their work, but she could feel bruises across her chest and shoulders where she'd been hurled forward and held. The engines coughed like the airplane's death-rattle.

Thick branches skewered the fuselage. A spear of wood had been driven straight through the windscreen, centimetres from her face. A bit to the left and she'd have lost her head. Instead Billi bore minute scratches from the twigs that had caught her.

Ivan was slumped in his seat, amid a tangle of cables and wires. Sparks jumped from the shattered control panel and there was a faint whiff of fuel mixed in with the cold air. One cable, still humming with electricity, hung perilously close over the hydraulic oil that pooled at their feet.

'Ivan?' Billi unclipped the harness and checked his

neck for a pulse. She couldn't see any blood, but that didn't rule out internal injuries.

'Ivan, are you OK?'

'Are we there yet?' he muttered. He had a fat new bruise on his forehead. He moaned and went pale as he tried to free himself. His right trouser leg was blood-soaked and Billi gasped when she saw the deep gash through his thigh.

'It's pretty bad,' she said.

'As they say in your language, "No shit, Sherlock."'

Billi raised an eyebrow – she obviously hadn't lost him quite yet. She pulled out a length of cable and wrapped a tourniquet round his leg as tightly as she dared.

'Do you know what you're doing?' asked Ivan, through gritted teeth.

'Yes,' Billi lied. She knew enough first aid to make a sling and deliver a baby – in principle. But major surgery hadn't been covered in the syllabus. 'The tourniquet will cut down the blood loss, but we've got to keep an eye on it and loosen the knot occasionally, otherwise you'll get blood poisoning.' Billi kicked open the crumpled door. 'Once we're out we'll put together a splint.'

'Then what?'

Billi sniffed. The acrid smell of melting plastic was filling the cockpit. The puddles of oil erupted in clusters of flames.

'We'll make you comfortable.' But first things first: they needed to get out, now. 'This is going to hurt. A lot.'

Ivan bit down hard as Billi dragged him out of the

cabin, hissing through his clenched teeth. Gaping holes punctured the fuselage and the rear of the plane had been torn away. Billi half-climbed out – using the aluminium frame and dense tree branches as a crude ladder. Unfortunately Ivan ended up bumping almost every branch on his way out.

'You did that on purpose,' was about all he could say as they reached the ground. She dragged Ivan away from the wreck, then clambered back up as flames began to spread across the seats.

Scrabbling in the rear among the thickening, stinking smoke, she tossed out the weapons and supplies before the heat became unbearable. Flames enveloped the front and Billi shoved herself out of the wreck on to the trees below. Dangling from a branch, she dropped the last few metres into the snow, just as the fire consumed the plane. Within minutes the tree itself was a tall burning torch.

Stepping away, Billi paused to properly examine their surroundings. They were deep in a forest, but it was unlike any forest she'd ever seen. The smell of decay was thick and pungent, even where dampened by the snow. The trees around her were thick-barked: their trunks' diameter was wider than she could put her arms around. Despite the burning plane a dozen metres away, the sense of nature's domination was overpowering. The old plane seemed like a toy next to the ancient strength of the huge trees.

'Where are we?' she asked as she cut a branch down with her kukri. Trimmed, it would serve as a crude crutch.

'On the Russian–Ukrainian border. There or there-abouts.'

'So this is it?'

Ivan nodded. 'The eastern tip of the *Belovezhskaya Puscha*. The primeval forest.'

Billi pressed her hand into the moss hanging from a giant oak trunk. 'It's beautiful.' She was awestruck, humbled, by her surroundings. The earth around her was alive. Like a dragon slumbering in winter, but huge, ancient and powerful.

Ivan continued. 'Once upon a time all of Europe was like this. From Ireland to Siberia.' He sighed as he leaned against the trunk. 'This was the world before man came along. This is what it'll return to, once we've gone.'

This is what Baba Yaga wants. A beautiful, empty planet. Billi could almost understand it. She gazed up into the dark canopy. 'We're not gone yet.'

Billi set up camp by a cave under a rocky outcrop. It was a house-sized boulder, all split by roots and covered in vines. She spread out a lattice of twigs so they were slightly off the ground, then added a layer of pine needles taken from the nearby conifers before covering it all with a plastic sheet she'd found in the plane.

She chopped down four straight sticks that she bound together on either side of Ivan's leg. But walking was agony even with the splint, and Ivan, leaning heavily on the crutch, ended up hopping to alleviate the worst of it.

'How does it feel?' Billi asked. She was starting to

241

regret sending Elaine back. She'd have patched Ivan up, no worries.

'I'm . . . fine.'

'You're such a liar.' Billi, kneeling in front of him, took a corner of the blanket and dabbed his face, wiping off the hot sweat. She smoothed the cloth over his forehead and softly over each eye. Her hand moved down his face, touching his bruised cheek.

'Ouch,' he whispered. He looked up at her. 'Now I'm not flying . . .'

'A kiss right now would probably kill you,' Billi said as she drew the cloth over his lips, slowly down his jawline to his neck. She could feel his pulse beating strongly now. 'There. All done.'

'Thank you.'

They sat facing one another, not speaking. She'd never thought she'd find anyone after Kay. Billi had buried her love under training and combat and now, with the end so near, here he was.

'There was so much I wanted to do,' Billi said, rocking back on to her heels. She raised her eyes to the stars. 'Funny, but you think it's all so endless.'

'Life is not measured in length, but in deeds.'

Billi laughed. 'More Chekhov?'

'My father.'

Billi shook out her hair. She must look a total bomb site. 'Not that I had any big plans, mind you.' She peeked at him from under the loose locks. 'Not like you.'

Ivan shrugged. 'Things didn't turn out so badly.'

'Glad you're so stoic about it. Last night you were sleeping in a four-poster bed with silk sheets; tonight you've got pine needles and snow.'

'But with you, *da*?' He smiled. 'You would have made a fine Tsarina.'

Billi scraped her hair back into a bun. 'I'm sure I would have. When you'd run out of your supermodels.'

Billi saw Ivan try to smile back, but all he could do was shake. He'd lost a lot of blood and was weak.

'We need to warm you up some more.' She picked up her kukri.

Billi quickly cut down some of the lower, drier branches and built up a fire at the mouth of the cave. It wasn't quite Davy Crockett, but it would do.

'We'll rest here tonight,' she said. She threw some more branches on to the fire. Damn it! They were so close. She stared into the forest. Vasilisa was in there somewhere.

She picked up her satellite phone and called her father.

The reception was awful, but she could just hear his voice. He sounded like he was down a mineshaft, shouting up.

'Billi? Where are you?'

'We've been delayed. Badly.'

'You OK?'

Billi looked at Ivan. His face was bloodless and his mouth drawn into a tight grimace. He wasn't going anywhere fast with that leg. She needed to find Vasilisa and he'd only slow her down.

'Don't worry about us,' she said. Ivan flinched as she

spoke. She couldn't risk the Templars wasting time looking for them. Vasilisa was the priority. 'Where are you?'

'En route. Elaine called and filled me in. But I found Vasilisa's granny.'

'And?'

'You know most of it. Baba Yaga disappeared right after the Tunguska meteor strike.' Arthur huffed, probably angry that they'd had the means to destroy Baba Yaga – the Venus figurine – and not realized. 'But the old granny gave us some useful advice. Baba Yaga is strongest in the wilderness; the deeper she lives in the forest the more powerful she becomes. So the opposite is true; she's weakest in cities. It makes sense. That's why she relies on the Polenitsy; otherwise she would have come for Vasilisa herself. Take her out of the woods and we may have a chance against her.'

'We could kill her?'

'We could try.' He sighed. 'But it's a bloody big risk if we're wrong. Stick to the plan, as agreed.'

Billi bit her lip. There was no escaping it. 'We still need to find Vasilisa.'

'There's a wolf reserve deep in the forest. And an extensive cave network in that region. If she's anywhere, it's there. I'll text you the coordinates.'

So many pieces were coming together – Baba Yaga's weaknesses, the location of the wolves – but was it too late? Without the Venus figurine, the small lump of meteor from Tunguska, they were missing the biggest piece. Billi looked at her dad's coordinates and checked the map. The boundary of the wolf compound was ten miles away. The sun would be up in a few hours and she could get going. Ten miles through dense snow? It would take four or five hours.

But that meant leaving Ivan. He sat quietly, gingerly settling his leg in the least painful position. They'd only known one another for a few days, but she'd come to depend on him. She wouldn't abandon him; she'd find a way to make him safe before she went. Maybe things would be clearer in the morning.

Billi turned and picked up her pistol and emptied the magazine, throwing the 9mm rounds into the bushes. The steel-jacketed bullets were man-killers, but she needed wolf-killers. She loaded in fifteen of Lance's silver bullets.

Ivan groaned as he eased himself against the rock. The alcove under the rock was cold, but with enough pine branches the worst of the wind was cut off.

Billi shuffled in next to Ivan and checked his splint. Then they huddled together under blankets while using the flight map and GPS to establish their approximate position. South was the Pripyat River that crossed through into Belarus and Ukraine beyond. Maybe, if the river wasn't totally iced up, they could organize a lift from a boat. Or at least Ivan could. Billi still had work to do.

The leg looked even worse in the firelight. Billi had done her best to patch the deep cut, but the crude bandages, torn strips of blanket, were already soaked. Ivan just lay there, eyes closed, utterly still. No breath stirred. Billi touched his hand.

Her heart seemed to stop. It was ice-cold.

'Ivan?'

'Mmm?' His eyelids fluttered and opened.

'Just checking.'

Thank you, God.

He looked up at her, grimly determined, grimly hanging on. Ivan wasn't going to die tonight.

Billi swallowed back her tears. Not like this. She'd already lost Kay – she wouldn't lose Ivan too. Whatever was ahead she would face it with Ivan, together. No matter what.

Then she sat, listening to the trees groaning in the wind.

'Tell me about Arthur,' said Ivan. He lay against the rock, gazing into the fire.

Billi lowered the scarf she'd wrapped round her face. 'What makes you think I want to discuss my dad with you?'

Ivan laughed. 'Billi, what difference could it possibly make now?'

The flames waved and hissed as the snowflakes danced. Her father had brought her up ever since her mother had been murdered. 'It's been him and me since I was five.'

'Is that why you wanted to be a Templar? To be like him?'

Billi shook her head. 'No. He made me join the Order. I hated him.'

Hated him. Yes, it was true. She had hated him for years.

Her training had begun at ten and it had been brutal. Most of the scars Ivan had seen had come from her countless hours in the armoury. *The more you bled in practice, the less you bled in battle.* That's what her father believed. So, she'd practised with swords, with daggers, with anything that could be called a weapon. Again and again she'd turned up at school with bruises or cuts, even with a broken wrist once. But her dad had only pushed her harder. So when the time came she'd be ready.

And the time *had* come, sooner than expected. She'd faced the Angel of Death and she had been ready.

'Then I understood why my father was the way he was. I saw things differently.'

'What changed?' Ivan shuffled closer, adjusting the blanket so it covered them both.

'Kay. The boy I killed.' She closed her eyes and there he was.

She stares into his eyes as creeping death turns them dull. His blood is warm on her hand as it trickles along the blade and his chest slowly rises, then sinks.

'It's OK, Billi,' he says. His breath is warm with fading life.

Then his breath stops.

'I loved him and I killed him. I had no choice.' Billi felt her chest tightening.

'Is that how you feel now? That you have no choice?' Ivan put his hand on Billi's. 'That to stop Baba Yaga you must kill Vasilisa?'

Billi sighed and gazed deep into the flames.

'This is what your father would do, yes?'

'Maybe my dad's way is the only way.' Billi blinked and drew her sleeve across her face.

Elaine's clues to destroying Baba Yaga were useless without the figurine, and they were running out of time and options. Billi had to prepare herself. She had to be more like Arthur: cold and heartless. That seemed to be her future, no matter what. To be like her father. Just like her father.

'That is a sad way to live, I think.'

Billi turned sharply, but she could see Ivan didn't mean it as a criticism. Just a fact. There was no arguing with the truth.

'For a Templar, it's the only way,' she answered. She was afraid of what he must think of her. But Ivan said nothing. He just put his arm round her.

'My father had noble ideals. He knew that evil had to be fought and that good men died.' Ivan stared into the flames, lost in old memories. 'I wish I had fought beside him.' He looked at Billi, smiling softly. 'I will fight beside you, Billi.'

He trusted her and Billi was grateful for that.

The night had become eerily silent. Billi hadn't noticed the gale die away, but now her breathing seemed to be the loudest thing in the forest. The fire was going well; the flames cast their caressing heat over them both and the rock face glowed with soft orange light.

Billi closed her eyes as Ivan brushed loose strands of hair away from her face and his fingertips grazed her cheek. He kissed her forehead, his lips leaving a warm imprint on her skin. Billi raised her head and felt Ivan's lips press down on to hers, as his hands went to the back of her head, urgently pulling her closer. If the world ended tomorrow, at least she'd have this.

The snow crunched as a weight settled on it.

The musty smell of the forest was joined with a new odour: the arrival of a hunter.

Billi sprang up, staring into the darkness. She held out her hand and without saying anything Ivan slapped the Glock into her palm. The flames from the aircraft had withered to a few smouldering embers, but the shallow circle was still lit by their dull, golden glow. Beyond it was a dark tapestry, impossible to penetrate.

'Get up.' The hairs on her nape stiffened as the barest breeze whispered out of the encompassing blackness like a curse. It was cold, and on it was the stench of blood.

A lone wolf stepped into the clearing. The tree branches overhead cast a net of phantom light and darkness over its silvery fur so it looked as if it was built of shadows. Its lips turned up on either side of its snout revealing long, ivory fangs.

Billi breathed slowly as she raised the pistol.

'You going to shoot it?' whispered Ivan.

'Just wait.'

It was pure wolf except the eyes. They were human, light brown and softly glowing in the darkness. A Loony then. Billi wondered why it wasn't in its monstrous form, half-man half-beast. Maybe over time the wolf aspect grew stronger until one day it awoke, forgetting it had ever walked on two legs. It patrolled back and forth in the shadows, wary but testing. There were about five metres between them, but Billi knew it could cover that in an instant. If the first bullet didn't kill it, then she was dead meat.

What are you waiting for? Billi cursed. *Just take a step into the light and give me one clear shot.*

But the creature's haunches stayed loose and relaxed, even though the hairs on its shoulders bristled with eagerness. It wasn't stupid.

Then it threw back its head and howled. It closed its eyes as it did, and the wild song was long, powerful and deep. Billi felt the chill sound down to her bones.

Eventually the beast dropped its head, tongue lolling in its black-gummed jaw. The sound of its cry echoed before disappearing into the sparkling night.

For a moment the forest listened silently. Even the trees stopped their incessant murmuring.

Then, out in the distance, the howl was answered.

More wolves called to the silver one, each cry adding on to and amplifying the one before. The sounds rolled over the forest like a wave, soaking them through with fear.

Ivan's fist held his crutch as if it was a club, but he stumbled, most of his strength gone. Billi scanned her surroundings.

'We have to move,' she said. She glanced at the wolf, but it was already retreating into the darkness; only its

250

glistening eyes could now be seen. It would wait for the pack, then they would attack together.

'I can't,' said Ivan. He lowered the crutch and Billi wasn't sure if he was asking for help getting up or pleading to stay.

'I can't protect us here.' It was true. The clearing meant the wolves could come, would come, from any and all directions. Even the rock she and Ivan were sheltering under was a risk; they could be attacked from above. She needed somewhere easier to defend.

'Where's this river?' Billi asked. If their backs were to the water, at least they couldn't be surrounded. It was still pretty desperate: she'd have no retreat.

'It's too far . . .' Ivan looked at her. 'You'll have to leave me here. Go without me.'

'Not bloody likely.'

Billi helped him up. She handed Ivan the pistol and picked up her knife.

'Lean on me,' she said. She pushed her left shoulder under Ivan's right armpit. He was heavy and they sank further into the snow as she took his weight. They weren't going anywhere quickly.

The howls started up again and gathered into a chorus. The wave gained in size and rose higher over the trembling forest.

How many of them are there?

They stumbled away from the crash site and into the darkness. The snow hid the roots, fallen tree trunks and potholes that covered the forest floor. Ivan barely supported himself and Billi was sweating fiercely after only a dozen steps.

They ploughed through the thick snow. Billi could hear the snapping of twigs and the crunching of paws on snow getting closer. She even caught snatched glimpses of movement beyond the tall avenues of trees. Ivan fired at the shadows, not hitting anything, but making enough noise to keep the wolves back. Billi stumbled blindly onward, ignoring Ivan's groans of pain as she resorted to dragging him by his coat. Sharp twigs scratched her, roots tripped her and branches grabbed at her. It seemed the forest itself was conspiring to hold her down.

They became tangled in the boughs criss-crossing their path and Billi fought hard to free herself. She pulled sharply and Ivan slipped. His feet cut hers away and suddenly they were both falling, sliding down an ice-coated slope. The stars spun above her head and Billi crashed on to a solid, rock-hard surface. Ivan landed beside her, groaning.

Ice. They'd hit the river and it was completely frozen. Billi glanced back at the steep bank they'd just tumbled down and saw that the trees had run right up to its edge. Beyond, maybe a hundred metres away, was the other bank and more of the same. If she could reach it, she'd have the high ground. It was a chance. A minute one.

Ivan pulled her sleeve and she followed his gaze back to the riverbank.

One by one they appeared like spirits summoned out of the forest itself. Their pelts shone pearly-white, and their eyes burned with hunger. Eight, Billi guessed, maybe more – it didn't matter.

More than enough.

One sniffed the grooved path Billi and Ivan had left as they'd slid. Its black snout wrinkled and it snarled, eager but wary of the steepness of the bank.

'Shoot it,' Billi urged.

'When it's closer,' muttered Ivan. 'This is my last bullet.'

Billi wiped her hand and settled the kukri into a good, firm grip. She peered across the ice at the wolf.

Their eyes met. It stood motionless, daring Billi to attack, its black lips curling up, revealing a sharp set of fangs. A low laugh rumbled in its throat.

C'mon, try it, it seemed to say.

Ivan cursed as he dragged himself over the ice. Billi backed up, sliding slowly, keeping the knife up and her eyes on the silver wolf.

The wolves started barking, howling and snapping; their quarry was creeping away from them and they didn't like it. The silver wolf's grin dropped and it put a forepaw on the muddy slope.

'Let's get going, Ivan,' Billi whispered.

'Don't wait for me.' But he'd got a rhythm going, a click and slide as he began to speed up, not fast, but steady. The ice creaked and Billi heard the rumble of the river beneath.

Silver ran down the slope. It slipped, its legs momentarily splaying out, and it spun slowly, unable to control its movements.

Ivan fired. The wolf rolled on to its belly and the bullet scraped across its shoulder, drawing only a yelp of surprise.

Shit.

Billi grabbed Ivan. With arms locked, they began slipping and sliding across the frozen river, their breath steaming out in sparkling clouds. Billi saw the fear in her eyes, reflected in Ivan's. The wild desperation to reach the other side.

Then Billi heard the soft patter of wolf paws and pushed Ivan away as she turned.

Silver leapt, smashing on top of her. The weight of the wolf blew all the air out of her and they crashed on to the ice. The impact jarred every bone in Billi's body and all she could do was ram her forearm into the beast's jaws as it sought out her throat. Burning pain erupted as its long fangs tore through the coat's fabric and into her flesh. Billi screamed and jammed her knife into its side; blood spurted over her hand as she twisted it. The wolf pulled her this way and that, ripping the muscle and sprinkling her blood over its coat and the ice.

'Billi!' she heard as the ice cracked like a pistol shot, sharp and sudden. The ground tilted under her and freezing water covered her face. She gasped for air and clawed for a solid hold before an orchestra of shattering sounded. Then the ice collapsed and she and the wolf vanished into the endless dark of the river.

CHAPTER 31

The freezing coldness crushes her, tightening round her lungs, squeezing the last few bubbles out, and she watches them rise like silver balls of life up through the blackness towards the vanishing light.

Billi rolled as the river surged around them, trying to twist free of the wolf's jaws. All finesse evaporated as the pair fought with desperate savagery. She clamped her teeth shut, fearfully hanging on to what little air she still held, and sank her fingers into the thick, slimy muzzle, forcing the jaws away from her face. Despite the enclosing, roaring darkness, the atavistic eyes of the wild creature bore into her. It shook her savagely, but Billi dug her knife in deeper. Claws ripped along her ribs, but she barely felt them now; her body was numb and her bones had locked into icicles.

The wolf's heavy pelt weighed it down and they began to sink. Bubbles shook out of the creature's trembling body and it jerked spasmodically, thrashing its limbs as panic took control. Its tongue lolled and its chest heaved. The fire in its eyes dimmed. As Billi kicked up she saw the wolf rolling away, loose and limp in the current. Her lungs screamed and blood pounded behind her eyes.

Vasilisa.

The stark, brilliant image of the young girl rose through her dull, slow mind. Billi kicked again, rising slowly.

She had to find Vasilisa. If Billi died now, they all died.

Still the river summoned her downward to join it.

Billi kicked again. Her limbs rose and sank limply, but the light above brightened. The river's surface was only a metre away. She could see the moon, bright and heavy and huge above her.

Billi pummelled the ice with her bare fists until her last breath ran out as a futile cry in the silent blackness of the waters.

Then the ice exploded. Jagged shards stung her face while hands dug into her arms and hoisted her out of the water. The cold air shook her back to life. Pain ran through every vein, filling Billi with beautiful agony. She curled up on the ice, shivering uncontrollably. She was in pain, and pain was for the living.

Ivan must have saved her. She turned over on to her back, her vision clouded with dizziness. A figure moved against the near-full moon and bent over her. Hot, feverish breath swamped her face, but Billi gazed up at her saviour, fighting the black sleep. She was so, so tired now, too tired even to shiver.

A pair of bright-green eyes gazed down at her. Fingers, hooked with talons, caressed her face, smoothing away her wet hair. A grey-pelted wolf, standing on two legs, spoke. Its voice rumbled as lips crudely mimicked human speech.

'Run,' said Old Grey.

CHAPTER 32

Billi ran. Teeth snapped at her heels if she slowed and rough fingers dragged her up if she fell. At first she could barely stand – she was battered and exhausted, her arm bleeding heavily. All around her were darting shadows and howling monsters. The pack, led by Old Grey, drove her into the black heart of the ancient forest. But as she went deeper into it, as the dawn sun slowly tinged the night sky with purple, Billi grew stronger.

Her heartbeat thundered and her skin burned with fever. Her body wasn't her own; something else growled deep in her guts and clawed its way through her chest, desperate to be free. Pine needles brushed her and she glowered at the fat moon face in the star-laden sky. Hot, panting breath washed over her and rough hands shoved her along the snow.

Old Grey faced her, her yellow fangs centimetres away. The other wolves gathered round her, each one eager and bristling with a hunter's fury. They bit at Billi's heels and if it wasn't for the older werewolf, she knew they'd like nothing better than to tear her to pieces. She stumbled over a half-hidden root and sprawled over the frozen earth. She wanted to stay there, push the burning fever out.

'Please,' Billi whispered. What was happening to her? A bone-chilling growl rumbled by her ear.

'Get up, Templar.'

Old Grey pulled her to her feet and pushed Billi on. They spilled into a small clearing and Billi fell under the moonlight. She stared up at the near-full orb. Its light shone down on her and passion seized her heart and she wanted to scream, to cry. To howl. Billi bit down hard; she wasn't going to free the animal raging in her breast. The Beast Within battered itself against the cage of her will.

I'm changing. How? She shook her head, trying to understand what was happening. She'd been bitten – when she was on the ice. She was infected.

Elaine had warned her that older wolves carried more potent infection. This was nothing like when she'd been scratched by the red werewolf.

I am not a beast.

She ran on. And how she ran. Suddenly the forest whispered to her. She glided over the uneven ground, her preternatural senses sniffing out the low branches, the twisted roots, the dense bramble walls. The claw wounds along her sides tingled and pulsed warmly. She felt free and flooded with power.

Bodies, hot, musty and animal, moved about her. A huge campfire blazed against the wall of trees. Billi was on fire and the cloth on her skin was suffocating. She wanted the snow to sting her skin; she wanted to feel the icy wind warp her body. She pulled at her coat, tearing off the cloth, not caring that her nails raked her arms. The fire rose higher and higher and the others danced and howled around her. A large wolf jumped at her, knocking her to the ground. It snapped at her, then scampered away. She squeezed her eyes closed.

'I am not a beast,' she whispered. She dug her long nails deeper into the iron-hard earth. 'I am not a beast.' She'd been clawed before, but she hadn't felt like this. She screamed as pain racked her body; the Beast was trying to come out, urging her to give in and transform.

No. Billi went rigid, forcing herself to stay unchanged, human. She would not give in.

The trees rustled and the ground around them trembled. A sigh stroked the fire and Billi saw the flames weaken, cringe even. An old, mangy crow perched itself on a branch above Billi, cawing. It flicked its head from side to side, watching Billi intently. One by one the wolves fell silent at the black-feathered herald's cry.

The shadows of the giant trees deepened as a figure – a darkness within the darkness – emerged.

Billi didn't need to be told – the awe and fear radiating from the Polenitsy warned her who it was. Their Dark Goddess.

Twice the size of any of them, she walked slowly, shuffling and hunchbacked, already old beyond measure. The wolves backed away from her.

Baba Yaga held out her hand. A finger uncurled and pointed a curved, black nail at Billi. Small, polished bones and stones hung from a bracelet on her bony wrist. Her face was lost behind a thicket of white hair tangled with more bones, twigs and shells. Only her eyes peered out, black and shiny as obsidian, and Billi stepped back, afraid.

Old Grey, back in human form, pulled her to her feet. The werewolf's naked body was covered with downy white fur. She squinted at Billi.

'She fights it, Great Mother.'

The witch smiled, her jagged iron teeth scraping together like rusty knives.

'She HAZZ a DaRKNEss IN herrr. *Freeeee* it. I want To hEAR *her* HOWL.' Hundreds of voices chorused the words together, all from one mouth. Voices of those she'd consumed over the countless centuries, still trapped deep within her soul. Billi clamped her hands over her ears, but the voices penetrated straight into her mind.

'The Beast is strong in her. A gift from her father,' said Old Grey.

The voices laughed.

'That GIFt did NoT *comme* from HER Faather.'

'I am not a beast!' Billi screamed.

The wolves pushed and beat her. Hard hands slapped her, pulled her hair and tossed Billi back and forth across the frozen ground. Everywhere she turned some creature barked and harried her. She was in the heart of the pack. The heady musk of the damp fur and hot breaths over-whelmed her. Women with wild, raging faces and bodies covered in woad patterns attacked her with their nails and claws. Wolves barged into her, knocking her down each time she rose. Others, half-human and half-beast, attacked her with blows and heavy cuffs, never letting Billi gather a breath. She spun in confusion.

Fight back! the Beast urged. Bite! Claw! Kill! Billi's eyes flooded red and a haze of fury roared in her head. Someone grabbed her coat collar and Billi bit deep into the furry hand. The other person yelled, but Billi shook her head savagely, tearing into the flesh. She felt the blood fresh and hot on her tongue. It tasted good.

Billi threw herself away from the melee, stunned, her head spinning and her legs weak and made of rubber. She spat the blood out, wiping out her mouth with her fingers to remove the taint of the rich, mouth-watering smell.

'I am not a beast!' she screamed.

Billi fought back, but steadily weariness took hold of her. There were too many. The dark-pelted wolves climbed over each other to get to her. The feral women formed a small circle round her and there was Old Grey, the leader of the pack, gazing at her with cold fury. Billi's arms became heavy and her reflexes dull. Unsteady but standing, Billi faced them, head low, breathing heavily, gasping down air. She flexed her fingers and snarled. The monsters crowded round her. But then Billi swayed as the ground under her pitched. Her vision became blurred and she sank to her knees.

'I am not a –'

CHAPTER 33

'Billi. Wake up.'

Billi groaned. She felt warm and safe like she'd been buried under the earth. She belonged down here. But the voice persisted.

'Billi. Wake up.'

She moved, but it was hard. Her chest throbbed dully and she could only take tiny sips of breath. She touched her ribs gingerly and found that tight bandages covered her chest. Every bone ached and every muscle burned, sending sharp spikes of agony along her nerves. Billi gritted her teeth and pushed, forcing herself up. It was hot work. Billi blinked as she emerged. The orange light from an oil lamp flickered on the walls of a nomadic Mongol tent – a *ger* – and weak sunlight shone through the partially open door flap. She hadn't been buried; she'd been lying under a pile of smelly sheepskins.

Ivan sat to one side.

'Welcome back,' he said, his face awash with relief. He looked tired, but well.

263

His leg had been reset and bound in a neat splint and there was colour in his cheeks again. He'd been given fresh, clean clothes. An embroidered shirt and heavy woollen trousers. Around his waist was a red sash. He wore a heavy Mongol coat draped over his shoulders – glossy, dark-blue silk with wool lining. He looked like he'd stepped straight out of some Victorian romance. An old wooden crutch lay on the floor behind him.

He handed her a ladle filled with water. Billi emptied it in a gulp and Ivan refilled it. She looked at her hands, almost expecting her nails to have turned to claws, but no, nothing had changed.

'You didn't give in to it,' said Ivan, passing over the ladle again.

But God, did that water taste delicious. She licked her lips, savouring the slight earthy flavour that lingered on her tastebuds.

There was also a bowl of steaming broth, chunks of freshly cooked mutton floating in the viscous gravy. Billi emptied it in seconds, then licked her fingers clean. She caught Ivan's disapproving look.

'Sorry.'

She closed her eyes and breathed deeply. The air swam with scents: of sweat and cooking, of the almost fruity perfume of leaded petrol and of deliciously smoky mutton.

'How long was I out?'

'Half a day. It's Friday evening,' replied Ivan.

'Running out of time,' said Billi. When the moon rose

tomorrow Vasilisa would die, and the world would die with her.

She'd fought off a change already, but tonight under the moonlight the urge would come again, stronger than before. And tomorrow, under a full moon? She'd transform.

Billi looked at the neat, clean bandages on her forearm, where she'd been bitten. But these weren't Elaine's poultices; these were plain cloth. 'I need my backpack,' Billi said. More than enough of Elaine's magic patches in there.

Ivan shook his head. 'They threw everything into a bonfire.' He leaned nearer. 'Just hang on, Billi. Don't give in. Your father knows where we are. He'll come and he'll bring more of Elaine's bandages.'

'And if he doesn't?'

'Then will it matter what happens? To any of us?' Ivan pondered the next bit. His chin rested on his fist and he looked at her. 'But I will stick with you. You know that, don't you?'

'Even if I become . . . one of them?'

'You will always be who you are, Billi SanGreal.'

She could hear voices around her, speaking in a mixture of languages and accents. People laughed and argued and coughed and cursed. The snow outside her tent crunched with approaching footsteps.

Svetlana threw open the tent flap wide and came in. She was holding a girl's hand.

Vasilisa gave a cry of delight and bundled herself against Billi. The two embraced.

265

'I knew you'd come, Billi,' she whispered. 'I just knew it.'

For a moment Billi just hugged the girl. Maybe all the pain and hardship had been worth it.

But then Billi pulled her back, away. Vasilisa continued to smile brightly. She trusted Billi totally.

She doesn't know why I'm here, Billi thought. *She thinks I've come to save her.*

In spite of the cold the child wore a white summer smock, beautifully embroidered with green vines and delicate flowers. Her hennaed hands were bound with golden bracelets and several necklaces hung from her neck. They were strung with beads, decorative stones and uncut gemstones. Her blonde hair had been arranged with seven or eight braids, each threaded with gold wire and old coins. On her feet she wore red slippers with curved toes, the felt decorated as lavishly as her smock.

The Polenitsy valued their Spring Child.

'Don't you feel cold?' asked Billi as she held out a blanket. The smock was as thin as a handkerchief and the girl's legs were bare. Vasilisa shook her head.

'Not any more.' She scratched her arm. 'She's shown me how, Billi. How to change what I am. It's like the wind, the snow.' She passed her hand over the lamp flame. 'Fire even. It doesn't touch me.'

'Baba Yaga?' Billi whispered. What other changes had the witch wrought on the little girl?

Svetlana hissed and Vasilisa shuddered. She glanced

over her shoulder at the Polenitsy, then nodded. 'Yes, the goddess has shown me what I am.'

Billi brushed Vasilisa's hair out of her face to get a good look at her. She was fresh and well-fed, but she had changed – she looked at Billi with wise eyes.

Vasilisa turned to Ivan. He'd been watching it all silently. Now he stood and gave Vasilisa a warm smile.

'They say you are a prince,' said Vasilisa. 'You look like a prince.'

'I am Ivan. It is a pleasure to meet you, Vasilisa.'

Billi's clothes had been swapped for a white shirt and baggy cotton trousers. She got out of bed and her legs almost gave way. Ivan grabbed her. She was still weak from last night's battering. 'I need something to drink,' she muttered. She licked her lips. 'More food too. Meat.' Her tongue ran over her teeth. She wanted to tear at a big, juicy steak.

Billi didn't miss the look from Svetlana. Billi was turning into one of them, but the young woman saw only a rival. If Svetlana wanted a fight, that was just dandy. Weak as she was, Billi's heart pumped with desire. She put her hand against her chest. She knew what would happen if she gave in to the anger. Elaine had warned her.

'It's the bite, Billi,' said Vasilisa. 'Silver Paws was one of the pack elders and her bite is particularly infectious. The other wolves are amazed that you've not transformed already. It takes a lot of willpower to fight it.'

'Are you OK, Vasilisa?' If Billi felt this bad, how must Vasilisa be feeling, with Baba Yaga so near?

The girl rubbed her head. 'SiCk, BiLLi. She *IZz*. InSide.' Her voice became distorted as dozens of others spoke through her. Billi heard the accents of other languages, of the old and the young, male and female.

Vasilisa's pixie face wrinkled and her big eyes filled with tears. Her body trembled. 'Oh, Billi. They won't stop talking.' She gazed at Billi, her voice quiet and intense. 'Please, don't let her eat me.'

Billi shot an angry look at Svetlana, but said, did, nothing. She didn't want to scare Vasilisa.

'She won't.' One way or another.

So Baba Yaga was in there, digging away. All psychics risked the voices until they grew powerful enough to shut them out. Being a telepath, Kay had had it real bad. As a child he'd spent weeks living in isolation, trying to cut off the invasion of other people's thoughts and dreams. Words and voices had spilled out of him, gibberish that had almost driven him mad. More than one asylum had a psychic patient deranged by all the voices that never quieted.

Olga entered. The old woman wore a long dress made of animal skin and decorated with beads. Her feet were in beautifully decorated fur-lined boots. Heavy, bronze bracelets rattled on her wrists and faded, blue tattoos covered her wiry, bare arms. 'The Great Mother wishes to speak with you, Templar,' she said.

The two Polenitsy put themselves between her and Vasilisa.

Olga stepped forward. 'We must go now.'

Billi stood, fixed to the spot. Baba Yaga wanted to see her. She thought of the dreaded power that had risen out of the forest. Then she'd only caught a glimpse of the Dark Goddess and it had overwhelmed her; now she was going to stand face to face with her. Goosebumps rose across her skin.

'What does she want?' Billi asked. Ivan tightened his hold on his crutch. He glanced at her and there was fear for her there.

Olga pulled back the tent flap. 'Come – now.'

They want us to be afraid.

Baba Yaga wanted to see her. That didn't sound good. She couldn't change that, but she could go either cowering, or head up. Billi steadied herself against Ivan, then let go and stood on her own two feet. Like a Templar should.

'No point keeping the old girl waiting,' she said. Olga pointed at a pair of fur-lined leather boots by the entrance. On the stool lay Billi's red coat, but it was badly torn and all the buttons were missing. She put it on and then pulled on the boots.

'You too,' said Svetlana. She grabbed Ivan and dragged him off his stool. He slapped her hand away and Red's hand sprang up, each finger tipped with an ivory claw.

'Svetlana!' snapped Olga. Slowly Red lowered her hand. Billi helped Ivan up and passed him the crutch.

'Ivan?'

Ivan wasn't listening; his attention was focused purely on Olga.

'Do you know who I am?' he snarled. Despite the injured leg, Ivan smouldered with anger; every muscle was tensed for battle and his eyes darkened like an approaching storm, like an advancing hurricane.

Billi stared at him and the old woman. *Oh Jesus*, she thought. *Olga killed his father*.

Olga nodded. 'The son of the old Tsar.'

'Son of the man you killed.'

Billi took hold of Ivan's wrist. 'We'll pick our moment, Ivan.' His head snapped in her direction and for a moment Billi thought he'd break free and attack. But then his rage cooled and he gave a single nod. He looked back at Olga.

She smiled wryly. 'And I will be waiting, boy.'

As they left the tent Billi's hair blew loose in the wind. Out of habit she tucked her collar round her neck, but she didn't feel the cold much. Was this part of the infection? The change was coming: first rage and bloodthirstiness, the emotions evolving into that of a predator. The physical change was last of all. But she couldn't give in yet. She still had work to do.

Ivan took her hand.

'Follow me,' said Olga. Billi and Ivan went next and Svetlana brought Vasilisa a few paces behind. Billi looked over her shoulder to see Vasilisa moving stiffly, eyes gazing into the forest ahead of her. Her breath came out like steam, in short, desperate gasps, clearly petrified of what lay ahead.

'Vasilisa . . .' Billi wanted to comfort her, but there

was nothing she could do. She knew it and so did Vasilisa.

The camp was large – about thirty or forty tents spread across a clearing within the heart of the forest. Lavish flags and totems hung from banners in front of most of the tent entrances. Others were customized with furs and beaded curtains, their exterior walls painted with shamanistic symbols that Billi didn't recognize.

A man with long, black hair and a heavily tattooed face stood in front of a tent that had stick figures being chased by giant wolves painted across the material, a sickle-edged moon hanging overhead. The man glanced at them, then turned his attention to a golden eagle watching from a high branch. Small, silver bells tinkled from tassels round its leg. The man raised his left fist, bound in a thick leather glove, and gave a curt whistle.

The eagle dived straight down towards them. At the last instant its wings spread, bringing it to a dead stop, and it landed delicately on the man's fist. The bird flapped its huge wings, tip to tip well over Billi's height and she wasn't short. Its feathers rippled, their sheen moving from gold to orange to deep, rich brown. Its head darted from side to side and it screamed angrily, bothered perhaps at having to come down from its royal perch high in the stars. The man gently stroked the irate bird, humming soothingly.

Next to the tattooed man were a couple of blonde Scandinavians, bearded bears of men, each wearing sleeveless body warmers. They tinkered with the engine of a twenty-year-old Land Rover.

'All werewolves?' Billi asked.

Olga shook her head. 'No. These men are merely consorts. Our bite awakens only women,' she answered with a hint of pride.

'Turns them into monsters, you mean?'

Olga smiled at her. Billi had thought she'd be angry, but the old woman seemed to find Billi's comment amusing.

'Tomorrow you will feel differently, I promise you.'

They left the light of the campfires and entered the surrounding forest. The darkness didn't bother Billi. She could see the black roots, the frost-coated rocks, the patterns on the bark. Large boulders, dropped here from some glacial retreat, bore ancient claw marks and faint traces of paintings – strange spiral patterns and images of beasts and witches.

Women were starting to gather round a huge rock. Old, young, something in between, they stalked through the trees, covered in paint, covered in tattoos, covered in beads and skins and power. They were of all nations and races. Fair Scandinavians and dark Africans. Black-haired Mongolians and brown-skinned women from the Indian subcontinent and the East. But they had abandoned their past lives when they'd become part of the Polenitsy, part of a more ancient, primeval identity. Their long locks blew wildly in the wind. One crouched above them on a branch, feathers and small bells hanging from her golden-brown hair.

The women came close, silently watching their

progression towards the rock. Billi felt giddy, drunk. She held tightly on to Ivan, shaking her head to stop the silent calling that rose from the women, the Polenitsy. It wasn't audible; she could only feel it in her deepest heart.

One of us.

Deep down inside her the Beast Within snapped at its chains, the links weakening. The clothes on her back were pulling her down. She wanted to tear them all off and go running and hunting and feasting with her sisters.

One of us.

Sisters? Billi stopped herself. No. She wasn't anything like them. They were monsters. The Beast Within was trying to trick her.

They parted as they came within a few metres of the house-sized black rock. Frost-covered moss and ivy shimmered on its surface. Billi spotted faded patterns and worn-out engravings under the ivy, but they were too weathered to make out. The Polenitsy retreated into the forest, but Billi knew they weren't far. She could join them whenever she wanted.

'Below,' ordered Olga.

At the base of the rock was an opening, a hole leading into the earth. It was almost invisible under the deep shadow of the boulder. Olga led the way, followed by Vasilisa. Svetlana pushed Billi, who spun and shoved the red-haired girl back.

Svetlana crouched, her loose hair framing her face. She had deep-red lips and was as tall as Billi, but more muscular. However, her powerful physique only made her more feminine, not less. Her features were strong and dominated by her green eyes, set above high, hard cheekbones.

Billi gritted her teeth and hissed. She wanted nothing more than to rip that mocking smile off her face. Ivan grabbed her wrist, pulling her back.

'We'll pick our moment,' he said. Svetlana snorted with derision. But he didn't let go until Billi had acknowledged him. Then he released her as she turned back towards the hole and slid down.

The passageway was too low to stand in, and the rocks it was made of were uneven and undulating, probably shaped by an ancient underground stream. The narrow channel was lit by candles that sat in small, chiselled-out alcoves. Above them was a gallery of artwork from prehistory. There were massive bulls with huge arched horns, and charcoal-outlined mammoths strolling across the ancient stone. Small, pot-bellied horses galloped over the rock, full of vivid detail and motion.

The animals were lavishly coloured with rich shades of ochre, reds and yellows. The outlines followed the shape of the walls so they seemed almost ready to break out of the rock and take living form. Matchstick hunters darted back and forth, throwing their puny spears and darts. The animals were drawn and painted with such love and beauty, but the humans were featureless and pathetic.

Feet scuffled overhead and Billi realized that the passage had opened up. More Polenitsy moved along natural ledges higher up on the walls, watching Billi and her party. All women, despite the men in the camp. They were marked by symbols, bones and decorations that were prehistoric and simply beautiful. Polished stones hung off twine necklaces and small, carved animals dangled from their braided locks.

'Babushka,' called Olga. She raised her hand and all movement ceased.

Water chimed ahead, echoing in the large space.

Billi caught her breath. The air trembled as though the Earth itself was sighing. Ivan came next to her. His own face was open with wonder as he gazed at the ancient artwork surrounding them. He touched the head of one of the bulls, tracing the curve of its horn with his fingertips.

Olga entered and they followed. Billi gasped at the size of the innermost chamber. The entire Temple Church could have fitted in here without touching the top or sides. The roof formed a high dome and around the widest part ran a deep ledge, decorated by huge crystalline formations that glowed deep ochre. Ten-metre-long stalactites dripped water into sparkling pools.

Olga led them down the ledge to the largest pool and they stopped at its edge. Thick columns of the same glowing crystal formed a forest of stone where the Polenitsy lurked. The walls were decorated with paintings and carvings of flying reptiles, man-beasts, huge monsters with wings and claws and humans with the heads of animals. The walls were marked with grooves where the wolves had sharpened their claws.

'Babushka,' repeated Olga.

Something moved through the crystal labyrinth. *Clack clack clack* went a staff of bone. Bare feet with leathery soles shuffled along the stone. The Polenitsy hissed and went to their knees.

Red shoved Ivan down on to his knees, and he stifled a cry. Billi knelt unbidden; it just seemed right. She was in the presence of the goddess. Only Vasilisa and Olga remained standing.

Invisible waves of energy rippled across the vast chamber and each one shook Billi to the core. She put her hands into the water, but fought to keep her head up. The weight of the goddess's presence was overwhelming.

This was why man feared the dark. From the earliest times he'd known something wild lurked just outside the flickering flames of his cave, with the beasts and the monsters. The Dark Goddess.

She shuffled into the faint candlelight and the shadows deepened around her. She walked hunchbacked, but even so was four metres high. Rags covered her skeletal frame, animal skins and ancient furs. Insects scuttled in her floor-length white hair that formed a veil over her face. Only the eyes peered out. Black, shiny, ancient. Her nails – long, curved daggers – clicked against her bone staff.

'*Com*e, MY **little** OnE.'

Vasilisa hesitated, and glanced back at Billi. But Billi

couldn't help her. Vasilisa crossed the pool to take the withered hand of the ancient witch.

Baba Yaga drew Vasilisa into her arms and laughed. It sounded like the crackling of dry sticks on a fire, or of river water battering against rocks and cliffs. It rose and now it was a bonfire, piled high and blazing. The surrounding stone bounced the laughter in from all directions so she laughed with a chorus.

CHAPTER 34

Billi entwined her fingers with Ivan's, holding tightly to try to stop herself from shaking.

Baba Yaga shuffled through the pool and peered at them.

'WhO Are *you*, DAughterrr?' she asked. There were ten thousand voices on her tongue. With Billi's acute hearing she could differentiate some. Men, women, children. Some were nearly articulate, while others screamed incoherently. All Baba Yaga's victims. No wonder Vasilisa was terrified, standing in the clutches of the witch.

'Billi.' Her own voice cracked with fear. She cleared her throat and tried again, pushing some courage into her lungs. It wasn't easy. 'Billi SanGreal.'

'A wolf-killer,' added Svetlana.

Baba Yaga's breath rolled like an icy wind over Billi's face. Her talon-like nails *click click clicked* and Billi was painfully aware of how any one of them could rip clean through her chest and out the other side. Ivan rose and took a step forward. His face was a mask of fear, but he stared at the Dark Goddess, determined and defiant.

'She did it to save me,' he said.

Baba Yaga's attention snapped towards him, and she stroked his throat with her cold nails.

Red spoke. 'They are to be punished, Great Mother. They killed Silver Paws, an elder.' She glanced back at Billi, smiling. 'Give me the honour, I beg you.'

'Babushka, she is my friend,' said Vasilisa, her small voice ringing through the cave. She looked up desperately at the old witch.

'We're here for the girl,' said Ivan. 'Let us take her and there will be no more trouble. It will be better for you.'

Billi looked at Ivan, shocked. *What the hell was he talking about?*

'There are hundreds of Bogatyrs on their way,' said Ivan. 'And Templars. With swords, axes and guns. You will be destroyed.'

It was one hell of a bluff, but Billi remembered the mural Koshchey had shown her back at the Ministry, and his tales about how the Bogatyrs of old had fought Baba Yaga before and driven her into the forests. If there was any fear in that black heart, maybe the memory of the Bogatyrs would reach it.

But if the old woman felt any trepidation, she did not show it. She swayed, her white hair trailing back and forth, and the twigs and bones knotted into the strands rattled and clattered together. She idly tapped her staff as she held Vasilisa.

'*Man* iZz a DEStroyer.' She tugged a small bone in her wiry hair, a curiously childish action. 'BuT so Izz

279

Nature.' Baba Yaga looked at Billi and there was a gentleness, a pity in her stony eyes. 'I gave BirtH to Maan, I DElivereD hIM to the World, OUT of his Fear and OUT of the *DARK*nez.' She glanced at Ivan. 'HIzz time iz OVER, Billi SANgreal. It is the way of THINGZZ.'

'You can't just wipe out mankind,' said Ivan. 'It's not for you to decide the fate of an entire species.'

'Is that not what you do? How many species, races too, have become extinct because of you?' snapped Olga. 'Mankind is a plague. Look at you. You rape and pillage, you suck the Earth dry and kill all your kindred. What species has prospered under man's dominion? Not one. This Earth is not *yours*. Its bounty was to be shared by all, not devoured by one species who claimed it as their god-given right.' She spat at his feet. 'Dominion over land and sea. You sought to enslave nature. You have poisoned the very air you breathe.'

'So your answer is annihilation?' said Billi.

'Nature always wins,' said Olga. 'With the blight of man gone, nature will reassert itself. The Earth will be reborn. It always has and always will.'

'The Law, Great Mother. What of the Law?' Red stepped closer to Baba Yaga. She pointed again to Billi and Ivan, more desperately this time. 'She is a wolf-killer and the Law demands her life.'

'The *Law*, YEzzz.' Baba Yaga pointed at Billi. 'She IZZ Like yoU, SvetLANA. No *Wonder* yOU Hate herr.' She looked Billi up and down, with no more interest than she'd look at a strange insect, curious for a moment. 'YeZZ, Kill Zem *b*OtH.'

Billi gasped. She backed away, knowing it was useless. Ivan scraped up his crutch. Heart banging away, she turned slowly, her fists ready. The Polenitsy blocked the only exit.

'Great Mother, I ask a boon!' Olga's plea stopped the Polenitsy in their tracks.

The old witch raised her head, the noise of her teeth grinding echoed within the limestone chamber and it made the hairs rise up on the back of Billi's neck.

Olga lowered her gaze respectfully. 'She has been blessed by the bite of Silver Paws. The change is upon her. She will be one of the Polenitsy by tomorrow.'

Baba Yaga pointed her claw at Ivan. 'AnD ze Man-ChilD, w*Ha*tt of him?'

'He is Tsarevich Ivan Alexeivich Romanov.'

'RoMannoFF?'

Ivan gulped as the witch stepped up to him, so close they were almost nose to nose. Her throat rattled with a laugh.

'WEl*comm*e, romaNOFF.' The old crone's eyes sparkled with amusement. 'The blood of MaNy princeZZ and kingzz runz in the veinZZ of the PoLenitsee. He wOULD make a FINE *consort*, do you not tHiNk, SVetlana?'

Svetlana hissed. 'I think we should kill them now.'

The old crone glided next to Billi. She took hold of her chin and turned her face towards hers.

'The BEASt Callzz, DOes it NOT?' Baba Yaga grinned grotesquely. 'Join Uzz, BILLi sanGREAL. Join your Siisterzz.'

Billi glared up at Baba Yaga. 'I am not an animal.'

Baba Yaga laughed.

By the full moon I'll change whether I like it or not. Everything hinged on tomorrow's moon. Billi would howl and Vasilisa would scream. The Earth would vanish under a sky of fire and brimstone.

'Have you told them of Fimbulwinter?' Billi asked. 'That the wolves will die beside mankind?'

Olga started. She shot a look at the old witch.

'I HONour MY PoliNNItZzee.' The witch drew a fingernail along her chin. 'YoU Humanzz *aRe* full of LYzz.'

'Then tell us how you can eliminate mankind while keeping the Polenitsy safe.' Billi crossed her arms; it was the only way she could stop herself from trembling. Any second now the old witch was going to kill her, but she had to make the Polenitsy understand that Baba Yaga was deceiving them.

Olga stepped forward, her head low and humble. 'Great Mother. How *will* we remove the curse of mankind and save the others who worship and honour you?'

Voices rose out of Baba Yaga, troubled and discordant, no longer driven by a single will. They babbled a thousand, a million things. Baba Yaga glowered, looming over them all.

Billi and Ivan backed away and even the Polenitsy

around them moved nervously, their bare feet scraping on the smooth stone. Many fell face down, kneeling in terror at the anger of their goddess.

'SILEnZZE!' She leaned close to Olga, her long, iron fangs just centimetres from the old werewolf's face. The witch hissed. 'iT Izz NOT YouRR place to QUesTion MEEE!'

Olga bowed low. But unlike many of the other Polenitsy, she did not kneel.

'I meant no disrespect, Great Mother.'

'ReMmember who zervezz wHo, Olga. Who zervezz Who.' Baba Yaga gazed deep into each of the werewolves' eyes, a gaze full of evil malice and anger. 'I Am YouRR godDD and iT is Not fOR morTalzz,' she hissed the last word, spiteful and contemptuous, 'to QuesTion the WiLL of theirrR godZZ.'

She swung around.

Svetlana, who had been beside Olga, shot a look of anger at her grandmother, then took hold of Vasilisa.

Baba Yaga tapped her way back into the darkness of the caves. 'Go Noww.'

Only when Baba Yaga had gone did the Polenitsy start whispering among themselves. Billi watched them, perched in the alcoves and ledges above. Some glared down at her, their hate clear. How dare she question the goddess? Others looked uneasy, whispering and arguing among themselves.

Svetlana met her grandmother as she crossed the pool, pulling Vasilisa behind her.

'*Ty dolzhna byla naklanitsa pered boginyey!*' said Svetlana.

Olga looked coolly at her granddaughter. '*My zhe Polenitsy, nye ryaby.*'

Svetlana turned abruptly and stormed out. Billi caught a glimpse of Vasilisa reaching out to her with a free hand as she was dragged away. She wanted to be safe, so she reached for Billi. Hadn't Billi crossed Russia to find her? To save her?

'What did she say?' Billi asked Ivan.

Ivan's eyes narrowed as he watched the Polenitsy depart. He whispered. 'The red-haired one said she should have got to her knees before the goddess.'

Yes, that had been strange. Olga, almost alone among the Polenitsy, had remained on her feet. She had been practically defiant.

'What was Olga's reply?'

'That they were Polenitsy, not slaves.'

'Come,' said Olga, sounding weary. Three other Polenitsy came down off the ledge and escorted them back out.

Billi's mind churned over the options.

Her dad was coming, but when? He had no idea how many Polenitsy were waiting here in the forest. The Templars would be slaughtered.

There would be no last-minute rescue. She and Ivan were on their own.

The sky was darkening as Billi crawled back out. But already the moon hung over the treetops, casting its pallid light over her. Sharp pangs shot through her stomach and across her chest. The Beast Within tore at her, trying to break out of her skin.

'I am not a beast.' The pain made her drop to her knees.

Ivan bent down beside her and locked his arms round her.

Eyes closed, Billi rocked gently in his embrace. She was not a beast, not yet. She had one thing to do before it was all too late.

'I'm all right,' she said. It wasn't true; she was anything but.

Vasilisa.

It hadn't been so long ago that she'd been at home with her family, safe and ignorant of the monsters outside. Through no fault of her own, through a freak of birth, she was now at the heart of the Bataille Ténébreuse.

I'm sorry, Vasilisa.

As the Polenitsy waited impatiently beside her Billi pressed her fingers into the snow, willing the cold to leach into her blood and freeze her heart. She had to turn whatever pity, whatever compassion she might have, to ice. There was no room for it now.

There was only one way to stop Fimbulwinter.

Billi would kill Vasilisa tonight.

CHAPTER 35

Olga walked beside Billi as they eventually made their way back to the camp, her brow furrowed. Ivan had fallen a few paces behind with the other escorts; it wasn't easy getting through the snow with his injured leg.

'I suppose I should thank you. For saving our lives,' said Billi. She didn't get it, though. With all that had happened, why had the old woman protected them?

'I was honouring a debt, nothing more.'

'A debt? You owe us nothing.'

'You saved two lives. Natasha and Maria. You helped them escape the Bogatyrs in Moscow.'

The Paisley woman and the young werewolf girl. 'They were friends of yours?'

'They were Polenitsy.'

'But the woman's dead. Koshchey killed her.'

Olga nodded. 'But Maria lives. For her life I saved yours.' She slowed down, pressing her boot-tip into the snow. 'And you are now one of us. We protect our own.'

Billi shook her head savagely. 'I'll never join you. Even if I transform, why would I want to be part of this?'

Olga grabbed Billi's arm and swung her around. 'Then where will you go? Do you think the Templars will welcome you? You that are Unholy in their eyes? You will join us and live a life you could not have dreamed of. What is better than this freedom?'

'It doesn't mean anything. With Fimbulwinter to be unleashed tomorrow, we'll all be dead soon enough.'

'Fimbulwinter so you say. Who told you about Fimbulwinter?'

'Vasilisa. You must know that Baba Yaga has been sharing her mind. Vasilisa found out all about Fimbulwinter from the goddess herself.'

'No . . . that cannot be true,' said Olga, her voice wavering.

'I don't know who's worse,' said Billi to the old woman. 'That mad witch or you, for worshipping her.'

If she'd wanted a reaction, she got it. Olga knocked her off her feet with a single swipe. She stood over Billi, flexing her fingers. The nails were normal, human. She didn't need claws to tear Billi apart.

'Get up, Templar,' Olga said. 'Why do you provoke me?'

Billi got up and dusted the snow off her coat. 'Provoke? You don't think kidnapping children and planning the apocalypse is provocation?'

'You should have stayed in London.'

'Why? Because it's safer? When Yellowstone goes there won't be a place on the planet that will be safe.'

'No. The Great Mother has promised to protect us.'

Olga shook her head. 'She would not unleash such devastation on us. If what you say was true, all the world's population would suffer near-extinction. Baba Yaga only wishes to protect the natural world.'

'She's lying, Olga.' Billi met the old woman's gaze. 'She wants to wipe the slate clean and start over. She only needs a few to survive. Even if it takes another thousand years for the world to repopulate, Baba Yaga can wait.'

'Baba Yaga has promised us a spring like no other, after the Spring Child's sacrifice.'

'Yes. But it's going to be a long, hard winter before it arrives and you won't be around to enjoy it. None of us will.'

This was a dangerous game. But she'd seen Olga defy Baba Yaga, so there was some doubt in the old werewolf's mind. If Billi could exploit that, might they not gain an ally and a chance to stop Baba Yaga? Maybe not all the Polenitsy blindly believed in their Dark Goddess. They'd seen the indiscriminate devastation of Vesuvius. There hadn't been any allowances made there – the volcano had wiped out everything.

'How, Olga? How is Baba Yaga going to save the Polenitsy?'

Olga glanced back towards the cave, then at Billi. She shook her head. 'It is not my place to question the wisdom of the Great Mother.'

'That's convenient. For her.'

'Does your god answer your questions?' Olga retorted. 'I think not.'

'Then we must find our own answers.' Billi stopped close to Olga. 'We are all going to die.'

Olga huffed and pointed towards the camp. 'Move faster.' She didn't want to discuss this any more.

A guard waited outside the tent. The man, a bulky, sword-armed Mongolian, pulled the flap back.

'Make sure they do not leave,' Olga ordered before departing.

'What exactly was that all about?' said Ivan.

'It doesn't matter.'

Ivan limped up to the fire in the centre of the tent. He rubbed his hands and warmed them over the flames. 'What are we going to do?' He stared at the fire and his eyes shone with amber flames.

'If you've got a cunning plan, now would be the time to enlighten me.'

'Plan? We're trapped, Billi.' He slapped the side of his leg in frustration. 'I'm going nowhere with this.'

'Just let me think.' Billi searched the room. Couple of stools, a bed and some pots and pans. Not much. She needed to move fast, before she changed her mind.

The stool.

'We need to get out of here now,' she said. She smiled at Ivan, picked up the stool and smashed it on the ground. 'Fight me.'

'What?'

Billi kicked the table over, sending the tray and cups clattering. 'Fight!'

Ivan grabbed the bed, shouting incoherently, and

tossed it over into the flames, sending burning embers across the carpet.

The tent flap swung open as the guard stormed in. Ivan screamed and threw his crutch at Billi, who caught it. She pointed at Ivan as the smoke began to rise.

'He started it!'

The guard glanced at Ivan and Billi swung the crutch into the back of his legs. He dropped to his knees. His hand went to his sword, while Billi spun the wooden stick around and whipped herself behind him. With the staff across his throat, she buried her knee into his upper back and pulled.

'Grab his hands! His hands!' Billi ordered.

Ivan lurched forward and did so. The guard hissed and locked his neck muscles as stiff as he could, but Billi had the staff under his Adam's apple, and pulled it towards her while pushing her knee further into his back, steadily strangling him. Ivan held the man's hands out in front of him.

The man coughed, then choked. He turned his head, trying to free himself from the suffocating trap Billi had him in. He twisted, but Ivan wouldn't let go. The struggles diminished in vigour, and after what seemed like a century, his body slumped.

Billi dropped the stick and the man fell face first on to the carpet. Ivan tipped a jug of water over the smoking edges of the carpet. He used the discarded blankets to smother the small fire.

'Thanks,' she said.

'It would help if you told me what you were planning in advance.'

'No time.' Billi checked the man's pulse. Still alive. 'He'll be out for ten minutes. Gag him and tie him to that.' She pointed at one of the two stout central tent supports. The post was about twenty centimetres thick, solid pine and dug in deep.

Billi unbuckled the man's weapons belt. The sabre was an old Cossack blade, sharply curved with a single edge tapering into a stiff dagger point. It was old and certainly sharp enough to shave a few hairs off a werewolf. As well as the sabre there was a plain stabbing dagger. Ideal for slipping between the ribs.

'I'm going after Vasilisa,' she said.

Ivan didn't ask what she was going to do with her; Billi's cold tone was explanation enough.

'And after?' he asked as he tied up the unconscious man. He stood up and smiled sadly, then leaned on the support column, worn out.

Billi shook her head. 'There won't be any "after", Ivan.' She could run, but how far would she get? The Polenitsy would be on her before she'd gone a mile. They would not treat her well for having killed the Spring Child. But whatever the werewolves did would be quick; Baba Yaga would want her to suffer a longer, crueller death.

'There has to be another way.' Ivan came up to her and put his hands on her arms.

'I'm sorry I got you into this mess.' Billi tried to laugh.

'I seem to have a fatal effect on boys.' But maybe they'd let Ivan live if she did the deed alone. It was a fool's hope, but at this point any hope was foolish.

Hope that Arthur and the Knights Templar would arrive and save the day.

Hope that the Polenitsy would defy Baba Yaga.

Hope that she could save everyone without killing a little girl.

Foolish, foolish, foolish.

Billi looked up at him and saw her reflection in Ivan's grey eyes. There was warmth in what Billi had once thought was a cold and guarded gaze, which matched the emotion behind his sad smile. Billi laced her fingers with his.

I am going to die. The thought hit her like a spear. Billi squeezed her fingers tighter round Ivan's. Once she let go that was it. She took a deep breath to quell the fear mounting inside. At least she wouldn't have to live with the guilt of murdering Vasilisa. Not for long anyway.

'Let's think for just a minute,' said Ivan desperately. 'Maybe your father –'

Billi pulled herself free. Time to get it finished. 'We can't wait.' She wrapped the belt round her waist, buckling it on the very last hole and checking her weapons again. The scabbard was worn smooth and the sword came free easily.

'Get the guard's coat and hat and stand out here; they'll notice if he's missing.' Billi went to the door flap. 'Wish me luck, Ivan.'

'I wish . . .' Then he stopped. The time for wishes had run out. He straightened his clothes; if this was goodbye, he'd do it properly. He started to smooth the creases, but faltered. He touched her face gently before letting his hand fall away.

'*Deus vult*, Billi SanGreal.'

Billi left.

She looked into the darkening sky. To the west the sun's dying light covered the clouds with deep-crimson smears, the shades turning to dark purple and black in the east. The moon had vanished behind the dense clouds, giving her some reprieve. She felt the feathery kisses of snow-flakes on her cheeks. The icy wind whipped at her tattered red coat and she pulled up the collar to protect her neck, but the cold air ruffled her hair and stung her ears.

She was fifteen years old. Funny, she felt older. She'd been shadowed by death and now it had caught up with her. The warm air of the *ger* warmed her back and for a moment Billi could have turned and rushed into Ivan's arms, but that was a foolish fantasy. She was a Templar. Duty always came first.

You shall keep the company of martyrs.

Billi closed her eyes and searched the air, seeking out a scent that she recognized. The air filled with emotions, hers, the Polenitsy's. They rolled like a melange of sharp spices. Fear was peppery, eye-watering. Chilli powder rage stung her lips. Musky love swam through her nostrils.

The world of the werewolf overpowered her senses.
Humans lived in such a dull, lifeless world.

I'm human.

Her eyes snapped open.

People waded through the dense snow, their vision limited by the flurries. Nobody paid her any attention. Billi peered into the snowy veil and saw a shock of red against the white field.

Svetlana.

Well, here I come, ready or not.

She was among the trees, twenty metres away. A smaller figure followed a few paces behind. Billi tightened her grip on the sword hilt. This was it. In a few minutes it would all be over.

Billi made her way directly towards them. Step by step she pushed, never taking her eyes off them. They'd come out of a tent on the opposite side of the clearing and moved onward, oblivious to her. Svetlana held out her hand and helped Vasilisa through the whiteness. The girl still wore only a smock. At times she was invisible; at others she shone brighter than the icicles dangling off the branches. She'd been given even more jewellery, multicoloured armlets, rings, necklaces, and small crowns of woven twigs and winter flowers.

Billi clambered over a four-metre-high boulder, hauling herself by the net of vines that ran over the grey rock like veins. She reached the top and stood, her scarlet coat flapping in the icy winds. She pulled out the sabre in her right hand and settled the dagger in her left.

'Vasilisa,' she said.

Vasilisa looked up and stared. She tried to pull free of Svetlana, but the red-haired girl was too strong.

'Billi . . .' Vasilisa pleaded. 'Help me.'

But the young Polenitsy understood that Billi wasn't here to save her and pushed the small girl on to the ground behind her. She smiled, revealing her long canines.

'Death in red,' Svetlana said. 'My favourite colour.'

Svetlana cast off her coat. She was naked except for the downy red hair that covered her broad shoulders and thick upper arms. She stalked forward, flexing her fingers. 'Come down here and die, Templar.'

Billi leapt.

Svetlana changed in a heartbeat. Two bounds and she had transformed into a raging monster, the beast Billi had first seen in Thetford. The hulking half-human, half-wolf creature had dense, heavily muscled arms and long, ivory claws, each tipped to needle-point sharpness. It threw back its shaggy head and howled. Billi slammed down in front of her and waited until she could feel the claws cutting the air, then dived sideways, slicing horizontally to open the wolf's belly. But Svetlana stopped dead and the blade's edge just scraped her furry pelt.

Billi rolled in the snow, but was up instantly. The Beast Within arose: pure rage flooded her and she stabbed. This was what it wanted. It smelt death and wanted it badly. Billi didn't fight with skill or grace; the battle was for blood, for blood's sake. Svetlana took a nick on her ribs while swiping at Billi's face. Billi stabbed upward with her dagger, but Svetlana dragged her claws across Billi's wrist, forcing her to drop it.

A red mist filled Billi's eyes and her human self shook under the assault from the Beast. She had to control it, bend that power to her advantage, use the Beast rather than let it use her. If she fought mindlessly, on Red's terms, she was going to lose. She focused her attention on her sabre, on her training, on fighting like a knight, not like a beast.

Something ripped at her leg and she vaguely saw three red lines through her torn trousers. Instead of backing off, Billi screamed and hurled herself at the young woman. They fell and Billi landed on top. She heaved the sabre down across Svetlana's neck. Svetlana grabbed the blade and held it, trying to force it away from her. Her fangs snapped centimetres from Billi's face.

Billi's arms quivered with fury and she forced her full weight on to the weapon, which sank closer to the were-wolf's throat. She grinned. She'd never felt so strong. Billi could see every hair on the werewolf's body and each bead of sweat on her brow. The blade began to break the creature's skin and a warm, single drip of red sprang from the wound. Billi wanted to lick it.

The Beast Within howled.

Svetlana hurled her off. Billi tumbled through the snow and crashed against a large rock, then scrabbled to her feet, hand still gripping the sabre. She raised the sword two-handed over her head. Her skin was burning from the fire within her. Bones ground together as they fought between human and wolf form. Her grip shook violently as the transformation spasmed through her.

Oh God, no.

The moon, almost full, shone bright within the blanket of black sky. Billi wanted to tear off her clothes and bathe in its ivory stare, to let it carry her away into the deep forest, away from humanity and all the ties that bound her. To be free.

Then Billi saw Vasilisa cowering under a boulder. She couldn't give in to the Beast yet, not until Vasilisa was dead. As a werewolf what might she do? Would she rip Vasilisa to shreds, or bow down before her, like the other Polenitsy? She had to stay human, to be sure she killed Vasilisa.

Still human.

Svetlana crashed into her, catapulting her into the air. The sword spun away as Billi crumpled into the thick snow. It hit a rock and the blade snapped. The blow should have broken her apart, but instead she just felt a hard jolt. Billi flipped back up and grabbed Red's face as the werewolf dug her claws into Billi's ribs.

Despite the roaring pain, Billi concentrated on sinking her razor-sharp nails into Red's face. Her thumbs were tipped with daggers and she pushed towards Red's eyes. Red grooves opened along the wolf's snout as she slid closer.

Svetlana screamed and twisted away. Billi stumbled towards the sword and, chest heaving, tried to lift it.

Even with only half a blade it seemed ten times heavier now, and she noticed the blood sprinkling the snow. Her blood. Her body was covered in cuts and her coat hung off her in tatters.

Every step was like dragging through lead. The were-wolf's eyes were filled with blood. She howled and swiped left and right blindly. Billi slashed at her legs, cracking the kneecap, and the red-pelted wolf buckled.

Billi stared down at Svetlana, who panted, her tongue dangling loosely out of her savage jaw. Blood smeared her face and her fur was blood-splattered. She tried to raise her arm to defend herself, but the effort was weak, defeated. Billi raised her sword and stiffened her grip. Svetlana stared up, eyes filled with impotent fury. Billi smashed the pommel on her head and the werewolf collapsed.

Vasilisa lay curled up in the nook of a boulder. She'd buried her face in her knees and had her hands over her head as if trying to blank out what had happened.

Billi looked at her own hands. The nails were thicker, but normal. She'd fought down the change again. The bloodthirsty rage subsided and with it she shook the Beast back into its cage.

Shouts rose out of the wind. Torches flashed in the distance and dark figures ran through the snow. The wind carried fearful howls.

Billi tossed away the broken sword. She groaned as she bent down to pick up her dagger. Every muscle screamed and her bones did too, each having been twisted and tortured out of shape and back. Her spine popped as each joint set back into its socket. It took a huge effort to grasp the dagger and lift it.

'Billi?'

She had to do it now.

Billi grabbed Vasilisa by her dangling necklaces and held her fast. She raised her knife.

Oh God. This is it.

Vasilisa stared up at her, not understanding. She shook her head like this might be some nightmare. She held on to Billi's fingers, wanting this to be OK, that she could still trust Billi, but she could only tremble.

Strike!

Billi willed her arm down, willed the blade to enter the girl's heart, but her arm wouldn't bend. Vasilisa gazed up at her, too terrified to move.

'Close your eyes, Vasilisa. You won't feel anything.' Billi's voice broke. She pressed her lips together, despite the tremor running through her. She had to do this.

It was her duty as a Templar. The life of one against the lives of billions. Baba Yaga would bring Fimbulwinter and humanity would suffer a long, slow death by starvation. A second of ruthless action and the world was saved. Billi wouldn't have time to regret it; the werewolves were going to tear her to pieces at any moment.

'God forgive me,' said Billi. She pushed Vasilisa against the rock and twisted the necklaces around her fist, holding Vasilisa still. The moonlight caught the little girl's petrified face, her bewilderment. It glistened off the brightly polished baubles and old flint arrowheads dangling from her neck. The small bones, lumps of precious metal, beads and a crude statue all jangled from Billi's grip.

Crude statue.

Billi's breath stopped. She held it between her fingers. The small, roughly carved shape of a woman, the big hips and small stub of a head, all veined with dark iron.

It was the Venus figurine.

A werewolf slammed into Billi, pushing her away from Vasilisa, and the necklace broke apart as it came free. The pair tumbled in the snow, knocking all the air from Billi's lungs. She lay limp under the snarling werewolf, its gruesome fangs just a few centimetres from her throat. Half-buried in the snow, Billi twisted enough to look at Vasilisa. Olga was already there, passing the girl to others. Two women helped Svetlana up.

Vasilisa was removed, quickly surrounded by the Polenitsy and carried away. Only when she'd gone did the werewolf move off Billi.

They lifted Billi up. Olga approached.

'Why didn't you kill her?' the old woman asked.

Billi smiled. She slipped her closed hand into her pocket, feeling the smooth, cold curves of the statuette made in Tunguska. The one thing that could kill Baba Yaga.

Oh, but I will.

CHAPTER 37

Ivan stared open-mouthed as they dragged Billi back. He shook his head like he couldn't believe his eyes.

It lasted a second before his face dropped. He was tied to one of the thick wooden posts in the centre of the *ger*. They did the same to Billi on the one opposite him. The leather straps bit deep into her wrists as Olga twisted and knotted the bindings around and around. She gave the knots a sharp tug, then stood between the two of them. The other Polenitsy had left, and Olga shifted from foot to foot, gaze moving from Billi to Ivan and back. Then she straightened her coat and left.

Ivan waited a few moments, then leaned over and whispered, 'What happened?'

'I couldn't do it.' Billi couldn't quite believe it. 'I think I've found another way.'

Ivan blinked. He leaned back against the column, shifting his shoulders to get more comfortable. A slow smile crept over his lips. 'I am glad you are alive.'

'Me too.' Billi tried to turn her hands, but the leather

seemed to cut into her skin. Already she felt her fingers tingle with numbness.

'I can kill Baba Yaga,' she whispered.

'That's impossible. She's immortal.'

Billi grinned, unable to resist the taunt. 'Let a Templar show you how it's done.'

Ivan raised an eyebrow. 'And how is that exactly?'

'You know Baba Yaga was badly injured in the early twentieth century?'

'*Da*. We learnt that from Rasputin.'

'But have you ever wondered why she fell ill?' Billi glanced to check there were no eavesdroppers. She could barely contain her excitement. 'It was Tunguska.'

Ivan frowned, then stared at Billi, understanding. 'Of course. The meteorite.'

'And it almost killed her,' added Billi.

Ivan laughed. 'So all we need do is wait around until the next meteor falls and make sure Baba Yaga is under it. Simple.' He bowed his head. 'No wonder you Templars have such a dread reputation. Baba Yaga's as good as dead.'

'I have a lump of that meteorite in my pocket.' Billi tried to get her hand in her pocket to show him, but failed; the bonds were too tight.

'But that was a huge meteor travelling at a thousand miles an hour.' Ivan shook his head. 'You've got a pebble.'

'A pebble slew Goliath.' Billi leaned back against the pole, hoping to work it loose, but there wasn't a millimetre of give. 'When Vasilisa felt the eruption of Vesuvius we covered her with snow. Just a few scoopfuls. But by cooling her, we cooled the volcano. It had the same effect as if we'd gone to Vesuvius and dropped a million tonnes of snow into the crater.' Billi searched the floor, hoping there might be a bit of sharp, broken crockery. No such luck. 'This rock is part of the element that almost killed Baba Yaga. So even a small impact from the same rock should replicate the huge impact of the original rock. It's the fundamental principle of sympathetic magic.'

'So let's do it,' said Ivan at last.

'We just need to get out of these straps.' She'd thought it through. The rock of the Venus figurine could be sharpened, chiselled away, until it became a crude stone knife. All she needed was to get close enough to deliver the blow.

'But even with this, why let Vasilisa live? You're taking a terrible risk.' Ivan struggled at his own bindings, but they were as tight as Billi's.

'If I'd killed Vasilisa, I'd have achieved nothing. I would be dead and the figurine lost, maybe forever. So what if Vasilisa died? Sooner or later another powerful Spring Child would come along, and we'd be back where we started.' After all they'd found Kay and Vasilisa within a few years of each other. Who knows who else might be out there, waiting to be found by the Polenitsy and brought to their goddess? She continued. 'Think about it. We have the means to kill Baba Yaga, and she's nearby. If Vasilisa had died right now, the Polenitsy would have ripped us to shreds and the only chance to kill Baba Yaga, once and for all, would have been lost. We need to get close to her. It's now or never.'

'So that's why you let Vasilisa live,' Ivan grinned. 'I thought you'd gone all sentimental and soft.'

'Then you've a lot to learn about me.'

'I hope I get the chance.'

The door flap flipped open and Olga came in to begin the watch, carrying a steaming wooden bowl. She took a stool and sat down on it. She blew over the steaming broth, scooped a spoonful into her mouth and ate in silence, watching Billi and Ivan.

Billi spoke. 'Olga, I don't understand why you're going to help her do this. You know she's lying to you.'

Olga lowered the bowl from her lips. 'Look at us, Templar. What do you see?'

Billi's first reaction was to say a bunch of howling monsters, but that wasn't true. The Templars had taught her to believe that werewolves were the Unholy, creatures who had to be destroyed at all costs, but why? She saw women, powerful warriors and a tribe of hunters. She saw the respect they had for each other, and the religious fervour of their beliefs. They were fighting for a better world too, just like the Templars.

They weren't so different. Billi laughed to herself. And tomorrow she'd be no different from them at all.

'We are so few. If mankind continues on his path, we will die.' Olga put down the empty bowl. 'Year by year the forests shrink and the trees fall. What is left for us?'

The old woman stared at the ash of the fire, nudging it with her boot. 'Baba Yaga will save us. The only reason you are being kept alive for now is so that you will see this.'

'If she knew how to save you, why wouldn't she say how?' Billi said. 'She'll summon the global winter and hibernate until it's over. Civilization will be gone. Every species of this planet decimated. She isn't just planning to sacrifice Vasilisa – she wants to sacrifice everyone.' Billi met the old woman's gaze. 'Trust me. I'm telling you the truth.'

Olga stood, snarling. 'Trust you? There is no trust between men and wolves.'

'I am not a man,' Billi replied plainly. 'There is only one way you can save the Polenitsy.'

Two tall women entered the *ger*. Each was nearly two metres tall and made of hard, wiry muscle. Both were dressed in long, ankle-length cloaks of hide and fur. One wore a necklace made of claws and animal bones and had her long, blonde hair strung with beads and feathers. The other, dark-skinned, had her face marked with tribal tattoos and she came forward.

'Olga,' she said. 'We must move the camp.'

'Why?'

The woman cast a hateful look at Billi and Ivan. 'These two humans must have been followed. Men come. Many men.'

Olga tossed the bowl away. 'What men?'

The woman's eyes darkened. 'Bogatyrs.'

CHAPTER 38

Vehicles jostled on the fringes of the camp. Fires blazed and tents collapsed as the Polenitsy prepared to leave. The night was thick with tension. Billi and Ivan were cut free and taken out of the *ger*, flanked by the two Polenitsy. One handed Billi a long, black nomad coat and a strip of red cloth to use as a sash. Billi wrapped it twice round her waist and knotted it.

'Where are we going?' Billi asked Olga.

'We cannot risk the ritual being disrupted by the Bogatyrs.' Olga pointed into the darkness. 'The forest is deep and we know how to hide.'

The Russians were coming for Vasilisa. Maybe if there were enough of them, they could overcome the Polenitsy, but it would be a bloodbath.

Could Billi escape if it came to a battle? Find Baba Yaga in the confusion and kill her? Unlikely. The Polenitsy would defend Baba Yaga to the last. She needed Baba Yaga with her guard down if she was going to succeed. And what of Vasilisa? The Bogatyrs still wanted to sell her to the *ghuls*.

'So Koshchey survived,' said Ivan as he joined her. He'd covered himself with his deep-blue coat and his hands were tucked into the sleeves. The Polenitsy didn't trust him with his crutch any more, but though Ivan moved slowly, he didn't show any weakness, just gritty determination. He squinted as the freezing air blew into his face.

'It could be one of the others,' Billi replied.

'No. He is Koshchey the Undying.' Ivan pulled out his hands and flexed his fingers. Despite the wounds he had suffered, Billi could see the power in his hands as he clenched them into fists. 'I let him escape once.'

'Baba Yaga's the priority,' Billi reminded him.

Ivan shook his head. 'No, stopping Fimbulwinter is the priority. Listen.' He held her arms and looked at her, hard. 'You go after Baba Yaga. But if you fail, we cannot permit her to complete the ritual.'

Billi nodded grimly. 'Then you'll finish the job for me?'

'*Da.*' He sighed. 'I am not happy about this, but while both Vasilisa and Baba Yaga live, we are in double the peril. We have a greater responsibility than just saving the life of a small child, no matter how innocent.'

'Wow.' It was like having Arthur addressing her. Ivan had 'leader in the making' written all over him. Billi smiled. 'You have got to meet my dad.'

Howls came from all over the camp. Figures moved like shadows on the fringes of the campfires, silhouettes creeping in and out of the stands of tall birch trees. The forest was thick with them. Billi watched as two of the Polenitsy threw off their cloaks, hunched down on all fours and went from human to beast within a few paces. Some children stood by their tents as their parents packed. Billi watched one child, his shaggy black hair decorated with strips of bright cloth and plastic beads, yelp with laughter as his mother lightly cuffed him into the snow. The boy rolled around happily, wearing nothing but a pair of cotton underpants. Then his mum hauled him up and kissed his eyelids.

Jesus. The Bogatyrs and Koshchey on one side and Baba Yaga on the other. Where the hell was her dad? She couldn't fight everyone alone.

'He's dead, you know that?' Billi said to Olga. 'That boy over there – and his mother. You're all racing off to your deaths.' Olga tried to turn, but Billi just blocked her path. 'Fimbulwinter is coming unless we do something.'

They'd stopped beside a rusty-looking van. Two men loaded chests and boxes on to the roof rack. A man in a parka attacked the deep snow with a shovel, hacking at the thick ice that had set round the wheels. The night echoed angrily with the bedlam of machines and wolves. Olga shoved the rear door open. 'What's your answer then?'

'All I know is that we need to stop this . . . madness.'

'It is not madness. It is the will of the Great Mother.' Olga held the door open for Billi. 'Do you not have a similar saying? *Deus vult?*'

Billi stepped into the van, followed by Ivan. A man was already sitting in the passenger seat, a big Swede. There was steel mesh between them. He glanced at Billi and Ivan, then pulled his thick parka closer round him. Olga climbed into the driver's seat and revved the engine. The headlights came on and the vehicle shook itself into action. Snow slid off the bonnet as the van climbed out of the snow-packed trench. Olga glanced at Billi through the rear-view mirror.

What is she thinking? Billi wondered. Olga wasn't like her granddaughter, a blind fanatic. She was the Polenitsy pack leader and took her responsibilities seriously. The survival of the pack was paramount, but loyalty to Baba Yaga had been bred into the Polenitsy for thousands of years. Olga looked away and the van began to move, bouncing over the rough snow.

Billi felt the Venus figurine in her pocket. She shifted closer to Ivan and put her head on his shoulder. His arm came up round her and they settled into silence together.

She sniffs the air and growls to her sisters. Mingled with the fresh scent of the forest is ash, the smell of burning, of man. She flexes her claws and peers into the veil of snowflakes that drift from the moon-bright sky.

There, at the edge of the trees. She sees light come from a window and hears the sounds of singing and music. But it is a harsh, false sound that hisses and crackles, man and their false voices and noises. A thin spiral of smoke rises from the stone chimney.

Billi steps over the low fence and comes to a wall of cloth. The human woman has hung out the sheets, though they are brittle with frost. Billi sniffs the white cloth and her head swims with the soft, milky odour of a suckling baby. She licks her lips.

Her sisters creep beside her as they approach the front door. Through the glass Billi sees the family sitting in front of their glowing box of colours. She blinks. The light is painful and the noise tears at her sensitive ears. No wonder humans are driven mad, in this pandemonium of hateful sounds and lights. The human woman laughs and the babe in her arms wails.

Billi reaches for the door. Her hands, covered in glossy black hair, touch the cold brass handle and her claws click together as she turns it.

Four humans gaze at her. The woman screams now, clutching the baby close against her heart. The boy stares, eyes blank with terror, and the acid sting of urine rises as he wets himself.

The man reaches for the poker beside the fire, though his hand trembles.

'Manflesh,' Billi growls. She and her sisters will feed well.

She leaps.

'Billi!'

Billi awoke. Ivan was staring anxiously at her. Her head was on his lap where she had fallen asleep.

God, she was boiling; sweat soaked her clothes and her hair stuck to her scalp.

'Are you OK?' He held her tightly and his face was close to hers.

'What happened?' she asked.

'Nothing. Just a bad dream.'

Thank God.

She was tossed and bounced as the van rattled across the countryside. Billi saw the lights of a convoy through the rear window; a dozen or so vehicles followed while wolves chased after, weaving in and out of the dense forest on either side of the road.

But where was Vasilisa? Billi caught a glimpse of something above her; a huge, cumbersome bat-shape that darted through the whirling snow. Ribbons trailed from the edges of its cloak and a scream of wild joy pierced through the wind.

Baba Yaga rode the storm.

Billi desperately fought the primordial feelings threatening to take her over forever.

'You'll make it, Billi,' whispered Ivan.

'No, I won't,' she answered. He wanted to reassure her, but she knew she didn't have long. 'Listen, you know where the stone is.' She nodded to her left trouser pocket. 'If I change tonight, I'll need you to take it and use it.'

'You'll make it. I know you will.' He stroked her hair while Billi hugged him, putting her head against his chest and closing her eyes. She listened to the steady beat of his heart and tried to forget the hunger she'd felt when she'd walked into that room.

This wasn't over yet.

*

The long night wore on and Billi sweated and shook with lycanthropic fever. The weather worsened and the only relief came when the moon went behind snow-stuffed clouds. Ivan stayed beside her, never sleeping, murmuring to her in Russian. Billi leaned her head on his shoulder, focusing on his gentle voice.

The engine rattled and gears screamed as the van came to a halt. Billi's eyes snapped open.

Olga turned the ignition off and on, but the noise was getting even worse, like the entire vehicle was having a seizure.

The big Swede swore and jumped out of the passenger door. Olga got out too.

The storm had lifted, but snow fell heavily from a dull, colourless sky. The sun was up, somewhere behind the clouds, and Billi was washed over with relief; she could rest now that the moon was no longer in the sky.

'What's going on?' she asked.

Ivan twisted his head and looked out. 'We've lost the others. Storm must have broken up the convoy.'

The Swede hauled out his toolkit as Olga popped open the bonnet. She held up a torch while the man rummaged around in the grease and steel. He leaned further in, complaining that Olga wasn't directing the torch properly.

Olga slammed the hood down on him.

He groaned and she did it again, making a hollow, clunking noise. The man's legs gave out, but he was

313

still conscious. He swung his arms, but Olga stepped back, then struck him across the forehead with the heavy metal torch, just to make sure. He hit the ground with a thud.

The rear door opened and Olga addressed Ivan. 'Tsarevich, I am going to have to trust you.'

Ivan said nothing, but his grim gaze spoke loudly enough. Olga sighed.

'I killed your father, but I meant him no ill-will. It is war and that is the way of things. Do you understand?' Billi hadn't noticed, but Olga wasn't wearing her tribal outfit any more, but a wool tunic and jeans, tucked into a pair of stout boots. Her grey hair was loose and swayed in the wind.

'I understand my father is dead.'

'We will *all* be dead unless you and I can work together.' Olga helped Billi out of the van. 'Though we are enemies, there can be respect between us.'

Ivan pulled himself out, never taking his eyes off Olga. Eventually he gave a curt nod.

'We will settle our differences another time,' he said.

Olga and Billi made their way to the front of the van, beside the unconscious Scandinavian.

'Take his legs,' Olga said and together they rolled the big man into the verge.

'What made you change your mind?'

Olga watched the man slide through the deep snow and come to a stop at the bottom. 'My first duty is to my Polenitsy. I managed to speak to the Spring Child alone after seeing you. She is truly innocent and has no guile in her. If the Spring Child says it is so, that Baba Yaga plans Fimbulwinter, then it is so.'

'Thank you,' said Billi. 'What about Vasilisa?'

Olga pointed back down the road behind them. Two weak headlights shone through the snow as a hulking Humvee lumbered towards them, part of the convoy that had fallen behind. Olga went to the footwell and pulled out a heavy revolver. The chunky Smith & Wesson's barrel was over twenty centimetres long and it looked like it had been built to hunt elephants.

'Ambush?' asked Billi.

'Ambush.'

Billi slid a metre or so down the verge and waited. Olga waved her torch at the approaching vehicle.

The car stopped, its engine still running. Peeking over Billi saw a man jump out of the back and approach Olga, smiling. He was still smiling when she swung the torch against his head.

Billi scrambled up the slope and ran to the driver's half-open window. There was a woman at the wheel, one of the Polenitsy still in human form.

Vasilisa lay in the back, asleep under a shawl. Billi poked the long barrel through the window.

'I'll take the Spring Child, if you don't mind,' she said.

Vasilisa woke up as Billi opened the door. She screamed and backed away, frantically wrestling with the door handle.

'No, Vasilisa, don't!' Billi reached out with her hand slowly. 'I won't hurt you, I promise.'

'You promised before and you lied.' She pressed herself hard against the far door, knees up against her chest and hand still on the door handle. Looking at her, Billi's heart broke. She had been dressed for sacrifice. Someone had combed out her hair and it shone like the gold necklaces that hung around her. Small wire armlets studded with gems covered her upper arms. Henna patterns had been applied round her eyes, spirals and delicate feather shapes that seemed to transform her into some fairy princess. Her dress was white and embroidered with gold thread; outlines of prehistoric animals and sorcerers covered the cloth.

Billi nodded; she had no answer. 'Please, Vasilisa. I need you to come with me.'

Olga ordered the other Polenitsy out of the car and confiscated her mobiles. Billi put the gun down on the car seat in front of Vasilisa and raised her hands.

Vasilisa snatched up the revolver and pointed it at her.

That would be perfect, Billi thought. *If Vasilisa blew my brains out.* She smiled at the irony of it. She could take the gun from the girl, but she needed Vasilisa to trust her.

'You're right to be angry, to not trust me, Vasilisa,' Billi said. Out of the corner of her eye she noticed Ivan limping towards them. 'But you can either come with me, or go to Baba Yaga with them. The choice is yours.'

With a sob, Vasilisa dropped the gun. 'Why, Billi? Why would you want to hurt me?'

There was no answer except that Billi was a Templar and that meant making life-and-death decisions. Maybe, if they survived this, Vasilisa would understand that once she too was a Templar. Whatever personal feelings she might have, she had her duty. Still Billi found it hard to face Vasilisa's tears and the distrust that now lingered in the girl's voice.

Billi took her in her arms and helped her out. Ivan grabbed the gun and then put a bullet in the radio transmitter and one in the radiator.

Billi carried Vasilisa to the van.

They drove on down a side road and away from the forest, planning to put some distance between them and the rest of the convoy. Ivan was up front with Olga, Billi in the back with Vasilisa.

'They will come after the Spring Child. The Polenitsy and the goddess,' said Olga.

'That's what I'm counting on.' Billi got out the statuette and handed it over to her. 'This is part of the meteor that struck Tunguska in 1908.'

One hand on the steering wheel, Olga inspected the small rock. 'Yes. It was from this element that Baba Yaga was sent into a coma. It hurt the Earth so it hurt her.'

'So we can use this against her. I just need to turn it into a weapon of some sort. A knife or something.'

Olga stopped the van. 'I have something better.' She checked the road was empty, then got out and climbed on to the roof and began unbuckling the straps holding the luggage on the roof rack.

Ivan and Billi came out and watched her.

'Vasilisa is bait,' said Ivan. 'But that's what you're counting on, isn't it?' He glanced back through the window at Vasilisa. The girl was under a blanket, staring out at the snowbound world.

Billi didn't like the idea of using Vasilisa like that, but it was the only plan she had. 'Yes. If anything happens to Vasilisa, Baba Yaga will just turn around. She'll no doubt send her Polenitsy out after us, for revenge, but she herself will not come. This way,' she nodded in Vasilisa's direction, 'we force Baba Yaga to make a personal appearance. We want Vasilisa alive.'

Ivan looked up at the sky. 'And tonight's the full moon.'

'Help me,' Olga ordered. Together they lowered a heavy trunk to the ground. Billi and Ivan gathered round it as the old woman lifted it open.

'You like?' asked Olga.

Billi grinned. 'Oh yes.'

Weapons lay neatly arranged in the trunk. Not guns or rifles, but swords, a bow and suits of chain mail. Each beautifully made and lovingly kept. It was like Christmas. Billi's sort of Christmas.

First she took out the mail armour. The suit was knee-length with sleeves that covered her to mid-bicep. The links shimmered in the bright-white light of the snow. The sword was a single-edged sabre, an Ottoman cavalry sword. Billi peered at the Arabic lettering along its mirror-bright blade.

'What does it say?' asked Ivan.

Billi frowned. 'Roughly translated it says, "Eat this, you Christian, *er*, seed-spiller." Or something.' She cleared her throat and slid the blade into its scabbard. 'It's a religious reference. Genesis 38, I think.' Then she saw the Mongol bow.

It was black, made of wood and horn, and formed a curved 'C' shape. Olga lifted it up and strung it.

'They called the Mongols the wolves from the east,' she said. 'They ruled Russia for over two hundred years. The blood of the Mongols is strong in the Polenitsy.'

Billi lifted the quiver. The arrows were neatly arranged in two rows. Wide-barbed man-killers at the front, narrow-headed armour-piercing bodkins at the back; all with eagle-fletching. Billi spotted a silver ring on a tassel off the side of the quiver. She put it on her right thumb. Olga handed her the bow, strung and ready.

The bow was a masterpiece.

'This will do,' said Billi.

They worked together to arm her. As Ivan laced up the mail shirt Billi tucked in the sword and a long knife. Finally she threw the quiver over her shoulder and notched her first arrow, hooking the bowstring round her thumb, then pulling back, slowly letting her back muscles do the heavy work alongside her arms. The draw was powerful. They'd use the figurine to make

319

arrowheads. She'd have no problem putting a meteor-tipped arrow through Baba Yaga's thick skull.

Olga stepped back and straightened Billi's armour. 'Maybe some Mongol blood runs in you, child. You are more wolf than you know.'

Ivan gave a low, admiring whistle. 'Now you are beautiful,' he said. He'd taken a mail shirt of his own and a plain, straight sword. But he seemed happiest with Olga's big revolver.

'They will have the advantage out here,' said Ivan, surveying the wild landscape. 'They'll come at us from all around. We need a better battlefield.'

'We'll find one,' replied Billi. She took one of the mobiles they'd confiscated and checked it. Barely any reception.

'Dad? Where are you?'

'Billi? Billi?'

'Dad, we've got Vasilisa.'

'Billi? Where are you?'

'We've got Vasilisa!' Billi shouted. Her dad sounded like he was shouting from the other side of the world.

'Where are you?'

Damn it! Billi stared around the road. To one side was a fenced-off stretch of rough woodland, picketed with spindly trees. Signs hung every ten metres along the fence. They were all a trisected black circle on a yellow background: the international warning symbol for radiation.

'Where are you?'

Somewhere made of concrete and choked with pollution, a place where Baba Yaga would be weakest. Billi read the dented road sign up ahead.

'Chernobyl, Dad.'

CHAPTER 39

They drove the rest of the day, stopping only to snack on dried meat, hard bread and water. Olga said nothing, but each time she stopped she spent the meal searching the horizon. But nobody came.

Using the toolbox, Billi disassembled the arrows. She cut the heads out and then, holding the Venus figurine between her boots, smashed it with a hammer. Vasilisa sat silently beside her as she chipped the shards of polished black stone into something that resembled arrowheads.

'What are you doing?' asked Vasilisa.

Billi handed her a rough triangle of meteoric stone.

'This is the meteoric rock from Tunguska I told you about. Your great-grandmother knew it had injured Baba Yaga before.'

The young girl inspected the stone, then handed it back. 'You think this will kill Baba Yaga?' Her voice betrayed her doubts.

'Bloody hope so.'

By the time they'd finished their meal Billi had three

decent, stone-tipped arrows. She used up a tube of super-glue to hold them into the shafts; they weren't particularly skilful and she should try shooting with them, to get an idea of how they flew, but time was too short; they needed to move.

The late-afternoon sun hung low on the horizon, bathing the landscape with pinks and oranges. Sparse woodland gave way to overgrown and abandoned fields, dotted with crumbling old farmhouses and empty villages. The signs of humanity increased as the day wore on. They'd reached the outskirts of Chernobyl.

Site of the worst nuclear disaster in history. Back in the 1980s a nuclear reactor had exploded and launched a huge radioactive cloud over most of south Russia and Ukraine. Tens of thousands had been evacuated overnight, taking only what they could carry. They'd never returned. It seemed like ancient history, but the town itself could have been emptied yesterday. The cars, the buildings, parks and gardens all remained. Not demolished like they would have been in a war – just empty. Only the humans had left.

So this was the world Baba Yaga wanted.

Silent, grey tower blocks stood like titans guarding a city of the dead. A flock of crows launched themselves into a cloud of black feathers, cawing angrily at Billi's arrival, their cries sharp and keen. Otherwise the streets were eerily empty. The snow-laden boughs of the trees lining the road sagged over them, their branches scratching the van's roof. Their roots had broken through the tarmac and pond-sized potholes pockmarked the road, each glistening with dark ice. Cars sat abandoned, rusting. Their bonnets had been thrown open and engines, tyres and seats all stripped out.

The van stopped. A large shadow loomed over the front windscreen and the air rumbled with a curious, threatening growl.

A huge, black bear with beady, brown eyes stood in the centre of the road. Olga left the engine running and stepped out of the van. The bear dropped down on to all fours and even then was still taller than the woman. It lumbered closer and raised its head to sniff her.

Olga just stood, watching it.

The bear rose on to its hind legs, towering over her. It threw back its head and bellowed.

Billi glanced at Ivan. He'd been in the back inspecting the weapons while Vasilisa had moved up front. He raised his eyebrows.

'Well?' he whispered. He moved forward and rested the pistol barrel on the back of the seat, pointing it at the windscreen. Vasilisa was squeezed next to Billi. The girl reached out and touched the glass, mouth open as she gazed at the giant creature in awe.

'Olga knows what she's doing. I think.'

Then the bear dropped back down on to all fours and wandered off into the woods. Billi stepped out and joined Olga.

'What was that all about?' said Billi after her heartbeat had returned to normal.

'He's the king here. He just wanted to make sure we knew,' Vasilisa said from out of the car window.

Ivan hopped out of the back and waved his pistol. 'We could have scared him off with this. It would have been quicker.'

Olga scowled. 'Just what a human would think.'

They drove on for another fifteen minutes, slowly rolling along the silent roads.

'Where are we?' asked Billi.

'One of the outlying towns.' Olga pointed ahead. 'The reactor's a few kilometres that way.'

Billi checked the surroundings. The town wasn't hugely built up and each residential block had plenty of space around it. No matter which direction the attack came from, she'd see it coming.

'Stop here,' Billi said. Olga drew up at the side of the road. Ahead stood a set of tall, iron gates, beyond which was a simple amusement park.

Billi wandered around the park. The yellow carriages of the Ferris wheel were filled with snow. Crystalline ivy covered the rusty steel legs of the main support and the steel creaked in the wind. A bit further were the bumper cars. The roof had long collapsed and long strips of plastic cloth and wood were scattered over the cars.

Opposite the park was a school building. It was about eight storeys tall, and would give them a good vantage point over the surrounding land. Vasilisa joined Billi as they went in to explore. They stepped through a door, its wood warped and the paint blistered and flaking, straight into a classroom. The paint on the walls and the desks had faded and blistered. There were posters of old Soviet leaders, a large, framed map of the USSR in faded red and drawings that had been made by the children, mainly of rockets and cosmonauts. Small rubber gas masks hung on the coat hooks.

They walked past the crèche, still filled with first-aid posters and old cots, and found the steps that led upstairs. Billi stopped dead as a shadow marked the wall. She tugged Vasilisa behind her.

The silhouette of a small girl with pigtails had been blasted on the wall by the atomic explosion. She was caught forever reaching up for the light switch.

They reached the flat roof and looked out over Chernobyl. The town was a cluster of concrete apartment blocks. Trees broke the outline as the woods had encroached from all directions. Billi saw branches poking out of the upper floors of some buildings and thick roots rippled over abandoned cars on the roadside.

'Didn't take long,' Billi said. Not long at all before nature stole back all that was once hers.

The chimneys of the nuclear plant stood up on the horizon. Three slim towers beside the curved shell of the reactor.

The silence was deafening. The abandoned town echoed with the sighs of ghosts.

They weren't here. The Templars hadn't made it. If her dad had hit Kiev that morning, when she'd called, he should have got here by now. Billi spent the next ten minutes scanning the streets and rooftops, hoping for some movement or light off armour or blade, but the snowfall made it difficult to see anything clearly. Maybe last night's storm had cost Arthur and the others an extra day. Maybe he never got to Kiev. And now they were out of days.

'Looks like this is it then,' said Billi.

Vasilisa stood beside her. Billi held out her hand, but she retreated, not quite trusting her. Billi put her hand down. The girl had good cause; they weren't going to be best friends after all that had happened.

Friendships were hard to come by in her line of work.

'She's near,' said Vasilisa. She scratched her head and frowned.

'What's wrong? She trying to get inside?'

'No.' Vasilisa lowered her hand. The henna covered her arms up to her elbows. She turned her palms over, staring at the strange patterns, then she looked at the reactor in the distance. 'Look at what we've done. We made the Earth so sick.'

'Sounds like you agree with her,' said Billi. Their eyes met.

'She is old and tired, Billi. She thinks she's the only one who cares for the Earth. She hoped mankind would learn, but it hasn't. That's why she won't die; she thinks no one else will look after it when she's gone. So she is trapped in winter, and it is always cold.' Tears ran down her cheeks. Vasilisa pitied Baba Yaga.

327

The sky was turning red. Billi watched the sun sink lower on the horizon. Up in the sky she saw the moon, a weak, indistinct circle for now. But it was full and perfectly round. Her skin itched and she loosened her collar, trying to let the heat out.

'Not yet, not yet,' she promised herself.

The thin birch trees were rustling when the first howl rippled across the snowbound town. Another joined it, then another, until the distant woods erupted with the chorus of hunters' songs. Olga waved at her from below and Billi ran down, Vasilisa a few steps behind.

They gathered in front of the amusement park gates. Olga had stripped down to just a thin T-shirt and shorts. Her bare legs and arms bristled with grey hair and already her nails had transformed into claws.

'How long do we have?' Billi asked.

'Five, six minutes,' growled Old Grey, listening hard to the sound of the oncoming army. She snapped her teeth as they grew in length and sharpness.

'We need to give ourselves some space.' Billi searched around; three roads led from this park, giving them options. 'Keep the engine running in case we need a quick getaway.'

Olga laughed. 'We are not getting away, young Templar. This is where we die.'

'Maybe, but we take the old witch with us.' Billi pulled out her stone-tipped arrow. 'I just need Baba Yaga out in the open and close, that's all.'

Old Grey growled as steel scraped across steel. Billi

spun around, arrow drawn, as a figure emerged from behind them.

Arthur drew the Templar Sword from his scabbard as he approached. He wore his own mail, covered with a patched-up leather coat. Snowflakes sprinkled his black beard and his scars were paler than normal, stark white in the frosty, weak sunlight. Gareth joined him, fingers in his composite bow. He saw Billi's own bow and nodded with approval. He had his quiver strapped to his belt, all the fletching made up of black eagle feathers. The Templar was short but broad-shouldered from years of pulling the heavy bow.

'Hope we're not too late,' said Arthur.

Mordred, the tall, elegant Ethiopian, stood nearby, his hands eager and anxious round his spear shaft. Hanging from his hip was a quiver and slung over his back a longbow. He'd wrapped a scarf round his face and had his woollen cap pulled low so only his deep-brown eyes showed. With him were Gwaine and Lance. They'd survived, thank God.

Gwaine had taken a battering; there was a clean bandage across his forehead and his mouth, usually so thin and grim, turned slightly. It could have been a smile, the first she'd had from the old warrior. On his back was a bow and quiver of arrows. In his hands he held a hefty battleaxe and had a dented steel breastplate strapped on. A crude red cross had been painted high on the left of it. A Templar to the last.

'*Bonjour*, Bilqis,' said Lance as he smoothed out his

long, brown moustache and bowed. The Frenchman had found a knee-length mail hauberk, older and heavier than Billi's, and on his left hip he had a longsword. He carried a shield, white with a black band across the top: the argent field and sable fess. The battle banner of the Templars. He looked like he'd stepped out fresh from the Crusades.

Billi's throat was tight, clogged with relief. She wet her dry lips. 'About bloody time.'

CHAPTER 40

Lance kissed her on both cheeks.

Billi grinned. 'You made it. How?'

Lance looked surprised. 'Why would we not make it?'

Mordred shook her hand. 'You look ready to cause trouble,' he said.

Billi laughed. She had her quiver and bow on her back, a suit of fine chain mail and sword and dagger tucked into her belt. 'Trouble's coming,' she said.

Gwaine stopped and looked down at Vasilisa.

'She still alive?' He spoke as though she wasn't there. 'Why haven't you killed her?'

Billi drew Vasilisa close beside her. 'I've found a way to kill Baba Yaga. But I need her close. If we hang on to Vasilisa, she'll have to come to us and give us our chance to be rid of the old witch once and for all.'

'She's bait then?'

Vasilisa flinched as he said it. She pushed Billi's hand away and stepped back, gazing at the Templars. Billi bent down and faced her.

'Vasilisa, we're here to protect you, I swear it. But

331

you'll need to play along.' She looked over at her dad, but he just watched impassively. 'When Baba Yaga comes we will destroy her.'

'And if you don't?' asked the Spring Child.

'Then we will have done our best.' Billi touched Vasilisa's cheek.

The other Templars gathered warily around Old Grey. She'd not fully transformed, but her skin was covered in fur and her skull had elongated to accommodate a snout and a line of fangs. She barely acknowledged them.

Arthur slapped Billi on the back and inspected her armour, nodding with satisfaction. 'Well done,' he said. He nodded at Lance. 'Get the car ready. I want to be able to make a quick exit, if needs be.'

'*Bon*,' said Lance. He took Vasilisa's hand and patted it between his palms. 'It is good to see you again, Vasilisa.' Then he slung his shield over his shoulder and disappeared down an alleyway.

Billi looked at her dad and held up her arrow. 'This is tipped with meteoric rock from the blast. I made it from the Venus figurine.'

Arthur took the arrow and pressed his thumb against the tip. 'Elaine told me the statue'd been left in London. You found it?'

Billi gestured to the small girl. 'Vasilisa had it all along.'

Arthur handed it to Gareth. 'What do you think?'

Gareth, the Templars' best archer, rolled the arrow in his fingers, testing its weight. He put the arrow to the string and the bow creaked as he drew it back to his cheek. 'Good for thirty, forty metres.'

Billi took out the other two stone-tipped arrows and handed them to Gareth.

'This all?' he asked.

'Sorry, it wasn't a big piece of rock.'

Gareth checked all three arrows and handed one back. 'The head's too loose on this one – won't fly far. I'll hang on to these two.'

'And if that doesn't work?' asked Gwaine. 'What about the girl?'

'If that doesn't work, we fight to the last man,' said Arthur. Unconsciously he ran his thumb over the engraved pommel of his sword as he scanned the battle-ground, tracing the emblem of the two knights on a single horse. Arthur pointed to the school building. 'What do you reckon, Gareth?'

'I'd prefer a grassy knoll, but that'll do.' He sprinted off, bow in one hand and his quiver in the other.

Billi held Vasilisa's hand and drew her sabre. 'Stick close to me.'

Vasilisa responded with a squeeze.

Arthur turned to Ivan. 'And you are?'

Ivan straightened. 'I am Tsarevich Ivan Alexeivich Rom–'

'But you can call him Ivan,' Billi interrupted. She wiped the sweat off her forehead. Arthur took her arm, seeing the bandages.

'You've been injured? How bad?'

'Werewolves. Pretty bad.' She pulled up a corner of the bandages. The bite marks were black circles now, but thin, dark veins ran just under the skin. 'She took a big bite.'

'Where are Elaine's poultices?' Arthur asked Mordred. The young squire sprang to attention.

'In the car, sir.'

'Then take Billi over there right now. Just get her –'

'Eyes front,' said Gwaine.

They came. Engines died as one by one the followers of Baba Yaga stepped out of their vehicles. Packs of wolves crept out of the woods and through the sprawling amusement park. Then the Polenitsy stopped and Billi watched their skin ripple as the wolves became women. They approached, chests heaving and blowing big clouds of steaming breath in the frosty air, eyes on Billi and the others. Closest was Svetlana. Her body shone with sweat as she stood on top of a car, staring down at them. Her face turned to horror as she saw her grandmother. Then the horror gave way to fury as she realized she was there of her own free will.

But the younger wolf didn't even have to voice her rage before the land around them came alive, silencing them all.

The trees trembled. Their burden of snow tumbled down over the gathered crowd. Their boughs creaked and their branches rustled as though whispering to one another.

'What's happening?' said Arthur as he backed away. He gestured to the other Templars and they formed a line alongside him, Billi and Vasilisa behind them.

'Baba Yaga,' said Vasilisa.

Old Grey crouched. Her hands had fully changed into claws and she flexed them, prepared for the attack. Gwaine took a wide stance as the ground trembled under him. Mordred's hands wrung the spear shaft while Arthur kept his sword low but ready.

Ivan had his revolver in his right hand and used his scabbarded sword as a stick to help steady himself. He quickly looked back at Billi.

'Now we will find out how right you are,' he said as he swayed on the pitching ground.

Billi pulled Vasilisa a little closer.

A powerful wind roared down between the buildings and in its howl there was the scream of a thousand voices. What Billi thought was a circling flock of crows was actually a single mass, a figure wrapped in long, streaming robes and a tangle of cloaks.

The ground shook and a crevasse tore along the pavement, hurling off sharp chips of concrete. The buildings groaned and Billi spun around as she heard the school's windowpanes creak, lines of fracture growing like spiderwebs across the glass, twisting with pain, but holding.

The Polenitsy knelt as one, all but Old Grey. She raised her head defiantly, her face now more wolf than human, long-muzzled and black-lipped.

The trees bowed, the thick trunks groaning as their branches touched the ground.

Billi covered her eyes as the wind stung her. She pulled Vasilisa against her, covering her as best she could.

Then the air stilled.

Baba Yaga stood among the Polenitsy. She drew her taloned fingers through her brittle white hair and her wrinkled, iron-fanged face darkened with rage as she slammed her bone staff on to the hard-packed snow. The ancient witch unbent, rising high over them, her shadow covering the Templars as she lifted herself to her full height, nearly six metres.

'Mother of God,' whispered Mordred.

'Steady, lad,' said Arthur, even though his voice was anything but calm.

Baba Yaga peered down at them, her black-diamond eyes glinting.

'The giRL. Give *herr* to MeEE,' she hissed.

'Come and get her,' said Billi.

Sixty metres, Billi reckoned, between her and Gareth. *Just come a few steps closer, you old hag.*

'Trust me, OK?' Billi whispered, then put her sabre against Vasilisa's throat. Vasilisa stiffened.

A few of the werewolves edged closer.

'No, not you lot.' Billi stared at Baba Yaga. 'Just her.'

'BacK, ZTay bacK.' Baba Yaga waved her hand. She turned her head slowly, searching the surroundings, not moving closer.

Did she suspect a trap? Of course she did. But Baba Yaga wanted the Spring Child, and what were they? Insignificant humans.

'Come on, take her,' Billi taunted. 'Or are you afraid of a few mortals?'

'YoU WiLL *dI*E SL*owe*St, L*itt*Le Templahh.'

Baba Yaga stepped forward. She moved slowly, each step churning the icy tarmac. Her fingers twitched on the bone staff, the bracelets and necklaces rattling. A deep, hellish hiss rolled from her cracked throat.

Just a few more metres.

She was thinking it. They were all thinking it. Billi's mind was focused on the arrowhead, that small sharp triangle of stone that would kill Baba Yaga. It all came down to the next few steps. She thought of Gareth in the armoury, sending arrow after arrow into the bullseye. The guy could put an arrow through the eye of a dormouse in the dark.

Just one more step and it's game over.

Billi couldn't keep the urge, the desire, out of her mind. None of them could. They were practically screaming for Baba Yaga to take another step.

'Noo, NoOO –' Baba Yaga stopped. She glared at Billi, her black eyes seeming to grow in darkness. Her teeth ground against each other.

Just one more metre.

Baba Yaga's gaze shot up to the school window. 'NOO!'

Oh no.

Baba Yaga was an avatar, but one who'd accumulated all the powers of the thousands of Spring Children she'd devoured. She could command the elements. She'd taught the first Polenitsy to shape-shift. *She could read minds.* She'd heard them – how could she not? They

337

were all screaming at her to step closer into the Templars' trap.

The twang of the bowstring seemed as loud as a thunderbolt, and like a thunderbolt, it covered the distance between Gareth and Baba Yaga in an instant. Baba Yaga screamed and fell backwards as the arrow entered her shoulder. The Polenitsy wailed and three scurried to aid their goddess.

My God, it works. The small arrowhead had done it.

The Polenitsy backed away as Baba Yaga stirred. She rose up again, her face twisted into a mask of horror. The iron-filled black mouth opened and she screamed, snapping the arrow off with a flick of her taloned finger. Bilious black blood spurted out of the wound.

The wolf pack leapt forward towards them. Dozens of Polenitsy moved from human to wolf in an eyeblink.

'C'mon!' Billi wrapped her fingers tight round Vasilisa's wrist as she backed away.

The second arrow flew, but Baba Yaga swatted it out of the air; it tumbled away and was lost in the snow.

Arthur grabbed Vasilisa round the waist as he ran, lifting her off the ground.

An engine revved and a jeep raced out from an alleyway, Lance at the wheel.

'Let's get the hell out of here,' he said.

The wolves charged towards them.

'Ivan!' Billi pulled him towards the jeep. She kicked one startled werewolf in the jaw, catching its tongue in its teeth. Old Grey leapt among the Polenitsy in a frenzy of fangs and claws.

Gwaine and Mordred sprinted into the school building while arrow after arrow from Gareth's regular supply flew in among the werewolves. Billi understood immediately: the three Templars would cover the retreat, forcing the werewolves to advance under a flight of arrows. Already two werewolves lay still in the reddening snow, arrows lodged in their throats and eye sockets. As Billi ran more arrows darted through the darkening sky as Gwaine and Mordred added their volleys to Gareth's onslaught.

Billi's heart raced as she threw herself into the passenger seat, expecting to have her back torn open to the bone any second. Arthur tossed Vasilisa in beside her and squeezed in next. Ivan slammed the front passenger door shut as a pair of claws ripped across the windscreen.

'Seat belts!' Lance shouted as the jeep's engine roared.

Two werewolves clambered on to the bonnet, then yelled as they were ripped off. Grey took one across the throat and hurled it into the pack. Its fur was criss-crossed by bleeding wounds and its jaw slavering red. Grey was defending them from her sisters.

The car jumped forward and accelerated away from the crowd of werewolves. Grey snapped at the arm of one, then she too turned and ran, loping easily alongside the jeep. Billi glanced in the side mirror and saw a dozen other wolves spring into the chase.

She checked Vasilisa, sitting beside her sobbing. She didn't look hurt, just scared. Beside the girl was Arthur, twisted around so he could watch out of the rear. His leather jacket creaked as he stretched his shoulders and his fingers fidgeted around the wire bindings of the sword hilt.

Ivan, beside Lance, put his revolver on the dashboard as he adjusted his sword belt. Then he wiped his hands on his lap and took up the big gun. He winked at Billi.

The car hit an ice patch and skidded sideways, the rear turning a full circle before bumping against a tree.

'Down!' shouted Ivan, glancing back at the were-wolves descending upon them.

Vasilisa screamed as werewolves slammed into the rear. The jeep jumped from the impact, then crashed back down with bone-jarring force. Billi dropped her head as Ivan shot out of the rear window. The glass blew apart and there was an ear-piercing cry as a wolf went down.

'Any time now would be good,' said Arthur to Lance as the wheels spun uselessly on the ice.

'*Merde*,' swore Lance, jamming the vehicle into reverse and barrelling the surprised wolves backwards. The jeep jolted, and they heard a crunch and a yelp from under it.

'Nasty,' muttered Arthur. Something slammed on to the top of the car and he shoved his sword through the roof. It caught something and he pushed harder. Blood trickled through the tear and a body tumbled off.

Lance shoved the wheel around and took them down a dark alleyway.

Arthur peered at Ivan. 'How are you doing, lad?'

Ivan was dripping with sweat and blood seeped through his trousers. All the running had reopened the wound on his leg, but his face didn't betray his pain.

'Not dead yet,' he replied.

'Where to?' Billi asked. They'd lost the chasing wolves, but it was only a matter of minutes before they were sniffed out.

'We patch you up, then fly you and Vasilisa right to Jerusalem,' answered Arthur. 'We've got the girl away from them. That is more than we'd all hoped for at this point. There's a helicopter parked near the reactor. The other team will keep the Polenitsy busy for a while longer.'

'And there's still this.' Billi pulled out the last stone-tipped arrow. Her bow was across her lap now and she plucked the taut bowstring. Maybe the arrowhead wasn't as well fixed as the others, but it could still do the job. They hadn't killed Baba Yaga yet – but they still could. It meant Vasilisa didn't have to die and for that Billi felt almost sick with relief.

Billi looked again at Arthur, Vasilisa and Ivan. She had three people she cared about right here. And she was going to do everything she could to save them.

CHAPTER 41

'Anything?' asked Lance.

Billi peered out of the rear window. No wolves. 'We've lost them.' They'd lost Olga too. She must have fallen back to fight her fellow werewolves.

'What about Gwaine and the others?' she asked.

Arthur wiped his sword with his sleeve. 'They should be retreating and will meet us at the rendezvous.'

'*Bon.*' Lance took his foot off the accelerator to get his bearings. Half the road signs were gone or too rusted to be legible. Arthur put his hand on Billi's arm and she winced.

'Show me your arm,' he said.

Billi rolled up her sleeve and looked at the wound.

Black lumps covered the bite marks and thick veins pulsed just beneath her skin. The wound itself smelt of damp, rotten earth.

Arthur drew a sharp breath.

'What d'you think?' Billi asked. She felt sick looking at the bite marks. It was like she had the plague. The skin around them was hot and red, feverish.

Arthur said nothing, but reached under the seat and pulled out a plastic box. The moment he took the lid off Billi sighed with relief. Elaine's stinking poultices. The smell made her eyes water, but right now the musky odour was sweeter than any perfume.

'We'll patch you up right and proper,' he said, but Billi could hear the tension in his voice.

Had they left it too late?

Just then Billi caught a sudden movement out of the corner of her eye. A tree – a thick oak – tilted. It twitched, shaking snow off its branches as though it was awakening. The pavement round it cracked and rose up in a shower of dirt and concrete as it leaned over. The boughs swayed, groaning as they bent like reeds, sweeping towards the approaching car.

A massive tree branch slammed across the side of the jeep, catapulting it into the air. Billi was tossed around as the jeep rolled over and over. The windows exploded and the metal frame screeched, flinging Billi against the back, then she was hurled forward, caught by the seat belt. She grabbed hold of Vasilisa, trying her best to cover the little girl's body with her own.

Then the car stopped. Billi hung upside down as it came to rest on its roof. Her ears buzzed and she tried to shake the fuzz out of her head. It took a few seconds for her focus to come back.

Outside Baba Yaga slammed down to the earth. The ground around her cracked and shockwaves spread out across the snow. She looked over at the upturned jeep, moonlight catching on her grinning teeth. She bent her arm, slowly flexing her fingers. The tree branches responded, bursting through the glass and piercing the car's bodywork. Baba Yaga pressed her hands together and pushed the jeep deeper into the ground.

Vasilisa lay on the ceiling, crying. Loudly. *That was good*, Billi thought. She sounded very much alive.

Shouting. People were shouting. Billi fumbled around for the belt catch and dropped out with a click.

Arthur reached in and grabbed Billi's hand.

'Are you OK?' He stared at her, terrified. Billi nodded.

'Vasilisa . . .' she said. Arthur understood. Billi crawled out as he wrenched the passenger door open. The metal buckled as the tree leaned its thickest boughs into the steel frame. Arthur lifted Vasilisa out.

'I'm OK.' Her smock was torn and she had small cuts on her hands and knees. Her necklaces and jewellery hung in tatters.

'Ivan?' Billi lay on her belly and desperately looked for signs of life.

Ivan groaned and unbuckled his seat belt. He dropped out of the jeep and yelled in pain upon landing. 'This is becoming a habit,' he muttered. Billi helped him up.

'Thank you,' he said. His sleeve had been ripped to the cuff so he took off his coat and threw it aside. His white shirt clung to his sweaty chest as he flicked open the gun barrel and checked the revolver wasn't damaged.

Lance crawled out the opposite side, pulling his sword

344

out after him. He held up Ivan's own sword. Ivan shook his head.

Lance took a sword in each hand and joined Arthur to face the ancient witch.

Baba Yaga stood at the far end of the street and she cried in victory as the jeep bent double under the pressure of the tree. The bonnet popped and folded like a book. Oil and petrol spewed out as the engine cracked. Baba Yaga shot up her arm and the oak tree sprang up straight. The branches shivered, then settled. They weren't getting away from her again.

The ancient witch flicked back her cloak and banged her stick on the icy ground. The sound echoed between the concrete walls and spread out across the still night sky. In the near distance it was answered by howls. The Polenitsy were on their way. From the calls they were coming from all directions. Baba Yaga lifted her stick and cried out to her werewolves.

Billi took a few steps before falling down. Her head felt heavy and swollen. Ivan slung his arm under hers and brought her to her feet. She rested herself against him, her head throbbing.

'Bloody hell,' whispered Billi. The moon rose, fat and full, bathing the tomb of mankind's nuclear folly with its dead light.

Chernobyl.

The old reactor was encased with huge concrete blocks. Millions of tonnes had been used to bury the radioactive heart of the disaster and the sarcophagus was thirty or forty metres high. Dark patches of leaked contaminants smeared the sides of the walls and some areas had been crudely patched with steel panels, themselves now deeply corroded. The perimeter walls were topped with rusty barbed wire.

The city, now the domain of beasts, erupted with fevered cries. Then from the sidestreets the Polenitsy emerged. Wolves, howling and snapping their yellow fangs, ran at them. The jeep's one unbroken headlight lit a bright path along the road straight to them. The wolves wove in and out of the darkness. Billi's hand fell on her bow and a handful of spilt arrows, but not the one she wanted. She needed the stone-tipped one and began searching. Where was it?

'Billi.' Ivan tapped her shoulder, the arrow in his hand. 'You should keep a closer eye on your gear.'

She could have kissed him. Instead she snatched the arrow and put it to her bow. The witch was over forty metres away. She needed to get a lot nearer.

Billi glanced at her dad as he stepped out between the wolves and the car. He'd cast off his coat so he could fight freely and the Templar Sword rested comfortably in his hand. Lance stood beside him, slowly turning his two swords, loosening his wrists.

'Billi!' shouted Ivan as the gunfire exploded.

Armed men ran down the road towards them. Koshchey led, flanked by two Bogatyrs, rifle in his hands. The other men drew hand weapons and met the werewolves, their steel against the lycanthropes' claws.

Koshchey pointed at them and a group of Bogatyrs broke into a run.

They've come for Vasilisa, thought Billi. She glanced at Ivan. *And revenge.* Koshchey had been humiliated and Ivan was still alive.

'Come on!' Ivan grabbed Vasilisa and Billi and they fled into a building across from the plant's main gate while Arthur and Lance fought back to back.

The moon's light shone through the broken wall of the single-storey office they'd entered. Billi stepped deep into the shadow, but the moonlight shone into her soul, on the Beast Within.

The arrow clattered on the wooden floor.

Her fingers curl. Billi stares, breath caught, as black hairs push through her skin and begin to cover the backs of her hands. She screams until her throat is torn and hoarse as her spine stretches against the mail. She wants to tear at the armour, desperate to rip it off, for the metal burns her and the clothes smother.

Ivan grabbed Billi's arms and held her up. He stared at Billi, but her eyes filled with a red haze and his face faded. She could see the heat rising from his exhalations, hear the warm blood running through his body. She smelt the adrenalin, the fear and the desire that soaked him.

'Stay with us,' he urged. 'You are not a beast.'

I am not a beast.

She repeated it over and over.

The floor trembled and long cracks broke along the wall and ceiling. Brittle plaster sprinkled down and the floorboards under their feet splintered. Vasilisa curled up and sobbed.

'The goddess is here.'

The fighting had stopped. Billi shook her head, trying to focus. The trees outside creaked and the wind rustled through the empty streets.

Billi's hair flickered as the breeze rose. The office quivered and the desks and chairs rattled and slid across the room.

Deep, long cracks opened along the walls and the roof rattled loose its tiles. The floorboards bent and snapped one by one. Then the walls exploded. Billi threw herself towards Vasilisa, but something fell from above, knocking her aside. Ivan shouted, but was drowned out as the building crumbled. All Billi could do was cover her head with her arms as the ceiling collapsed and she vanished under the avalanche of tiles and timber. She choked on the dust that filled her lungs and a deep drumming echoed in her ears.

The avalanche seemed to go on and on. Billi, submerged in debris, had managed to crawl under a gap made by two cupboards landing on each other.

Where's Ivan?

Where's Vasilisa?

She tried to call out, but could only cough. Eventually, when the noise had subsided, Billi began to drag herself out. A layer of broken roof slates covered the rubble and Billi started sliding them aside.

'Vasilisa?' Billi called.

A deep, black mass rose among the ruined building. *Tap tap tap* went a staff on the cracked concrete and rotten wood. Black eyes, old and so full of evil, glistened with victory. Baba Yaga used her claws to dig through the rubble. She tossed large lumps of brick and block behind her like they were polystyrene.

'Vasilisa!' Billi cried as she struggled to push herself free of the debris.

Baba Yaga reached into the dark pit and dragged Vasilisa out of the devastation.

CHAPTER 42

Arthur and Lance were surrounded by wolves. A Bogatyr charged Baba Yaga, his rifle blazing. The bullets merely sparked against her skin. With one hand she snapped her fingers round his neck and popped his head off. The body stumbled another two steps, then slumped, its severed neck pumping scarlet into the dirty snow. Vasilisa screamed as Baba Yaga dragged her away from the collapsed building.

The Bogatyrs were retreating. Men and wolves lay dead, some killed fleeing, others locked in their death fury. But the wolves were slowly gaining the upper hand. Billi watched as two werewolves broke through a gap and launched themselves at her father. His sword took one in the gullet, but the second knocked him down. Lance's swords stabbed into the wolf's side and the monster was tossed away.

Gwaine, Mordred and Gareth came charging down the street. Their arrows all spent, they launched into the melee, Gwaine swinging his axe in great skull-smashing arcs as they fought their way to the Templar Master.

Billi tried to heave herself up, but every muscle felt shredded. She managed to slide a beam far enough to crawl out of the rubble. Her armour was in tatters and blood dripped from a cut on her forehead, blinding her momentarily. The taste of it stung her lips.

Baba Yaga took her prisoner away from the ruined building as Vasilisa screamed and struggled in the old crone's grip.

Red leapt across the broken rubble. She sniffed the ground and her emerald eyes rose to meet Billi's.

Rage filled Billi's heart. Her head swam with fury.

'Get out of my way,' Billi snarled.

Red stalked closer. Then the broken concrete between them parted and Ivan reached out, revolver in his hand. He fired at Red, point-blank and straight into her belly. She stumbled back and he put two, then three bullets into her.

But she did not fall.

Ivan rose to his feet, both hands on the gun, as she sprang. He pushed the revolver barrel against Red's stomach and two muffled explosions went off in rapid succession. Red rammed her claws into his chest as she roared with savage hate. Ivan tilted backwards, firing again and catching the werewolf in the chest.

Red spasmed and bright blood spilled from her abdomen as her body changed. The hair began to sink away into her pale flesh and the limbs twisted under the pulsing skin. Ivan lay on his back, fingers still locked round the gun, his chest torn and bleeding heavily. Billi stepped towards him and touched his face. His eyes closed and he sighed.

Then nothing.

'Ivan?' She put her fingers to his still lips. 'Ivan!'

No no no. Not again. Billi pressed her fists against her head, though she wanted to scream.

'Billi!'

Vasilisa raised her head. She stared at Billi, eyes gigantic with terror. Baba Yaga lifted the girl and licked her great iron fangs. Her jaw ground like steel plates as she opened her mouth wider and wider, almost bending her head back like a mantrap.

Billi looked once at Ivan, then searched the dusty ruins frantically. She got on to her hands and knees and looked among the broken slabs and bricks for her weapon. Then she saw it, wedged under the fallen cupboard.

Somehow the bow had survived. A long crack ran down the wood, but the string was still wire-taut.

The arrow lay beneath two slabs a metre away. Billi spotted it through the narrow gap left as the wall and roof had collided. Vasilisa screamed and Billi glanced back. The little girl was trying to fight, but she couldn't resist the strength of the ancient crone. Vasilisa kicked furiously as she was lowered head-first into the old monster's wide maw. The moon was full and with one snap of her jaws Baba Yaga would consume all of Vasilisa, her flesh, blood and her powers.

Billi wanted to run and tear at the witch, but she fought the mindless urge. She screamed in anger and frustration as she reached through the gap, her fingers outstretched, vainly grasping for the arrow. A tremor ran across the ground and the slabs slid closer together and pinched Billi's arm. If they moved much more, it would be severed.

Billi watched the two avatars. One ancient, decrepit, wise and evil, the other a frail child. She pushed her shoulder into the hole and stretched her fingers to their utmost. Dust fell over her as she wormed deeper into the rubble. The slabs slid another centimetre closer together.

She touched smooth wood and jerked her hand out as the two huge chunks of concrete slammed together.

Billi raised her bow and notched the arrow.

Thumb ring hooks round the string and she pulls with the right as she pushes with the left. Her arms and shoulders shake under the strain. Baba Yaga is twenty metres away, holding the small girl above her, and her teeth begin to close round the girl's head.

Vasilisa screams.

Billi shoots.

CHAPTER 43

The arrow flies.

CHAPTER 44

Baba Yaga stumbled back and lifted her hand to her throat. Vasilisa fell to the ground, motionless. The old crone coughed. It was a small, weak noise as if she was shaking a small seed out of her gullet.

Her hand touched the arrow shaft jutting out just under her chin. She snapped it and tossed it to the floor, then sank to her knees. One by one the werewolves paused in battle.

The blood was flooding out of Baba Yaga's neck, great gushes with every heartbeat, spraying over Vasilisa's limp and exhausted body. The young girl blinked, awake.

Billi stumbled over the broken wall to try and reach her.

Vasilisa slowly rose and wiped the blood out of her eyes. Then she saw Baba Yaga.

'I am here, Babushka,' she said.

Baba Yaga hissed as she lowered her head; blood covered most of her chest. Vasilisa reached up and stroked the monster's face, carefully drawing the broken arrow out.

Billi cautiously made her way towards them. She could hardly breathe after having been crushed under the collapsed roof and her head swam with exhaustion and pain.

Blood formed soapy bubbles round the old crone's mouth. Baba Yaga stretched out her fingers and Vasilisa put her hand in the Dark Goddess's.

'Vasilisa, get away from her!' Billi dropped her bow and began to run towards them.

'Child . . .' said Baba Yaga. She gazed at her huge palm. Then, through the crevasses of wrinkled skin, a thin, green shoot unfurled itself. Baba Yaga gasped.

The green veins spread along Baba Yaga's fingers and up her arm. Billi watched as a string of flowers sprouted across the witch's fingertips. Vasilisa kept her small hand in Baba Yaga's, even as it began to transform, her skin thickening into deep, wrinkled bark. Her arms turned into thick, long boughs and her fingers burst with bright green leaves until her body was covered in lustrous foliage. Baba Yaga's black eyes flowered with purple irises. Her iron teeth closed forever and her blood turned to moss.

A wolf crept up to the bent oak tree. It sniffed round the trunk. It whined and moulded its body from wolf back into human. Others gathered around, some as wolves, others transformed back as women. Olga was nowhere to be seen.

'My God. It's over,' whispered Billi. Baba Yaga was gone. Vasilisa stumbled towards her and they hugged.

Billi bent down and cupped Vasilisa's bloody face. 'We did it, Vasilisa. We –'

Koshchey strode towards them, surrounded by what remained of his army, ten or so men. The Bogatyrs had been decimated in the battle, it seemed. They stopped six or seven metres away and Koshchey pointed his pistol at Billi.

'Give me the girl,' he said.

No, not after all this. He was too far away for her to attack and at her first move he'd put a bullet in her head. But she didn't care. 'Forget it, Koshchey. You can kill me, but you won't get a dozen metres before the werewolves rip you to pieces. If they don't, the Templars certainly will.'

'You have cost me too much, Templar, for me to walk away empty-handed. I have lost half my men getting here. Give me the girl. What I get from the vampires for the Spring Child will barely cover expenses.'

'You will not have her.' Billi's heart pounded in her chest and hot blood began to course through her body, filling her muscle with fiery strength. The Beast Within sensed victory.

Koshchey gazed at her, then at the werewolves gathered round him. Nobody would come out of this a clear victor. The bloodbath wasn't over yet.

Koshchey nodded. 'You are right, Templar.' He raised his pistol. 'But if I can't have her, no one can.'

A shot rang out and Billi gasped. Vasilisa let go of Billi and put a hand to her chest. She looked quietly surprised.

A red spot grew on her white smock. She tilted away and fell.

Koshchey fired once more and Vasilisa twitched. Then stopped.

'She's all yours,' he said.

CHAPTER 45

What?

What?

Billi stared at Vasilisa. Then at Koshchey.

What?

A deep, threatening growl rumbled in her throat as she stood and turned towards him. Koshchey backed away into the protective circle of his Bogatyrs.

'Do not try it, little Templar.'

Billi stepped forward. It really didn't matter now, but she was still going to kill him. Koshchey pointed the pistol at her head. At this distance he could hardly miss.

'I will warn you only once.'

Billi had a weapon left, her dagger. She pulled it out and held it in her fist. If she died, she'd make sure she took him with her. The power racing through her meant she'd leap the few metres between them easily.

'*BILLI.*' A hand, wet and sticky, touched Billi's arm and she turned. '*STEP AWAY.*'

Vasilisa stood in the red snow. She was covered in blood and there was a burnt hole in the centre of her smock. She looked up at Billi and smiled, a guileless child's smile. But the eyes were aged, not just a few years, but many, many thousands. They were black and as deep as eternity. Billi glanced at the Bogatyrs, then stepped away, retreating from the young girl who'd now become so much more. Baba Yaga had tried to consume Vasilisa, but instead Vasilisa had consumed her. All the Spring Children now inhabited the body of a nine-year-old. And so did all their powers.

Vasilisa stepped forward and faced Koshchey.

'KOSHCHEY THE UNDYING,' she said in a chorus of countless souls.

Koshchey fired. His men fired. Bullets shattered against Vasilisa's body as she held out her arms. Billi ducked behind a rusty car as the bullets rebounded off the invulnerable avatar. The gap between them filled with smoke and the stench of gunpowder. When Vasilisa lowered her arms Koshchey was staring at her in mute horror.

Vasilisa looked to the surrounding Polenitsy. 'COME, DAUGHTERS, FEED ON MANFLESH.'

'Wait!'

The command was clear and imperious. Ivan hobbled out of the rubble. His chest was a mess of tattered cloth and blood and he dragged his leg as he walked.

'Ivan?' Billi blinked. He was alive. She reached for him, but his eyes were on Koshchey. Her heart trembled. Koshchey's men outnumbered him – he would lose.

Couldn't he see that? Billi bit her lip and stopped. She wanted to run to him, help him, but this was not the time. He had a score to settle. All she could do was stand by and watch.

Vasilisa raised her hand, stopping the Polenitsy.

'TSAREVICH.' She acknowledged his presence and his right.

Smashed and battered as he was, there was almost demonic determination in Ivan's eyes as he gazed at Koshchey. 'We have unfinished business, you and I.'

Koshchey's eyes narrowed. 'A duel, perhaps? For what, *Tsarevich*?'

'If you win, then you go free.'

One of the Polenitsy shouted, but Vasilisa nodded in Ivan's direction. 'SO BE IT.'

Koshchey laughed. Hands on hips, he threw back his head and bellowed.

'You want to fight me? You can barely –'

The gun boomed once and Koshchey fell. The thunder of the gunshot echoed across the city. Ivan stood, big revolver perfectly still in his hand, the smoke whispering out of the long, shiny barrel.

'I want you dead,' he said. 'And that is all I want.'

The Bogatyrs stared at the body of their leader. Then back at Ivan. They were a tight unit, but suddenly they looked lost and not a little frightened.

'Go now,' he ordered. He tossed the empty gun aside and cleaned the sweat from his forehead. The Bogatyrs, throwing their weapons away, fled.

Billi ran forward into his arms. 'Thank God. I thought you were dead.'

'Me? Dead? Do you know who I am?' Ivan winced. 'I am Tsarevich Ivan Alexeivich Romanov. It would take more than a couple of scratches to kill me.' He wobbled and would have fallen if Billi hadn't hung on to him. 'Not much more, though.'

One of the wolves howled. A woman climbed on to a wall and cried at the moon. The victorious Polenitsy gave full voice to their joy and the city echoed with their feral calling. The sound trembled in Billi's soul and her ears pricked at the cries of celebrating beasts.

She sighed and stepped back from Ivan. She raised her head and stared at the moon. The brightness of it hurt her eyes, but she didn't blink.

The Beast Within stepped out of its cage.

She pulled off the broken remains of her mail armour.

Ivan took hold of her arm. 'No. Not after all this.' He shouted at the Templars. 'Quickly!'

Billi twisted, but he wouldn't let go. She stared at her coat, bloodstained and ripped. She drew her long, sharp nails, talons now, peeling it off.

They had won. Her sisters.

Dimly she watched her father run towards her, backpack slung over his shoulder. His blue eyes were open and fearful. Why?

'Billi, your dad's coming, just hang on,' said a man, a man called Ivan.

No, he was the enemy. He smelt of blood and wolf and gun and smoke, the stench of civilization.

'Let me go,' Billi said. Oh, how ripe he looked.

'No.'

Billi snarled and her tongue touched the needle-sharp row of fangs in her mouth, all the better for tearing out his throat. She smiled, smelling the fear dripping through his pores.

'You are not a beast, Billi.'

He did not flee as prey should. He stood facing her, daring her.

No. This was Ivan. He'd saved her life. Billi faltered.

The howls drowned out her thoughts and Billi screamed. She collapsed, curling up as her body began to break its human mould. Arthur dropped beside her.

Human and Beast fought for domination. Billi's soul split in two, each eager to rule the other. Muscles flinched and jerked as the Beast Within tried to force its will over body and flesh.

I am not a beast.

No matter what she'd done, she'd not given in to it.

Billi stared hard at Ivan, digging her nails into his skin, hanging on to him like she was drowning.

Arthur ripped open his backpack and the stench within made Billi want to vomit. The werewolf part recoiled and snarled as Arthur pasted the thick herbal poultices over her arm and side. But her blood boiled and her skin burned.

Then a stream of coolness began to spread through

her. First Billi sweated, then shivered as the herbs did their work.

Billi slumped in Ivan's arms and gave in to the comforting chill coursing through her veins.

CHAPTER 46

Billi felt the trickle of cold water across her forehead. Drops fell on her eyelids, making her blink.

'Thank God,' whispered Arthur.

Billi blinked again, wiping the water away, and gazed around.

'It was looking a bit hairy for a moment,' said her father. He dropped the cloth into a plastic bowl.

'Is that a . . . joke?' she asked. 'Please, no more. I don't think I could take it.'

Arthur brushed her hair away from her face as Billi sat up. A few blankets had been tossed over a tiled floor and she lay under a heavy coat.

'What happened?' Billi saw the fresh poultices on her arm and felt them against her ribs. It was still dark outside and she flinched as she saw the moon hovering over the buildings, but then she relaxed. It had no power over her.

'A truce, of sorts,' said Arthur. He looked weary and the Templar Sword stood up against the wall. 'Vasilisa, if she is still Vasilisa, has permitted us to stay in Chernobyl while you were resting. I think she was curious to find out if you might change.' He pointed at the moon. 'Join with the Polenitsy. I think she'd like that.'

'She's with the Polenitsy now?' Billi asked.

'Oh yes. They have lost their old goddess and found a new one.' Arthur scratched his chin. 'It looks as though all the power Baba Yaga had has now passed to her.' He didn't sound entirely happy about it.

Billi swung her feet in front of her.

'You should rest a bit. Lance is sorting out some transport.'

'Where's Ivan?' Billi stood and wobbled, grabbing the wall to steady herself. Then she slowly let go and stood on her own two feet. 'I want to see him.'

'As stubborn as your mother.' Arthur handed Billi a coat. 'Outside. He's been waiting.'

Billi smiled as she slung the coat over her shoulders. 'Thanks, Dad.'

Outside Billi watched Lance and Mordred busy with one of the large Humvees the Bogatyrs had abandoned. Gwaine and Gareth stood on the roof, packing. Gareth's arm was in a sling and he winced as he shifted a box of food with one hand and one boot. To the edge of the buildings, just beyond a rough strip of brushland that might once have been a park, were the Polenitsy. Even from here Billi felt the stir of the Beast. It wanted to go and join them. Billi turned away and saw Ivan.

He sat on a pile of bricks, staring at Koshchey's body. Ivan's chest was wrapped in bandages and someone had given him a bulky winter coat.

'Penny for your thoughts?' Billi asked.

'They aren't worth a penny.'

The big man still had his eyes wide open, a faint expression of shock frozen on his stark, white face. There was a large, blood-encrusted pit in his chest.

'How do you feel?' Billi wanted to embrace Ivan, but she kept back.

'Honestly? Numb. Cold. Nothing in particular. I thought I would feel . . . more.'

'It's done now, Ivan.' Billi held out her hand. Ivan glanced at it. Silently he slipped his fingers into hers.

'It has been an honour to fight beside you, Billi San-Greal.' He smiled and Billi helped him up.

'What are you going to do now?'

Ivan shrugged. 'Get adopted.'

'What?' She must have misheard. She tapped her head; perhaps she was still delirious with all that had just happened. It sounded like he'd said 'get adopted'.

Ivan smiled slyly. 'England's royal family. We're related, you know. I may decide to come to London and impose on my cousins' hospitality.'

Billi laughed. 'Well, if you have no luck at Buckingham Palace, we might be able to find some space for you at the Temple.' They began walking back to the building, both supporting each other. Billi clung close to Ivan as he limped along and he likewise had his arm round her waist, holding tightly.

A plaintive howl made them both look up.

A mangy grey wolf, its pelt bloody and torn, licked

the still face of Red, of Svetlana. Its green eyes searched the girl's body for some sign of life, whimpering softly as it sniffed the deep chest wounds. It licked the girl's cheek, but she did not stir.

'Olga,' Billi said. The wolf lifted its head in her direction and Billi raised her hand. She wanted to thank her. The old werewolf, more than anyone, had saved the world from Fimbulwinter.

The old grey wolf watched them, blinking. Then it touched its nose against Svetlana's still lips and jumped down. With what could have been a nod or a bow, it turned and disappeared.

'Sister SanGreal,' said a voice from behind them.

A woman with scars and tattoos waited a few metres away. 'The goddess wishes to speak with you.'

Goddess? Billi looked at the Polenitsy gathered in the distance. She saw Vasilisa sitting among them.

Ivan turned to go with her, but the woman's hand shot up. 'Not you.'

Billi smiled at Ivan. 'It'll be fine. Vasilisa and I are friends.' But as she turned towards the werewolves and the young girl she wasn't so sure. The spirits of all the other Spring Children were in the small, pale body of the nine-year-old girl. There was no knowing who was in charge.

Vasilisa sat on the wreck of an old car with the Polenitsy around her. They'd found a plain white dress for her. The material was brittle and threadbare, but still elegant. Round her head she wore a crown made of bound twigs and decorated with leaves and small bottle-tops. Her face was spotless and her hair had been cleaned and woven with small, white flowers: snowdrops. Vasilisa seemed to glow under the moon. Some of the Polenitsy had changed back into human form, but most, about twenty or so, still kept their beast form as wolves or half-humans.

'DON'T BE AFRAID,' said Vasilisa to her. The group of women parted to let Billi through.

'We're going home now, Vasilisa.' Billi met the black eyes of the small girl and a chill fear grew in her heart. She was afraid. 'If you still are Vasilisa.'

'OH YES, I AM STILL HER. AND MANY OTHERS. ALL THE OTHER SPRING CHILDREN.' Vasilisa smiled. 'THEY ARE AT PEACE, BILLI. IN TIME THEY WILL ALL FADE.'

'Then what's next?' Billi asked.

'FOR YOU, BILLI SANGREAL, A SAFE JOUR-NEY.' Vasilisa held out her hand and touched Billi's fingertips. 'UNLESS YOU WISH TO STAY HERE, WITH YOUR SISTERS.'

The Beast Within. It would prowl the cage of her soul forever, and she could hear its call echoing deep inside. It had tasted freedom and Billi had fought it down. She checked the bandages on her arm, praying they would cure her, praying it wasn't too late.

Vasilisa smiled slyly, understanding. 'DO NOT FRET. THE BEAST IS CAGED.' She raised her fingers to touch Billi's heart. 'BUT THE WOLF WILL ALWAYS

BE WITHIN YOU. COME TO US AND WE WILL FREE IT.'

Billi shook her head and stepped backwards. 'I'm sorry, but I know where I belong.' She frowned. 'Did I do right, Vasilisa? In saving you?' She'd thought she would defeat Baba Yaga and save an innocent life. Instead she had replaced the old goddess with a new one. Would this one be friendly towards humanity or side against it?

Vasilisa took off her crown. She held it lightly and green buds swelled along the twigs, rapidly growing into ripe, round cases that cracked open, unfurling petals of yellow and soft orange and red.

'NATURE WILL ALWAYS WIN.' Vasilisa put the crown back on. *'CHERNOBYL IS PROOF OF THAT.'*

'So you're saying Baba Yaga was right? That mankind is best out of the picture?'

'I AM SAYING WHATEVER HUMANITY DOES, NATURE ALWAYS TRIUMPHS.'

'And Fimbulwinter? Is Yellowstone planning to erupt?'

'FOR NOW, THE VOLCANO SLEEPS AGAIN.' The girl climbed off the car. *'ONE DAY IT WILL AWAKEN, THEN EVEN I WILL NOT BE ABLE TO STOP IT. THAT IS HOW NATURE IS.'* The Polenitsy began to wander away, disappearing into the birch tree woods surrounding the town. Like sylvan spirits they melted in among the branches and trunks and snow-layered earth. Vasilisa walked with them, then paused at the line of trees, on the edge of the darkness.

'WHEN YOU WEARY OF YOUR WORLD COME TO US, BILLI. WE WILL BE WAITING.'

'What about Baba Yaga? What did you do with her?' Billi shouted. The girl was a white shadow now, barely visible in the snow as though she was already melting into the elements.

Vasilisa lifted a finger to her endlessly dark eyes. 'CAN'T YOU TELL?' Then she laughed and among the multitude of voices Billi heard the brittle cackle of the witch, Baba Yaga.

DEVIL'S
KISS

BY
SARWAT
CHADDA

The incredible prequel to

DARK
GODDESS

Kissed by a devil. In love with an angel.
Let your fear take flight . . .

www.devilskiss.co.uk

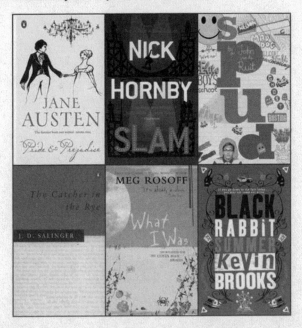